Murder in an
Irish Garden

Books by Carlene O'Connor

Irish Village Mysteries

MURDER IN AN IRISH VILLAGE
MURDER AT AN IRISH WEDDING
MURDER IN AN IRISH CHURCHYARD
MURDER IN AN IRISH PUB
MURDER IN AN IRISH COTTAGE
MURDER AT AN IRISH CHRISTMAS
MURDER IN AN IRISH BOOKSHOP
MURDER ON AN IRISH FARM
MURDER AT AN IRISH BAKERY
MURDER AT AN IRISH CHIPPER
MURDER IN AN IRISH GARDEN
CHRISTMAS COCOA MURDER
(with Maddie Day and Alex Erickson)
CHRISTMAS SCARF MURDER
(with Maddie Day and Peggy Ehrhart)

A Home to Ireland Mystery

MURDER IN GALWAY
MURDER IN CONNEMARA
HALLOWEEN CUPCAKE MURDER
(with Liz Ireland and Carol J. Perry)
IRISH MILKSHAKE MURDER
(with Peggy Ehrhart and Liz Ireland)
IRISH SODA BREAD MURDER
(with Peggy Ehrhart and Liz Ireland)

A County Kerry Mystery

NO STRANGERS HERE
SOME OF US ARE LOOKING
YOU HAVE GONE TOO FAR

Published by Kensington Publishing Corp.

Murder in an Irish Garden

Carlene O'Connor

KENSINGTON PUBLISHING CORP.

KENSINGTON BOOKS are published by

Kensington Publishing Corp.
900 Third Avenue
New York, NY 10022

ISBN: 978-1-4967-4445-6

Printed in the United States of America

Murder in an
Irish Garden

Chapter 1

If you've never had the pleasure, let me assure you that a quintessential Irish garden in the height of summer is a magnificent sight to behold. Vibrant blooms in a kaleidoscope of shapes and colors, shrubbery crafted by artists, playful fairies, gnomes, and angels, all forming a path to an ornate fountain in the center. Imagine if you will, a stately manor house beckoning in the distance, proudly standing behind sturdy limestone walls. But if all you see is the beauty, then you're a fool. Because did you know that many of those manor houses exist because of the violent dissolution of monasteries? Wealth thrown to the aristocracy and Tudor men, eager to feast on someone else's lands while the Irish farmer toiled and struggled? You might dislike me for educating you, but can you fault me if some people prefer their roses in the form of little colored glasses?

Besides, you are liable to point out, an Irish garden can exist anywhere. They can flourish in front of sweet little cottages with thatched roofs. In the back of semidetached flats in town. Even windowsill boxes can be transformed into a flowering bonanza. I'll give you that—gardens are for everyone, and they can flourish everywhere. But do you know what else gardens hold? Weeds that choke and drown. Secrets that are burrowed deep into the rich, dark soil. Sharpened weapons: spades and rakes and stakes. Oh, my. Butterflies that flutter with beauty in front of your face while darting bees sting you in the back. Yes. One must look closely at Irish gardens, for one never knows what lurks amongst the blades. I know someone who purports to be a nature lover and to nature she will return. Would you like to know my favorite time to visit a garden? At night, of course. When it's shrouded in a cloth of dark. Danger can lurk. Danger can strike. Do you see the resemblance? Manicured lawns, objects made of stone, angels hovering about, and things buried deep in the earth? If you haven't figured it out, I'd be happy to spell it out. One man's garden might be another man's grave.

Chapter 2

"Would you please read that one again?" Siobhán O'Sullivan drummed her fingers on their farmhouse kitchen table, something Macdara had already somewhat politely asked her not to do. Her study-weary husband sighed. They had been at it all night. Morning had announced itself through the kitchen window, bold and uninvited, blinding them with a ray of sunshine. At least there was coffee, and Macdara had warmed blueberry scones in the oven. The rich smell of the heavenly concoctions filled their small kitchen and took the edge off the torture.

Normally Eoin would have stepped in to make them brekkie, but he was ensconced with his restaurant opening. Ann was away at her first year at the University of Limerick, even though the summer had barely begun, she'd moved to campus upon returning from their holiday at sea because she was on the camogie team and practice would start soon. At least she was close to home. Gráinne and James, on the other hand, had stayed behind in Lahinch to renovate Gráinne's new inn, and Ciarán, who had just passed his Leaving Certificate had concluded (against Siobhán's will) to take a "gap year." It meant he was technically still living at home but more often than not was out with friends or fellow musicians. She fully supported his fiddle playing, and he was fierce talented at that, but she was bracing nearly every day for him to announce that he was running away with a band. As usual, life was changing faster than Siobhán could keep up. And with all this chaos swirling around her, the task of passing her detective sergeant exams was daunting.

Camped out next to her, a pile of textbooks teetered like the Leaning Tower of Pisa. Preparing for the exams from home had been challenging enough, but now there was commotion going on outside, and this went way beyond rattling wind and chirping birds. Chainsaws, drills, workmen barking orders—it was madness, and for once it wasn't all taking place in Siobhán's poor head. But it was too late to find a quieter place to focus; she'd promised Eoin that she would keep an eye out for a special delivery. His restaurant, The Six, was going to have its soft opening in two days. If that wasn't enough, he had rented out the field in front of it to a contestant for Kilbane's Top Garden Contest. Cassidy Ryan. Tomorrow was the first day of the contest and the town was abuzz with excitement.

Siobhán's mam had had a green thumb, and their back garden in town had been an oasis of fresh herbs and flowers. Often, Naomi O'Sullivan would dry and hang the herbs in the kitchen of the family bistro and adorn the tables with fresh cut flowers. How her mam would have loved the garden competition, maybe even taken home the coveted prizes of ten thousand euro and The Golden Rose.

"Officer Healy is on patrol," Macdara was saying. "It's evening and he's nearly finished for the day. He's strolling down the street—"

"I thought he was *walking*."

Macdara gave her a look. She had a dreadful feeling they were building up to their first big fight as a married couple.

He took a deep breath and she had no doubt he was counting to ten in his head. "Walking, strolling, there's no difference."

"Of course there's a difference."

"Do tell."

"Why is he strolling if he's on duty? He should be less relaxed and more alert."

"Fine. Officer Jennings—"

"Healy—"

"Right. Officer *Healy.* It would be easier to remember if I could get through the question at least *once* without interruption." He stared at Siobhán as if daring her to say something. She was doing a lot more than counting in her head, but she kept her gob shut. Exams were hard, but there were days that marriage was even harder. "Officer Healy is walking down the street, as alert as he can possibly be at the end of a very long day, and here comes your fella Mike. Mike waves Officer Healy down—"

Macdara was paraphrasing and talking too fast. These questions were ridiculous. There was no choice but to interrupt again; she was the one who would be taking the test, and she needed clarification. "Why does Mike need to wave Officer Healy down if he's already approaching him?"

Macdara threw the manual down on the kitchen table. "We're not getting anywhere! I haven't even gotten to the accident." He stood and headed for the kettle.

Siobhán glanced at the practice manual and imagined setting it on fire. "What accident?"

"Exactly!" Macdara said, as he rummaged around in the cupboard for a box of tea. He continued to talk as he set about preparing two cups. "Mike tells Officer Healy that he saw a man named Joe plow into a cyclist and take off."

Apparently her overachiever husband had memorized the entire scenario. There were days she would have found this an attractive quality. Today was not one of them. She tapped her pencil on the table; it helped her think. "Does this Mike fella wear glasses?"

Macdara frowned as he dropped tea bags into the mugs. "That's nowhere in the scenario!"

Siobhán crossed her arms and stared at her notes. "It should be. I would think that would be very important, don't you?"

"For the love of curried chips, will ya please just shut your gob until I finish the question?"

Siobhán's jaw tightened. She was going to blow before the kettle. She didn't even bother to count this time. "Did you just tell your wife to shut her gob?" She lasered him one of those looks only a wife can give. "And before you answer, I'll be adding me own crime question to the list if your answer is yes."

"You will, yeah?"

Siobhán nodded. "If a wife kills her husband but he totally had it coming because he egged her on by telling her to *shut her gob* when she's trying to study for one of the most important tests of her career—is she really responsible for his death?"

"Yes," Macdara said. "She most certainly is." He paused and cocked his head. "How would you do it?"

"I'd slip something into your tea." Macdara stared at the mugs on the counter. Siobhán grimaced, pulled the manual toward her, and skimmed the inane passage. " 'Joe saw Mike plow into a cyclist and drive away. Luckily the cyclist is not harmed. His name is Kevin. Mike chats with him and finds out he's forty years of age, with a wife and two sons.' " She pushed it away again, disgusted. "What on earth does that have to do with being hit by a car?"

"I didn't write the question and you didn't finish it." She gestured for him to do so. "He chats with your one, then fifteen minutes later Officer Healy is driving about, and he sees the vehicle—"

"Wait. How could he see the vehicle? You didn't even say the color, make, or model."

"He obviously knew all of that."

Siobhán shook her head. If only she could meet with these men—and she knew it was men who designed nonsensical practice questions, she'd murder them too. "It's not obvious at all."

The kettle whistled and Macdara wet the tea. He stirred in milk and sugar and brought them to the table. "Sans poison, dear wife." He set hers in front of her and gently touched her shoulder. "I know you're nervous. But this is never going to work if we can't even get through a single question."

He was right. She hated when he was right. "Fine."

Macdara eagerly sat down and supped his tea before pulling the manual toward him. " 'He stops the car, they pull to the side of the road, and he orders him to get out.' Now. Ready for the question part of the question?" She pursed her lips and nodded. " 'Is Officer Healy within his rights to conduct a breathing test?' "

"Yes, if—"

Macdara held up his index finger and wagged it. "It's multiple choice. I haven't read the choices." Siobhán crossed her arms, slouched in the chair, and patiently waited. " 'A: No. He has no right to tell him what to do and he shouldn't have stopped him in the first place. B: No, he has no proof the accident even happened—he only suspects it happened. C: Yes. But the test must take place within or close to an area where the requirements for Joe to cooperate can be imposed—' "

Siobhán pounded her fist on the table. "What in the world does that even mean?"

" 'Or D: Yes. Officer Healy can do whatever he wants because he's a police officer.' " Siobhán opened her mouth, and there was her husband's index finger again. It wasn't the first time she thought about biting it. "Don't do it, Siobhán," Macdara warned. "Do not say D."

"I cannot answer the question if I do not understand what in the world they're trying to say in answer C."

"Well, that's unfortunate because explanation C is the correct answer."

"What?" She was starting to wish there was whiskey in her tea.

Macdara began to mansplain. "Since Officer Healy has spoken to the cyclist hit by the vehicle and confirmed the accident—"

"It didn't say he confirmed the accident. It said he confirmed your one was forty years of age and married with two sons."

"If the cyclist didn't confirm the story, I'm sure it would have said that cyclist denied it. Why would they even write up this question if there was no accident?" By now they had both risen to their feet and were competing to project their voices over the commotion outside. Siobhán was wondering exactly where this argument was headed when someone pounded on the front door. Had they disturbed the workers outside? Saved *by the bang.* Siobhán hurried to the window above the kitchen sink and peered outside. Planted at the front door was a baby-faced deliveryman and next to him was an enormous wooden crate. It had to be for Cassidy Ryan and her garden design. Siobhán opened the window.

"That goes to the white tent," she said, startling the poor man. He whipped his head around and raised his cap. He was so young. Nineteen at the most.

He glanced nervously in the direction of the large tent. It was big enough to house a traveling circus. All the gardens in the competition had tents erected around them so that their creations would be hidden until the official unveiling. "Where exactly would you like it?" His voice started off deep and then squeaked.

"You're not going to like me answer," Siobhán said.

"Join the club," Macdara piped up.

The poor lad looked terrified. "I'll take you over to the tent," Siobhán said. "If the recipient isn't there, I can sign for it." She glanced at Macdara. "I need some fresh air."

Macdara rose and grabbed the manual. "Not a bother. I can walk and talk."

Ugh. He was relentless. They headed outside and Siobhán once again glanced at the enormous person-sized crate. It was propped up on a rolling dolly. "Is it an elephant?"

The lad leaned forward and glanced at a sticker on the crate. "Statue."

"She's going all out." Cassidy Ryan had already caused quite a bit of trouble with the other gardeners, and not just because she was a blond bombshell who flirted with every male in sight. She was the only *professional* landscape designer of the group, and the other gardeners were incensed. Unfortunately, no one had thought to write a clause barring professionals into the bylines, so they were stuck. It wasn't just the test questions that were aggravating. It was life. Rules and regulations. Everything revolved around rules and regulations. As Siobhán led the way, she could hear the wheels of the dolly squeaking and bumping, not to mention a fair amount of grunting as the delivery lad strained under the weight.

Macdara continued to yammer behind her. "If Officer Healy has reasonable grounds to believe Joe hit the cyclist, then he can ask for the breath test." He was committed to her passing these exams and using tough love to accomplish it. Was he worried it would be a poor reflection on him if she didn't pass the first time around? And why was this flustering her so much? She was normally an excellent student. Her head just wasn't in it. Did she even want to be a detective sergeant? Wasn't one in the family enough? "Can we put this on hold?" She called over her shoulder. "I need a break."

"The Road Traffic Act basically states that if an accident happens as a result of a motor vehicle on the road, and the officer believes that this person was in charge of the vehicle when the accident occurred, then the officer has legal authorization to administer a preliminary breath test." Macdara waited for her to respond.

"There was an accident?" the delivery lad asked when silence stretched. He sounded worried.

"See?" Siobhán said. "That's what I said."

"I didn't write these questions," Macdara said. "You asked for my help."

"*You* took the test, didn't you?" Siobhán asked. She was getting her back up, but she couldn't help it.

"I wouldn't be a detective sergeant if I hadn't taken the tests." He paused. "And you won't be either."

He did not just say that. In front of this delivery-baby no less. Siobhán eyed the crate again. It was big enough to stuff her husband into—maybe she could convince the lad to haul him away. "You could have at least given headquarters feedback on how idiotic these questions are."

"You're blaming me for *taking* the test? I don't have to help you study, you know. I do have other things I could be doing."

"Like what?" Macdara was off for the week following their holiday and he was still trying to be a "man of leisure."

"Don't you worry about it."

"Consider yourself officially dismissed." They reached the tent. It was situated across from Eoin's farm-to-table restaurant, a short stroll away. Once the garden was unveiled, restaurant guests could walk through the installment either before or after their meal, and it would remain on the property throughout the summer for folks to enjoy. It was ingenious of Eoin to think about doing this, even if it had gotten him in some hot water with the other contestants. Now that they were near the tent, Siobhán was surprised that all was quiet. "Hello?" she called out. "Cassidy Ryan? There's a large delivery here. Some kind of statue?" There was no reply. "She must be on break," Siobhán said. "Would you like me to sign for it?" The lad glanced at his paperwork. "It clearly states that only Cassidy Ryan can sign for it."

"A rule follower," Macdara said. "Good man." He gave Siobhán a pointed look.

"Wait here then and I'll see if me brother knows where she is." Siobhán ignored Macdara and headed for the restaurant.

Macdara followed her. "Let's try another question. Susan is walking to work one morning—"

"Not strolling?" Siobhán shot back.

"Two men suddenly come up behind her—Harry and Joe—"

"Is this the same Joe who struck the cyclist?"

"They say, 'We won't hurt you as long as you give us the bag!' " Macdara was getting into it, acting out the role. Just as he was speaking, the restaurant doors opened and a young woman with long brunette hair emerged with a camera slung around her neck. She had not only caught the tail end of his statement, but Macdara was acting as if Siobhán had a handbag and he was going to snatch it.

The woman's eyes were panicked. "Leave her alone!" she yelled, running toward Siobhán. She started to tug on Macdara as she screamed at Siobhán. "Where's your bag?"

"I'm not carrying one," Siobhán said. She glared at Macdara. "And neither was the person in that scenario."

The woman let go of Macdara and stepped back, confusion planted on her pretty face.

"Of course she was carrying a handbag," Macdara said. "How could they try and rob it off her if she wasn't?"

"Then why doesn't it clearly state that she's carrying a handbag? Good old Harry and Joe just said, 'Give us the bag!' For all I know it was a SuperValu bag."

The woman's eyes ping-ponged between them, her shiny pink lips agape. She was slim and her dewy face was dotted with freckles. "Do either of you want me to call someone?"

Macdara turned to the young woman. "We're reading test questions," he said. "My stubborn wife is studying to become a detective sergeant." He shook his head. "Or should I say she's actively *avoiding* studying."

Siobhán put her hands on her hips, realizing that to this young woman she probably looked like a typical wife nagging her husband. But some things couldn't be helped. "And my detective-sergeant husband is drilling me with practice questions that do not make an ounce of sense because they were written by men with limestone for brains!" Siobhán could feel her blood pressure tick up. She wanted to hit something. Preferably him.

"Stop overthinking every single little detail," Macdara said. "When you become a detective sergeant, you can lobby to change the questions. But if you don't get out of your own stubborn way, you're never going to pass the exams!"

"How many times are you going to call me stubborn?"

"As many as it takes to get through to you!"

The woman backed away slightly, her hand going to her camera. If she started to film them, Siobhán was going to yank it off her neck and stomp on it. She was dying for the woman to start filming them. The young woman held up her right hand and flashed a diamond on her engagement finger. "Should I take this as a warning?"

"Yes," they said in stereo.

Siobhán tried to calm herself by staring out at the fields. Summer was here and everything was green. Maybe it would help her see less red. "Please excuse my rude husband."

"Rude?" Macdara said. "Rude?!"

"We just returned from our honeymoon. Isn't it obvious?" Siobhán said.

"The honeymoon's over," Macdara said, throwing his arms out.

The woman was studying her engagement ring as if she'd just realized something deadly was wrapped around her finger.

"We're sorry we frightened you," Siobhán said to the woman. "I swear. We're normally not like this."

"Not a bother." She looked around as if she wanted to flee.

"We're looking for Cassidy Ryan. But first things first. I'm Siobhán O'Sullivan-Flannery and the rude old goat behind me is my husband, Macdara."

"Fantastic," Macdara said. "I'm a rude old goat. Noted."

"And I'm a stubborn wife. Noted."

"Say less and you'll hear more," Macdara said.

"You know what?" Siobhán whirled around. "I will say less. In fact, for the record, I am officially giving you the silent treatment." She mimicked locking her lips and throwing away the key.

"It's my lucky day," Macdara said, throwing his arms open. "I love the silent treatment!"

"Molly Murphy," the woman said, taking out a pad of paper and biro. "For the *Kilbane Times*. I'm the reporter and photographer for Kilbane's Top Garden Contest."

"You are?" Siobhán blurted out. She looked like a baby too. A baby with a job and a fiancé. Everyone looked like babies. Twenty-something and bright-eyed. Siobhán was getting old. And cranky. "Brilliant." They had just had their first big row in front of an engaged reporter. *Typical.*

Molly jotted something down on her pad, her tongue sticking out of the corner of her mouth. Siobhán could hear Macdara breathing. No doubt he was fuming. But he was the one who just couldn't give things a rest. This wasn't her fault.

Eoin emerged from the restaurant. His ginger hair was slicked back, and he was wearing a white apron, white shirt, and black denims. He looked sharp. Long gone were the days where acne dotted his face and he wore American baseball caps backward. He was a man now, clear complexion, nice hair . . . *handsome.* And she was bursting with pride. All her siblings were grown up, although she still thought of Ciarán as a baby. "What's the story?" he asked. "Did I hear arguing?" He raised his eyebrow and took in the pair.

"There's a delivery lad by the tent who needs Cassidy Ryan's signature," Siobhán said, gesturing. "Would you look at the size of that crate?"

They began to walk back toward the crate, and the young reporter tagged along. "I haven't seen her since the wee hours of this morning," Eoin said. "Saw her pop in and out of the tent but she didn't stay long. Just long enough to berate her garden crew. She's not answering calls or texts either."

"These aren't the wee hours?" Macdara asked.

Eoin laughed. "You weren't the only pair up all night. With the competition opening tomorrow, I bet all the gardeners have been at it 'round the clock."

Siobhán nodded. Everyone had been putting in a lot of preparation for this event. Every year it brightened up the town with flowers and ambition. "And with your restaurant opening, you've been working even harder."

They reached the outside of the tent and the delivery lad looked at them expectantly. "Sorry, luv," Siobhán said. "Cassidy Ryan isn't here."

The lad stared at the crate and groaned. "If she doesn't sign for it, I have to take this back." He lifted his cap and stared at it with dread. Sweat glistened on his forehead. "It's really, really heavy. Even with the dolly." "I don't know what to tell you," Siobhán said. "But if you'd like to wait a bit, you could come into the restaurant." She turned to Eoin. "Right?" "I can get you a tea or coffee," Eoin said. "And maybe whip up an Irish brekkie if you're hungry." The delivery lad glanced at the crate again. "I really can't leave it." He gazed at the restaurant. "But a coffee would be nice." "We'll all wait then," Siobhán said. "Although not *everyone* needs to be here," she said to the field. "It's a grand fresh day," Macdara said. "I think I'll stay." He was the stubborn one. *Stubborn* old goat. "I'll put the coffee on," Eoin said. "Anyone else?" Siobhán raised her hand. Eoin nodded.

"Thank you, Eoin, for the very kind offer," Macdara said. "I will use my words and politely decline."

Oh, no, he didn't.

Eoin laughed. "Whatever the pair of ye are smoking—don't pass it on." He ambled away.

"She's the only gardener who turned down my last interview, my last word with them before the competition opens," Molly said, staring at the tent. "She must have been extremely paranoid about me trying to peek at her garden. Last night she went so far as to deliver a cease and desist letter to my doorstep. Can you believe it?"

That sounded odd; Siobhán couldn't imagine anyone having that kind of reaction. Was Molly exaggerating? "An actual cease and desist letter?"

"I don't think it was drawn up by a solicitor, but in essence she was telling me to back off."

Macdara seemed just as confused. "All this over an interview?"

Molly threw her arms open as if reliving the frustration. "Everyone agreed in advance that I'd be touching base with them just before the unveiling. She's a piece of work, that one." Molly stared at the crate. "In my first interview I could tell she was thrilled to be in the spotlight. Then suddenly she's threatening me with legal action over another interview?" Molly gestured with her head to the crate. "I bet whatever is in there is the reason why."

Siobhán edged closer to the crate. "What do you mean?"

Molly sighed. "She was very paranoid about the other gardeners getting even a whiff of her garden plans. Like even if I knew what they were, I wouldn't give away any surprises in my interviews. She was basically insulting my integrity."

"Like a magician afraid you'll learn their tricks and spoil it for everyone," Macdara said.

Molly laughed. "Exactly." She turned to him twirling a strand of her hair, her tone suddenly flirtatious. "What's the rest of that test question?"

Seriously? Was the entire universe conspiring against Siobhán? The reporter was a little instigator. Siobhán wanted to throttle her too.

Macdara didn't hesitate. "Harry grabs Susan, he puts a knife to her throat while Joe tries to snatch her handbag." He began to act out the scene. "She fights back. She starts to run away—they chase her—she trips and bangs her head on the pavement. She's dead."

Molly gasped.

"What?" the delivery lad said, joining the party. "Who's dead?"

"She should have just given them her bag," Molly said. "Even if it was designer." She threw a look to Siobhán.

Did she *want* a punch in the face?

Macdara nodded his consent. "The question is—"

"Somebody tell him we all know what the question is."

Siobhán held up her index finger. "The answer is *yes*. They can be considered liable for murder if their actions led to her action of running away, which it obviously did."

"I knew it!" Macdara turned to Molly. "Someone knows all the answers. She's just being stubborn because she doesn't like how they're worded. Now. Which one of us is the real goat?"

Fuming. She was absolutely fuming. She needed to go for a run. Otherwise she was going to get in her vehicle and *it* was going to go for a run. It was going to run over her stubborn rude goat of a husband. And then she'd be the one liable for murder. Road Traffic Act, her arse.

"You two are an interesting couple," Molly said.

"You can be liable for murder, even if you don't actually murder someone?" the delivery lad chimed in, his voice squeaking.

"If your actions lead to the murder, absolutely," Siobhán said. "You can be prosecuted at least."

"Jeez." The lad grimaced. "Tough break."

Molly cocked her head and stared at the lad with a smirk. "Did we ruin murderous plans of yours?"

"What?" He looked and sounded stricken. The world was going to eat him up. "No. Of course not." He gulped.

Eoin returned with two mugs of coffee. Just after he handed one to the delivery lad, his phone dinged. Siobhán took the other mug and wrapped her hands around it. She loved the rich smell even if she didn't need another cup. "A text from Cassidy Ryan," Eoin said, flashing his screen. "*Finally.* She's given me permission to sign for the crate and she says a crew is on its way to install"—his eyes lingered on the crate—"whatever it is." He showed the text to the lad and then grudgingly the lad handed him the paper to sign.

"Cassidy won't even tell you what's inside?" Siobhán asked.

"Other than it's a statue, no," Eoin said. "And before you suggest it, we are not going to take a peek."

"It's against the rules," Molly said.

Siobhán so wanted to peek. She was starting to wonder if she was a bad person compared to this rule-following lot. Maybe that was another reason she wasn't fit to be a detective sergeant. And wasn't it just more paperwork? Did she want more paperwork?

"I cannot wait until tomorrow," Molly said. "We kick off in the town square." Her eyes shone with excitement. "This is my first feature assignment."

"Well done," Macdara said.

"Congrats," Siobhán added. She knew her tone was lackluster, but it was the best she could manage.

Eoin whipped a ticket out of his pocket. "Speaking of which—Siobhán, I was given a VIP ticket for the opening garden tour, but with my restaurant set to open as well, I just can't spare the time."

"She has to study," Macdara said.

"I would love to go." Siobhán snatched up the ticket. "One has to stop and smell the roses."

"Or get pricked by their thorns," Macdara muttered.

Siobhán threw open her arms. "Who doesn't love flowers?" She could act as well as the rest of them.

"Not just flowers," Molly interjected. "This year, each garden has to incorporate a water feature—and there will be shrubbery, and statues and garden sculptures—I can't wait to see what everyone has created!"

Everyone slowly turned to stare at the crate.

"Whatever it is," Eoin said, "Cassidy Ryan swears it's a real showstopper."

Chapter 3

Kilbane's town square was brimming with folks gathered to celebrate the competition's opening day. And even though Siobhán was the lucky VIP who could accompany the judge and the gardeners on the opening tour, the event kicked off in the town square so that the public could get into the spirit of things and cheer them on. Siobhán was thrilled to be there on her own. Macdara had spent the night on the sofa. Maybe some time apart would heal their rift. That is, if he apologized profusely, of course.

In the distance, the bells of Saint Mary's chimed. It was ten in the morning. Horticulturist, and this year's judge, Larry Lorcan stood on a bespoke stage at the top of the square, grinning as Finnoula Connor stepped up to the podium. Despite being a slip of a woman in her sixties, she was a force of nature clad in a floral print dress. She lifted her hands, at ease with the spotlight, and the crowd hushed. "Welcome one and all to Kilbane's Top Garden Contest!" Applause rang out and the crowd leaned in eagerly. "Every year we see the passion of the community and our gardeners blossom before our very eyes." Laughter and more applause rang out. "Today we are honored to have with us a man who needs no introduction in the plant world, esteemed gardener in his own right and owner of our beloved Lorcan Nursery, Mr. Larry Lorcan."

Larry bowed and then waved as polite applause rang out. Standing side by side they made a funny pair. Finnoula seemed almost like a child planted next to a big old bear. Finnoula pinned a blue ribbon on Larry's broad chest and stepped back to admire it. JUDGE was embossed in shiny gold. Larry stood tall and proud as Molly took his photo after which Larry gently pushed Finnoula out of the spotlight. "I look forward to the creativity and designs our gardeners have cultivated this year." His voice, deep and booming, echoed through the town square. Finnoula grinned and gave a thumbs-up. "And I promise to be an impartial judge."

"Even when it comes to Cassidy Ryan?" a man yelled out. Rumor had it that Larry Lorcan had a crush on the vixen. Then again, the same could be said for many men in town.

Larry turned seven shades of red. "I will treat everyone *equally*." He certainly flustered easily. Folks were already dishing out the dirt. It would certainly be an interesting competition.

Finnoula waved a pair of gardening gloves as if trying to settle the crowd. Surprisingly it worked. She had their rapt attention. "The first garden we will tour is Sean Bell's." She grinned as she looked to the contestants gathered in the front row. Finnoula's smile evaporated as she began to count them. "Sean Bell?" she yelled. Apparently he was not among them. She lifted her chin to the crowd. "Are you hiding out there?" Heads began to turn as folks searched the crowd for the missing gardener.

Finnoula glanced at her watch, then at Larry Lorcan. "It looks like someone overslept."

"If he's still working on his garden, he's disqualified," a

female gardener said. "Right?" She was heavyset with rosy cheeks. Her hair was in braids and her apron read: I'M SO EXCITED I WET MY PLANTS.

"He's not the only one missing," a thin older man beside her said. Siobhán recognized him straightaway. Teagan Moore. In his late fifties and spry, he generally kept to himself except until his roses were in bloom. Then he became a social butterfly as throngs of people stopped by his garden on a daily basis to fawn over them. "I'm sure you've all noticed Cassidy is absent as well."

"Indeed, we seem to be missing Cassidy Ryan and Sean Bell," Finnoula observed. "I suppose we should wait. But no more than five minutes."

"In the meantime, can I film the rest of the participants?" Molly asked, aiming her smart phone in their direction. "Would you mind giving your names and a brief description of your gardens?" The gardeners just stared at her. "Without giving too much away, of course."

"I'm sure we can accommodate that," Larry Lorcan said with an infectious grin. "All publicity is good publicity!"

"Fantastic." Molly held up her hands and peered at the gardeners as if getting a picture into frame. Given King John's Castle was behind them, it would make for a nice photo. "Mr. Lorcan," Molly said, dropping her hands, "I'd like to begin with you."

Larry Lorcan removed his cap, and smiled, then nervously put it back on. A slight wind had kicked up and the sun was hiding behind gray clouds, but there was no sign of rain, and a floral scent from nearby planters hovered in the air.

"Mr. Lorcan," Molly said. "I understand this is your first year judging the Kilbane Garden Contest?"

Larry poked at his ribbon. "*Judge* Lorcan," he corrected.

"And it's Kilbane's Top Garden Contest, dear," Finnoula added.

Molly turned red. "Of course. *Judge Lorcan*. Kilbane's

Top Garden Contest." She flicked Finnoula a look, who responded by pursing her lips and nodding as if resigning herself to Molly's incompetence. Siobhán wondered if she'd won the past three years in a row by bullying everyone. Then again, a reporter did need to be factual.

"It is indeed my first year judging the garden competition," Larry said, flashing his teeth. "But I've always been a big fan."

"Did these gardeners purchase any of their flowers and plants and accessories from your nursery?" The spirited reporter glanced at her notes, her lips curling into the smile of someone about to catch an animal in her trap. "Lorcan's Nursery?"

Larry's mouth dropped open and his full cheeks reddened. "Are you suggesting impropriety?" His left eye began to twitch.

"Of course she's not," Finnoula said. She treated Molly to another look. "What are you playing at?"

Molly was unfazed. "I understand you were first nominated by none other than our front-runner, Finnoula Connor," she continued. A few in the crowd began exchanging glances. Past coverage of this event had been light and fluffy, but Molly seemed to have other plans.

Larry's eye twitch became more pronounced. "I'm honored to be this year's judge," he stammered. "Although with this esteemed group, I have a feeling there's going to be stiff competition."

"Thank you, Judge Lorcan," Molly said. "I'm sure you will be able to be impartial despite the fact that the contestants are purchasing goods for the competition directly from your nursery."

Larry seemed startled, then grinned. "Judge Lorcan," he said. "It really does have a nice ring to it, doesn't it?"

Molly frowned then turned to the gardeners. "Finnoula Connor, would you step up next?"

Finnoula switched places with Larry, but before Molly could ask a question, she held up her hand. "I know I need no introduction. I am Finnoula Connor, the first-prize winner of the garden competition three years in a row." She caught Larry's eye and winked. "But don't hold that against me."

Larry laughed nervously and began looking around as if trying to suss out whether or not it was okay to find Finnoula's comment amusing.

"You've certainly set the bar for the competition," Molly said. "How do you feel about a professional designer taking over the competition this year?"

At the mention of Cassidy Ryan, Finnoula's face soured. "If she's so professional, she would have shown up on time."

"I find it fascinating that both Sean Bell and Cassidy Ryan are missing," the heavyset woman with the jokey-apron said. "Do you reckon they're knocking boots?"

"Nessa O'Neill!" Finnoula said. "Language."

Nessa put her hands on her hips. "I might have said it, but we're all thinking it."

"Are you all upset with Cassidy Ryan?" Molly asked. "Is she like a bad weed?" Siobhán hadn't been imagining it earlier; Molly Murphy enjoyed stirring the pot.

"Let the best garden win," Finnoula said. "Remember, each garden is a book, waiting to be opened, a story to be read. That said, I do think it's only fair to mention that those of us here are *amateur* gardeners. We don't make our living in landscape design. We're just ordinary folks doing extraordinary things." She glanced at her watch several times as if she had somewhere else to be.

"Do you have a favorite flower?" Molly asked. "Anything poisonous growing in your garden this year?"

Finnoula's mouth dropped open. "What are you implying?"

"I'm referring to your blog post," Molly said. "Recently

you wrote about 'the big herb,' alus mór." Molly had done her homework after all. She might be taking the job a bit too seriously but nevertheless Siobhán was impressed. Last year's reporter covered it like the assignment was punishment by plants.

Finnoula visibly relaxed. "Who doesn't have a little foxglove in his or her garden?" she said. "They're beautiful. And they attract bees."

"Bees sting," Molly pointed out.

"Are you introducing us or interrogating us?" Finnoula said. "We have a garden tour to begin. Let me quickly introduce the others—Nessa O'Neill." The heavyset woman grinned and waved to the crowd. "Nessa will be showcasing flowers native to Ireland." Molly didn't look happy to be thwarted, but she didn't interrupt. Finnoula pointed to a tall woman with nice curves standing next to Nessa. "Here we have Alice McCarthy . . ." Alice was a beautiful woman in her thirties with ink-black hair that fell past her shoulders in waves. She lifted a spade in greeting. "Teagan Moore," Finnoula continued. The slim older man didn't bother to address the audience; he simply nodded.

"And there you have it," Finnoula said. "Folks, we will now commence with the private garden tour; however, our dogged reporter, Molly Murphy, will be filming it live, and they'll be playing the recording on big screen in the Kilbane Theatre." The crowd cheered. "The first garden on the list is Sean Bell. And we'll be unveiling it—with or without him."

Chapter 4

A shuttle van ferried the gardeners and Siobhán to the first
stop. Sean Bell lived in a townhouse development that
shared a back field with the other homeowners. They had
given their permission for him to commandeer a large portion of their communal space for his garden installation. It
seemed a bit hypocritical to Siobhán that they were giving
Eoin a hard time about leasing to Cassidy when Sean had
done something similar. But she supposed the fact that he
lived here and wasn't a professional landscape designer was
the major difference. Then again, he was a contractor, with
mad building skills, and everyone was expecting to see his
construction talents in full display. The group exited the
shuttle and were soon standing in front of a white tent,
identical to the one on Siobhán's property. A garden shed
was situated behind it, and it looked as if it had been a recent build.

"Sean Bell?" Larry Lorcan called out. "Are you in there?"

"If you are, you're disqualified," Nessa called out. Alice and
Teagan kept quiet, but the pair exchanged a glance. Finnoula
sighed and twisted her watch around her thin wrist. Molly stood
back, filming them.

Larry pressed his ear to the tent, then turned to the crowd. "I can hear water running—but nothing else."

"I bet he went to town on the water feature," Teagan said. "Typical."

"We should proceed as if Sean is here," Finnoula said. "The rest of us shouldn't be punished for his inability to tell time."

"Maybe he should be disqualified," Alice said quietly. Larry Lorcan held up his index finger. "Let me guess," Alice continued. "Not in the bylines."

Larry nodded and then shrugged.

"We are so rewriting the rules after this," Finnoula said.

Molly dropped her arm and shook it out. Even though she was filming with her smart phone, which certainly wasn't heavy, she seemed to grow weary of holding it in position. Her impatience was palpable. "Shall we begin then, Judge Lorcan?"

"Sean?" Larry called again. "We're going to begin without you." He sighed and nodded to Molly. "Take it away."

Molly held up her selfie stick and spoke into her smart phone. "I'm Molly Murphy with the *Kilbane Times* and we're here at the tent of the first contestant for Kilbane's Top Garden Contest. Sean Bell. Sean's theme is that of a Japanese garden. Will he incorporate a temple? A shrine? A tea ceremony? Let's find out, shall we?" She angled herself for the best view into the tent and nodded at Larry. He reached for the golden rope holding the flaps shut. "One, two, three." Larry pulled on the tassel and the front of the tent fell away.

At first there was silence, and then a collective gasp rippled through the small group. Where there should have been the serenity of a Japanese garden, before them sprawled a chaotic scene. A red temple with a golden bell was situated at the back of the tent, and it would have been a showstopper had its gate not been broken and hanging from its hinges. The golden bell that had presumably once been attached to the top of the temple had crashed to the ground. Stones that laid a path around a gurgling creek were chipped, and more than a few were missing, leaving gaps like neglected teeth. Where there should have been curated plants and thematic sculptures, there was nothing but gaping holes. The shrubbery that presumably had been planted in them were flung to the side in a giant pileup. Tools were strewn around the tent, along with discarded Styrofoam cups and take-away bins. A worktable was still set up on the right side of the tent, covered with more tools, and plants, and dirt, as if Sean had destroyed his own garden and simply walked away.

"Do you think he did this in a mad fit?" Nessa whispered.

Heads snapped toward her. "Why on earth would he do this to himself?" Teagan asked. Apparently everyone was having the same thoughts.

Nessa shrugged. "One never knows what's going on behind closed tents."

"Ladies and gentlemen of Kilbane," Molly said, holding up her selfie stick and speaking into her phone. "What happened to Sean Bell's bell?" She turned it around and zeroed in on the golden bell on the ground before whipping it back to her. "And like Nessa O'Neill wondered—did he do this to his own garden?" She panned the group. "Or is someone amongst us the vandal?"

As the camera panned the gardeners, Nessa looked smug, but the rest of them seemed genuinely perplexed.

"Do you think he's on a bender?" Finnoula asked.

"Sean?" Alice scoffed, flipping a strand of her long dark hair over her shoulder. "Don't be ridiculous."

"I agree," Teagan said. "Sean was very dedicated to this contest." He looked to Siobhán. "There must have been some kind of emergency."

"We could knock on his door," Finnoula said. "Maybe he's in his flat."

Alice wandered over to the creek and knelt beside it. "These poor dears!" she cried. Everyone rushed over to see what she was on about. As they drew closer, Siobhán spotted koi fish swimming in murky waters. "You poor, poor dears," Alice wailed. "They deserve better than this."

Just then Siobhán heard what sounded like someone pounding on a wall. She snapped to attention. "Does anyone else hear that?"

Everyone began to look around and murmur. And then it sounded again, a faint but definite pounding.

"The shed." Siobhán exited the tent and hurried toward it. The pounding grew louder and more frantic. A rake lay across the door, barring it shut. Siobhán quickly removed it, and before she could even open the door, Sean Bell stumbled out with a yell. He plowed into Siobhán, who was still holding the rake, and the pair of them fell to the ground. Sean was a big man and she was crushed by his weight. "Off," she managed to say. "Get off."

"Sorry, sorry." Sean rolled away, and Siobhán pushed the rake off before getting to her feet. Nothing about this morning was going the way she had imagined. The rest of the group hurried over and Teagan Moore helped Sean stand. His overalls, not to mention his handsome face, were covered in sweat and dirt. "Where is she?" Sean demanded, his voice rising. "Where is Cassidy Ryan?"

"Why are you asking for her?" Siobhán asked. "And why didn't you call out for us earlier?"

Sean took in the gardeners and frowned. "I'd been pounding on the shed and screaming for hours. I took a wee break and I must have fallen asleep."

"I think you would know whether or not you fell asleep," Teagan Moore pointed out.

"I just told you I fell asleep. Thankfully I heard Alice cry out." He ran a hand through his mussed-up hair. "Cassidy Ryan locked me in here—I'm sure of it."

"Do you know that for a fact?" Molly Murphy asked as she closed in, recording with her phone.

Sean ignored her and barreled over to his garden. As he took in the destruction, his mouth dropped open. He put his hands atop his head, and for a moment Siobhán thought she was about to see a grown man pull his own hair out. "Look what she did!" He pointed as if they couldn't see the destruction for themselves. "It's ruined. Me garden is ruined." He whirled around, his eyes wild with rage. "I'm going to kill her."

"Take me through what happened," Siobhán said, fumbling in her handbag for a notepad and biro. Molly Murphy wasn't the only one that could take notes.

He stared at her. "Is that why you're here, Garda?" He took in her civilian clothes and frowned. "Are you on duty?"

"No," Siobhán replied. "I'm simply a guest of the garden tour."

"I've been locked in that shed since last night," Sean said. The others gasped. "And look what she did to me beautiful shrubbery!" He walked over and hovered over the discarded pile. "I'm so sorry, my sweet, sweet shrubs." He spoke as if talking to a beloved child. "The bad, bad woman will pay for this. She will pay!"

Alice moved to the creek and put her back to it as if she was trying to hide the stressed-out koi. Given his emotional state, it wasn't a bad idea.

"The temple is class," Teagan said, stepping forward. "I like the gold bell." He gulped. "We can help you rehang it. We can help you fix all of this." He turned to his fellow gardeners. "Isn't that right?" Reluctantly they all nodded their agreement.

Sean stared at the bell on the ground. "It wasn't gold," he said. "It was *black*." He advanced toward the bell, shaking his head. "It's not mine. It's not my bell." Once again, he looked at Siobhán. "Who did this to me?"

"You were working on the garden last night, and then what happened?" Siobhán asked.

"It was finished. It was *perfect.* I only had to clear away me worktable and tools, but everything else was on point." He suddenly noticed the creek, moved Alice aside, and then screamed. "My koi!" He fell to his knees and peered in. "You poor things. This water was crystal clear. Now look! I'm going to kill her," he sobbed. "I'm going to kill her."

"Look," Nessa O'Neill said, gently helping Sean to his feet. "They're okay, and we'll definitely get them moved." She glanced at the fish as if waiting for them to contradict her. "Everyone knows I'm not on Team Cassidy. But why are you so convinced that she's the one who messed with your garden?"

"Because I got into a row with her yesterday morning," Sean said. "She came by and was trying to snoop into my tent!" The others began to murmur.

Finnoula stepped up. "Now *that* is definitely against the rules." She looked to Larry Lorcan. "Judge?"

"Do you have any proof?" Larry said.

"Did you *see* her tampering with your garden?" Molly asked.

"How could I see her if I was locked in the shed?" Sean retorted. Molly hunched her shoulders and took a step back. Sean wiped his forehead with the back of his arm. "I'm sorry," he said. "I didn't mean to snap at any of you. But who else would do this to me?"

"Snooping into your tent is one thing," Siobhán said. "But can you think of any possible motive for this kind of destruction? I'm not saying it excuses what's been done. But if I'm to accuse anyone, I'm going to need hard evidence."

"As the judge of you all, I concur," Larry said.

Sean stared at his feet, his face reddening. "After she came sniffing around, I kind of gave out to her."

Siobhán nodded and jotted down a note. She couldn't help but notice Molly Murphy was edging closer, no doubt doing a little snooping of her own. "What exactly did you say to Cassidy Ryan?"

"I told her she had no business being here and that I was going to make sure she was disqualified."

Teagan turned to Nessa. "And you thought they were knocking boots," he said with a smirk.

"What?" Sean said. "You said that?" Nessa turned twelve shades of red and shrugged. Sean shook his fist at the heavens. "Outrageous!"

"And surprise, surprise, Cassidy is nowhere to be seen," Alice said. "She must have known the trouble she'd be in for locking you in the shed."

"See?" Sean said, pointing toward Alice and nodding. "Cassidy is missing. There's your proof!"

"Can you please take us through your day just before and up to being locked in the shed?" Siobhán asked.

Sean crossed his arms. "I had just put the finishing touches on me garden, and I was wearing headphones. Cranking me music. I entered the shed and was putting away me tools, and the next thing I knew the door had slammed shut. No matter what I tried I couldn't open it."

"Someone barred it with a rake," Alice said.

"Not someone," Sean cried. "Cassidy Ryan!"

"Wait a minute," Siobhán said. "I'm missing the part where you caught Cassidy snooping."

"That was earlier."

"How much earlier?"

Sean shook his head. "I suppose she was here around noon yesterday. It was nearly half-three when I was locked in the shed. She must have left and come back. Or maybe she only *pretended* to leave."

"You've been locked in that shed since half-three yesterday and your wife didn't notice?" Alice asked. It was an excellent question. Siobhán was irritated with her husband at the moment, but she always knew where he was. And if he didn't come home, she'd be heading up a search party.

Sean frowned, then looked toward the apartments. "It was the final evening," he said. "I told her I was pulling an all-nighter." But Alice had planted a seed of doubt in Sean. He was now wondering if his wife shared the blame; it was written all over his face.

Siobhán glanced at the side of the building that faced them. "Are there any security cameras on the grounds?"

Sean nodded. "But they all face the building and the car park. No one ever saw the need to watch the field." He gave her a look as if she should know better.

"What if Cassidy is snooping on everyone else's gardens as we speak?" Teagan said. "If she touches me roses, she's dead."

"Are you going to do something, Detective Sergeant?" Sean said.

"She's not a detective *yet*," Molly said. "She still has to pass her exams."

Siobhán glared at her. "Not helpful."

"Sorry," Molly said. "Just trying to be factual."

"This is theft—and . . . and *kidnapping!*" Sean cried out. "Locking me away adds up to kidnapping, does it not?"

It certainly did. "We'll get to the bottom of it," Siobhán said.

"I can keep the koi in my pond until Sean figures out a better home," Nessa volunteered.

Siobhán glanced at Sean. "Would you?" he said. "Thank you. I won't forget this."

Nessa blushed. "Not a bother."

He glanced at his shed. "I don't have plastic bags."

"I'll tell the guards to bring some and they can scoop them out and give them to you," Siobhán said to Nessa. "I still cannot have you walking around the crime scene." Nessa nodded and took a step back.

"Do you hear that, ladies and gentlemen?" Molly announced. "We have ourselves a crime scene." She looked all for it. "Viewers ratings are going to soar!" She was brimming with excitement. This time several gardeners threw her a dirty look.

"We'd better check on the other gardens," Siobhán said. "Just in case."

Chapter 5

"I live the closest," Teagan said. "And I can't concentrate knowing me roses could be in danger."

"Distance is irrelevant," Finnoula said. "I've nearly spent my entire savings on my garden!"

Alice McCarthy made sure to join in. "I have sculptures to check up on."

Nessa stepped up. "We're *all* worried about our gardens."

"But there is only one shuttle van," Teagan said.

"It's more than likely that someone did this to Sean Bell and only Sean Bell," Siobhán said. "There is only one shuttle van, and if Teagan lives the closest, we'll go there first."

"Torture!" Finnoula said.

Siobhán understood how they all felt but there was nothing she could do. In the end, everything *did* come down to law and order. "If your gardens are destroyed and you want me to catch the person who did this, I can't have you trampling all over the crime scenes."

"Crime scenes," Molly said. "Did you hear that, folks? *Plural.* Crime *scenes.*" She beamed as everyone stared at her.

* * *

Siobhán had called into the station on the ride to town, and as promised Garda Aretta Dabiri was waiting on the footpath on Sarsfield Street with a protective suit, booties, and gloves. Teagan's garden was nearby. *Just in case.* Aretta handed everything to Siobhán.

"Thanks a million." This wasn't what she had in mind when Eoin gifted her the VIP ticket. Lucky her.

"Dubious start to the garden competition," Aretta said, taking in the crowd developing on the footpath. "I have a call out to your other half, but Eoin said he went for a run."

Siobhán gave a nod; she didn't want to discuss Macdara. The sooner he apologized, the better. "Did everyone hear Molly's reporting?" Even as Siobhán asked the question, she knew the answer. The glory of live streaming. Sarsfield Street had filled up quickly, and she could already feel the gossip broiling.

Aretta nodded. "If there's a soul in town who missed it, we should do a health check on them."

Siobhán glanced down the small pathway to the back of Teagan's property. "Here goes nothing."

Siobhán pulled the golden tassel and the flap on Teagan Moore's tent fell away. Her first reaction was awe. The ground was covered in rose petals. Red, orange, pink, yellow, white. It was as if the Irish skies had rained rose petals. But one look at the actual rosebushes, heads firmly plucked off, leaving nothing but stems and thorns, and she knew that indeed she was looking at another vandalized garden. His fountain, which housed a cherub balancing on one foot and spitting water out of its mouth, now spewed mud as if the poor thing had a terrible case of food poisoning. The concrete base was choked with roses and making gurgling sounds. At the base of the fountain lay a golden rose. Was

that the official golden rose that was supposed to be given
to the winner at the end? She lifted it and held it up. It certainly looked like the one given to the winner. Siobhán
thought of the golden bell. Sean insisted his original one
had been black. Slightly odd . . . She dropped the golden
rose into an evidence bag just as someone cried out from behind her. Siobhán whirled around to see Teagan Moore taking in the destruction. He fell to his knees and started to
sob. "Why did I ever sign up for this? Why? Why? Why?"
She knew he wanted to race inside and touch them. She was
proud of him for restraining himself. Siobhán helped him
up and accompanied him to the footpath where the other
gardeners waited. The others gasped and gathered around
to comfort Teagan. "My roses were innocent," he crooned.
"They were so innocent!"

"We'll get Cassidy," Nessa said. "She won't get away
with this."

Someone gasped, and Siobhán turned to see Finnoula
pointing at the evidence bag. "Is that . . . the golden rose?"
Her mouth dropped open and she flicked a look to Teagan.

He was already shaking his head. "I didn't have anything
like that in me garden," he said. "Someone must have put it
there. That is *after* destroying all me rosebushes!"

Alice gazed at Siobhán with pleading eyes. "She'll be arrested, won't she?"

"Absolutely she'll be arrested," Finnoula said.

Sean Bell, still dirty from being locked in a shed overnight, looked feverishly around the crowd. "Where in the
world is she hiding?"

"Please," Siobhán said. "I do not want to hear any more
accusations without proof."

Nessa pursed her lips.

Everything is certainly not coming up roses, Siobhán
thought.

Siobhán pulled Teagan over to the side, away from the others. He was still crying. She felt a deep well of empathy. These gardeners were artists, and it must be soul crushing to have their months of hard work destroyed. And Teagan's roses were like his children. "I'm so sorry for your loss," she said. Teagan blew his nose and the tears started up again. "When is the last time you saw this garden intact?"

"Last night," he said. "I shut the flaps around six in the evening, just as the sun was setting. It was perfect. It was a winner."

"You're sure it was six P.M.?"

Teagan nodded. "I heard the bells of Saint Mary's chiming. It was six."

At half-three someone had locked Sean Bell in the shed and destroyed his garden. Had this been his or her second stop? "Was there anyone else around?"

Teagan glanced up at his building, a semidetached two-story limestone. The back garden was not visible from the front. But everyone knew about the garden, and when his roses were in bloom, folks would walk down the narrow passageway to the left of the building. Teagan had eventually made his peace with that, and for this year's contest, he had even constructed a mosaic of roses leading directly to the back, and a sign out front pointing to it. Those tiles had been scratched and shattered. There was no doubt it was an act of hate. Siobhán glanced at the ground floor of his building where Raven, a charity shop, resided. The signage, no surprise, was a rendering of a raven, a gleam in his eye as if he was plotting revenge against an unknown enemy. It was actually a lovely shop and their proceeds went to a local bird sanctuary. She was going to have to pop in at some point and see if anyone saw Cassidy Ryan sneaking around.

"There were a few heads in the shop," Teagan said, gesturing to it. "Finnoula Connor, for one. I could see her through the window." He shook his head. "But there was no one in me back garden, if that's what you're asking."

"Did you see Cassidy Ryan yesterday?" Finnoula asked, barging into the questioning.

Siobhán had a feeling she was going to have a number of green-thumbed-sleuths involved in this case and she was going to have to nip them in the bud. If this wasn't such a serious moment, she would have laughed at the unintentional pun.

"I've barely seen or spoken to Cassidy Ryan since this entire thing began," Teagan said. "If she's guilty I'll be the first to condemn her, but I'm not going to join some kind of a witch hunt." He crossed his arms and lasered in on Finnoula. "However . . . I did see *you* in the shop."

"Is that a crime?" Finnoula narrowed her eyes. "I was dropping off a bouquet of flowers. Cut fresh from my garden."

"I'm sure your roses were beautiful," Nessa said. "I'm so sorry, Teagan."

"Do you think all of our gardens are ruined?" Alice said. "I spent so much time on my *Alice in Wonderland* sculptures!"

"Please have spared mine," Nessa cried. "Please!" She looked as if she wanted to take off running.

"The guards are now going to examine the rest of the gardens," Siobhán said. "You can accompany them to the outside perimeter of your tents, but no farther. I know you're all tempted to have the first look, but if you want this perpetrator caught, you cannot enter your gardens. If there has been vandalism, then it is an official crime scene."

It wasn't what the gardeners wanted to hear; she could feel their anxiety building. Nessa grabbed a hand on each side of her—Alice's and Finnoula's. She must have squeezed hard, from the expression on their faces. "We'll get through this together," Nessa said. "Bless our gardens, each and every one."

Molly began to circle them. "We've now discovered the second garden to be destroyed, that of Teagan Moore who is known for his prize-winning roses."

Siobhán gestured for Aretta, who came over straight-away.

"I think after they check on their gardens we should shuttle everyone to Eoin's restaurant while the guards divide and conquer." This way Siobhán could check on Cassidy Ryan's garden and see if they could find her to clear this all up. "Can you also assign a few guards to each garden—inform them not to enter, just release the flap and report back with photos as to whether or not they've been disturbed?"

Aretta gave a prompt nod. "I'm on it."

"Would you also organize the shuttle to the farm when they're all ready? I'm going to take a garda car."

"Not a bother."

Siobhán placed a hand on her shoulder. "You're the best."

Aretta grinned. "Just remember that when I'm calling you Detective Sergeant O'Sullivan."

By the time Siobhán pulled into their farm, her phone was already blowing up with texts. The first photo was from the guard assigned to Nessa O'Neill's garden. Siobhán sat in the car, staring at the photograph, gobsmacked. Someone had released a herd of goats into the small space, and predictably, they had gone to town. Apparently flowers native to Ireland were yummy, for the goats were chomping away. Her water feature was a bathtub filled with floating flowers—and in the midst of it were two goats, who looked as if they were taking the bath of their lives.

"Could any of these be poisonous to them?" Siobhán texted.

"Nessa O'Neill has already called a vet," the garda texted back immediately. "But they seem happy-out." And then a hand reached for the camera, yanking it away with a war cry. Nessa's face filled the screen.

"Whoever you are—you're going to pay for this. You're going to pay." Siobhán groaned. Apparently her command that they stay quietly in the background was being ignored. Just as Siobhán exited her vehicle, her phone dinged again. She pulled up the next video as she began walking to Cassidy's tent. Alice McCarthy's garden. Siobhán stopped and pressed Play.

It was obvious that the scene in front of her was supposed to have been an *Alice in Wonderland* theme, clever and delightful. But it too was destroyed. A tea party had been set up at a table in the middle of the tent. But now the table was lying on its side along with all four chairs. Shattered remains of delicate teacups and plates adorned the tipped-over furniture. A beautiful figurine of Alice herself was lying sideways under a waterfall, as if she'd passed out cold. The rabbit figurine stood over Alice, his pocket watch falling out of his little paw and dangling over her face. The pocket watch was swaying back and forth as if he was hypnotizing the prone Alice into eternity. And like the other gardens, all the beautiful flowers had been shredded and— most shocking of all—someone had ferociously carved a message into the shrubbery: EAT ME. This wasn't just vandalism; this was bordering on psychotic. Whoever had done this either had a team of helpers, or he or she had been at it all night. Who hated these gardeners this much and why?

All was quiet as Siobhán reached Cassidy Ryan's tent. The enormous crate had vanished. The crew must have arrived to set up the statue. But if they had found the garden destroyed, why hadn't they called the guards? Or why hadn't Eoin called her?

The video of Finnoula's garden was the last to come in. Siobhán once again clicked Play. She didn't think she could be shocked anymore, but Finnoula's video almost made her drop her phone. The entire garden was flooded. Everything was floating. Water could still be heard running in the background along with frantic yelling as people tried to figure out how to turn it off. And strangely, golden trophies were floating all over the place—as if every first-place contest Finnoula had won had been tossed into what could only be described as a lake. It was devastating. If Siobhán didn't catch this perpetrator, there was going to be war. She cut off the feed; it was time to face the garden in front of her.

As she took hold of the tassel, she glanced toward the restaurant. Eoin had no doubt heard from Aretta and was preparing to host the distraught gardeners. He was probably tempted to be out here to have a gawk at the tent, and she was proud of him for his restraint. Macdara was nowhere in sight; he would be in for a surprise when he returned from his run. Siobhán grabbed the tassel, took a deep breath, and pulled. As she took in the scene before her, she was shocked yet again.

In front of her was a garden that looked as if it belonged in heaven. Bursting with color, and shapes, and meticulous design. Not a blade of grass was out of place. There was a lot to take in, but what was stealing her attention at the moment was the jaw-dropping centerpiece—the statue from the crate. It was a full-size golden statue of a woman. She stood in the center of all the glory, hands outstretched, and little birds resting in her palms. Above her hung a chalice, tipped toward a second chalice below her. Water flowed from the one above to the one below, and then finally splashed into a puddle at the statue's feet. And then she noticed something else. Something strangely familiar. Scratch that—several somethings strangely familiar. There was a small Japanese temple with a black bell in the left-hand corner. Hadn't Sean said his bell was black? Magnificent rosebushes lined the right-hand side. A nod to Teagan Moore? Another grouping in the upper left corner had a sign that read: NATIVE TO IRELAND. A nod to Nessa O'Neill? Was there anything reminiscent of Alice McCarthy's garden? And sure enough, as she looked, she finally spotted it—a rabbit with a pocket watch. This one seemed to be staring straight at Siobhán and grinning. He looked as if he wasn't late to the party at all; he'd been early. The reason Cassidy Ryan—or *someone*—had snooped on the other gardens became apparent. It appeared as though Cassidy Ryan was a copycat.

Even though not a single thing in this garden looked disturbed, Siobhán played it safe and quickly suited up again. She approached the golden statue, holding up her phone to record. If Cassidy Ryan had destroyed the other gardens—what in the world did she hope to gain from it? She couldn't possibly think she'd take the prize—especially when everyone suspected her of being the vandal. She had to know this would end in her arrest. To what end? Siobhán couldn't help herself; she had to get a closer look at this stunning statue. It couldn't possibly be real gold, although hadn't the delivery lad said it was heavy?

Up close it was even more remarkable. Such a human face. But now that Siobhán could see every detail, she knew immediately it wasn't real gold—it was spray paint. And something else. Beneath the gold, she saw bits of . . . frost? Had this statue been frozen? How odd. Portions of it were already beginning to melt. Siobhán studied the flowing hair, also spray-painted gold. There was at least one spot that the painter had missed. Sticking out from all the glittered paint, was a strand of platinum blond hair. Just like Cassidy

Ryan's. Was this supposed to be a replica of her? Had she given this statue a wig? Now that a comparison had been made, Siobhán realized that the voluptuous statue indeed looked like a statue of Cassidy Ryan. Her height, her curves, her cleavage. Although it was stunning, there was no doubt someone would point out it was quite a vain thing to emboss yourself in gold—and place it in the center of your garden. Siobhán found herself walking around the statue. When she reached the back, she stopped cold. A trellis of flowers had been shimmied against the back of the statue as if she was leaning on it. Siobhán made her way all the way around, then stopped when she reached the statue's left side. That's when she saw a wedding ring on the middle finger of the statue's left hand. Odder yet, it was a man's wedding ring. Someone had wrapped twine around it so it would fit. Siobhán reached up to touch it.

Her fingers brushed the ring, and as she tried to move the band back to the end of the finger, chips of ice and then paint scraped away with it. Beneath the layers, Siobhán saw skin. Human skin. Instinctively she backed away. "No," she whispered. "No." She then did what she'd done to all her siblings, something they each despised when they were younger, except Ciarán, who tolerated almost anything. Siobhán brought her gloved thumb up to the statue's cheek and began to rub. "Please, no," she said as she gently smudged the golden paint. *Please let me be wrong.* But underneath, a grotesque truth emerged. The cheek was cold, but there was no faking human flesh. As she rubbed, additional pale skin flashed. Siobhán stepped back as her heart thudded in her chest. "No," she said aloud. "No, no, no." Her cries did not alter the reality in front of her face. The gentle curves of Cassidy Ryan's body had been forever immortalized in a posture of fairy-tale joy. There was no denying it. Siobhán was looking at none other than the spray-painted, frosted-over corpse of Cassidy Ryan.

Chapter 6

Siobhán and Macdara stood with Aretta in front of The Six as guards cordoned off the tent. The gardeners were going to gather here soon, but it was taking longer to coordinate the shuttle van, and there had been no need for Aretta to wait around with the gardeners. Eoin, who had understandably freaked out over the incident, had bummed a cigarette off one of the waiters and was out back puffing away. It took everything Siobhán had not to rip it out of his mouth and tell him he was grounded. But he was a grown man (whether she liked it or not), and these were extreme circumstances, to say the least.

Eoin had been fond of Cassidy Ryan—maybe her only friend in this competition—and now he was dealing with some dark emotions. Grief because she had been murdered, but also guilt—for how could he help but feel crushing disappointment for himself? He'd worked so hard and waited so long for his restaurant to open. He'd waited ages for all the permits, and he had tackled obstacle after obstacle and prevailed. This was supposed to have been his time to celebrate. Murder was hardly ever convenient. They had also taken his mobile phone off him to have a look at the text

Cassidy Ryan had sent him yesterday when he'd tried to reach her in regard to the crate. But of course it wasn't actually Cassidy Ryan who texted him, was it? They had all gathered around the crate, not knowing what lay inside. The killer must have used her phone to reply to Eoin. Why? Not that everything killers did made sense, but why wouldn't he or she just ignore his calls and texts?

This killer wanted to delay the "unveiling." He or she wanted to make a grand show of it. Most likely with everyone in town gathered around to be awed by the golden statue before horrifying them.

Siobhán relayed her thoughts to the team and Macdara agreed that finding Cassidy's phone would be a top priority. "Maybe it's at her place," he said.

Cassidy had been renting a cottage just outside of town. A warrant to search the premises would be requested, and they would try and get ahold of the landlord.

Given that Dr. Jeanie Brady, the state pathologist, wouldn't arrive until tomorrow afternoon at the earliest, they would have to focus their attention on the other gardens. And the gardeners themselves would have to be relocated to the Kilbane Inn, for even their homes were now part of the investigation. They had reached the owners of the inn, identical twin sisters Emma and Eileen, and they had confirmed rooms were available and said they would hurry to get them ready.

They would also need to question "Judge" Lorcan. All the gardeners had used his nursery to procure items for their gardens. They would need to comb through the security tapes in his nursery as well. And what of the lad who delivered the crate? They would need to speak with him. But how? Siobhán realized that his uniform had been plain—there had been no identifiers at all. What company was he with? He'd taken a signature from Eoin, but she had been standing right there and the lad hadn't given him any kind of receipt. Was he truly a delivery person, or had he helped pull off a crime right in front of their very noses? If that was the case, it wasn't going to look good for either herself or Macdara.

"Given we now have multiple crime scenes," Siobhán said, "do we have the resources?" She addressed her question to Aretta, who was wedged between herself and Macdara. No doubt she'd picked up on the tension between them.

"This is how we're going to play it?" Macdara asked, also speaking to Aretta.

Aretta squinted and shook her head. "Has it frozen over below?" she said. "I did not expect this." Siobhán knew Aretta wanted to be with Eoin right now, comforting him. They were a new couple, still flying under the radar. But she had a job to do—they all did—and finding the killer was the best way to help Eoin.

"If *someone* would like to profusely apologize, now would be the time," Siobhán said.

"I second that!" Macdara said. Both waited.

"There are times I wish I drank," Aretta said. She turned to Macdara. "Detective Sergeant, do we have enough guards to oversee each tent?" There was only a trace of sarcasm as Aretta paraphrased Siobhán's question; she was a consummate professional.

"We're going to be stretched thin," Macdara said. "But we'll manage."

"Brilliant," Siobhán said. "Tell him we shall proceed as normal."

"This is normal?" Aretta asked. She was answered with silence on either side of her. "Do you think one person could have done all this?" Aretta asked. "Or are we looking at multiple perpetrators?"

"I was wondering that meself," Macdara said.

"Ditto," Siobhán said. "I think we need to figure out how

someone destroyed these gardens without anyone knowing, and how many people were involved." *Or used as pawns.* It was possible the delivery lad and who knew how many others had been unknowingly wrapped into this murder plot. "According to Sean Bell, Cassidy Ryan visited him at noon." She shuddered as the image of the golden corpse flashed in her mind. "I'd be tempted to say Sean Bell was lying, because of course it couldn't have been Cassidy who stopped by, but Eoin thought he saw her Thursday morning as well."

"Eoin saw her from a distance," Macdara said. "You said Sean Bell actually exchanged words with her?"

"I believe he said he caught her trying to peek in on his garden. I'm not sure how many words they exchanged."

"Someone had been impersonating her," Aretta said. "And whoever it was, she fooled both Eoin and Sean."

Siobhán nodded. "Unless Cassidy Ryan has an identical twin, that's the only explanation." Siobhán began to pace. "Then, at half-three, someone locked Sean in his shed. He claimed it had to be Cassidy, but of course he was inside the shed when the door was barricaded, so he was only making an assumption. Teagan Moore said it was six P.M. when he closed up his garden. He mentioned seeing Finnoula Connor in Raven as he was closing up his installation."

"Someone did not have much time to pull this off," Macdara said. "It had to be planned well in advance."

"It was quite elaborate," Siobhán agreed. It would have required coordination and helpers. That actually bode well for them—the more people that were in on this, willingly or not, the higher the chance that information would leak. It was human nature; bottled-up secrets were like poison. "Just turning Cassidy Ryan into a golden statue, not to mention putting her in a deep freeze somewhere, then placing her in a crate and having it delivered would have taken time." She chewed on her lip. "We also need to figure out how to find that delivery lad. I didn't even catch which service he worked for." *If he worked for one at all.*

Macdara mulled it over. "His uniform was tan and plain, but Garda O'Sullivan is correct. It didn't have any logo on it."

"Should we look at who had the simplest garden?" Aretta asked. "Maybe that person had time to finish theirs and destroy the others."

"I think we'll find that all of these gardens were complex," Siobhán said. "But it's something to keep in mind."

"They were also each allotted a crew to help with the garden," Macdara said. "We could find out who used help the most—interview the crew members, see who was absent the longest."

"Could one of the crew members be guilty?" Aretta asked.

"At this point anything is possible," Siobhán said. "But whoever did this had a strong connection to Cassidy Ryan. And I believe the damage they've done, not to mention the fact that they turned Cassidy Ryan into a statue—that shows rage."

"And showmanship," Macdara added.

"Exactly." Siobhán couldn't help but agree.

In the distance, she saw Eoin heading back to the restaurant, his shoulders slumped. He would be forced to perk up once all the gardeners arrived and gathered in his restaurant. It would at least keep him busy.

Macdara stared at Cassidy's tent. "Do you think it *was* Cassidy who destroyed the other gardens? Maybe one of the gardeners caught her in the act."

"That's an interesting theory," Siobhán said. "But between the elaborate spray paint and the crate . . ."

"It seems too planned out," Macdara finished. "And someone wanted us to believe that she was alive yesterday at noon."

"I'll be eager to hear from Dr. Jeanie Brady as to the cause of death, not to mention the time," Siobhán said. There had been no blood, and even though she'd been painted gold, there were no visible wounds. Poison? Something like foxglove or nightshade? Every single one of these gardeners had poison at their fingertips.

"A killer has sewn darkness into the soil," Macdara said. "Pun intended."

"And it's going to be up to us to root them out," Siobhán tagged on. "And ditto."

Chapter 7

Twilight had descended by the time the remaining gardeners and judge assembled in The Six, splashing the skies with strips of lavender and pinks. It was as if the heavens were paying homage to the garden competition, or perhaps Cassidy Ryan herself. Eoin and his sous-chef were in the midst of preparing the dinner he had planned for his soft opening. Not only had these gardeners gone all day without a proper meal, Eoin informed Siobhán that otherwise all the food would go to waste. And given the grim news they had to deliver, the least they could do was feed them.

Heads swiveled around the old dairy barn-turned-restaurant, and those who were familiar with its former state were amazed by the transformation. The beamed rafters, the white brick walls with black-and-white photographs of the Irish countryside, the lovely wide-planked pine floors. A pink neon sign hung behind the hostess table read: THE SIX. Instinctively, many gathered around the centerpiece, a gas fireplace encased in glass that could be viewed from all sides. Even though it was summer, evenings cooled down, and it was hard to beat the comfort of a fire, even if it wasn't wood burning. It even crackled, a sound which always soothed Siobhán. Communal farm tables were set up all throughout the restaurant while floor-to-ceiling windows invited the outside in. One could see green fields and sloping hills, and given the fact that windows were situated on all sides, they would catch both sunrises and sunsets. The restaurant was going to be a smash hit, even if things were once again delayed. Siobhán joined the gardeners while Macdara and Aretta strategized at a nearby table. A hush fell over them as Siobhán approached, and she could see the curiosity in their eyes.

"Did you find that wicked woman?" Finnoula asked.

"Did she confess?" Nessa said.

"There's crime scene tape around her garden too," Sean said. "She could be a victim along with the rest of us."

"Victim?" Finnoula said. "That will be the day."

Teagan sniffled; it appeared he wasn't finished crying over his roses. Larry Lorcan's eyes were glued to the opening into the kitchen, as the smells and sounds of fine dining wafted out. They were going to hear the grim news sooner than later, and there was no use putting it off any longer.

"We did indeed locate Cassidy Ryan," Siobhán began. They all began talking at once. Siobhán held up a hand, blocking the myriad of questions that were poised to fly her way. "There's no easy way to say this. Cassidy Ryan was murdered." At first there was silence; even Molly Murphy put her selfie stick down as her mouth dropped open.

"You're joking, right?" Nessa O'Neill said. "This is some kind of sick joke." She looked around as if to suss out who was in on it.

"What do you mean 'murdered'?" Sean said, as if the concept was foreign to him. "How?" His eyes fell to the tent, and before Siobhán could stop him, he'd rushed to the window. "Is she . . . in there?" He turned back to the group. They all turned to the window that faced Cassidy Ryan's tent.

"She is in the tent," Siobhán said. The group let out a

collective gasp. "The state pathologist will arrive tomorrow to examine the scene. Given that this is now a murder investigation, we will not be able to discuss the details with you just yet." She took in the faces around her, wondering which one of them was a killer.

"You couldn't have waited to deliver this horrific news until after we ate?" Larry said.

"Are you saying you no longer want a meal?" Siobhán asked.

He shook his head. "Carry on."

"We've arranged for all of you to spend the next few days at the Kilbane Inn."

"What?" Finnoula sputtered. "*Why?*"

"Because guards will be crawling all over our properties," Teagan Moore said. "Does this mean you're going to enter our residences?"

"Not a chance," Alice McCarthy said. "What does my home or my garden for that matter have to do with Cassidy Ryan's murder?"

"They can't enter our homes without a warrant," Nessa said.

"We do want to search your homes," Siobhán said. "And we do need a warrant—but only if you refuse to cooperate."

"Are you saying that if we don't cooperate, that will cast suspicion on us?" Nessa chewed on a fingernail.

"It would be greatly appreciated if you give us permission to search your homes," Siobhán said. "If someone broke into your gardens, who's to say that they didn't also break into your homes?" The contestants began eyeing each other. "After dinner, a guard will accompany you to your places so you can pack a bag for your stay at the inn."

"You can search mine all you like," Sean said. "I for one have nothing to hide." He held up his index finger. "But I would appreciate it if you wouldn't linger in the drawers of me bedside table." The side of his neck flushed red.

"Surely you don't think it's one of us?" Finnoula cried.

"We've all been working on our gardens," Alice agreed. "Who has time to murder anyone?"

Finnoula seared her with a look. Apparently she wasn't finished. "I know this was gearing up to be a very competitive year—but murder? Why would any one of us want to murder her?"

Alice tucked a strand of her long dark hair behind her ear. "I *just* said that."

Finnoula glared. "You interrupted me, and I was *about* to say that."

Teagan Moore came between them. "Really? You want to take this moment to have a petty argument?"

Finnoula and Alice made eye contact then each mumbled an apology, neither of which sounded sincere.

"The prize is only ten thousand euro," Nessa said. "I wouldn't kill over that."

"Is that right?" Molly Murphy said, turning to her with a smirk. "At what price would you kill?"

Nessa put her hand on her hip and wagged her finger at Molly, but if she had planned a retort, none came out of her mouth.

"Do not forget the golden rose," Finnoula said. "It's worth something." Her gaze flew to Teagan.

He shook his head. "I did not place that rose in my garden!"

Finnoula shrugged and broke eye contact with him.

"What about our families?" Sean said. "I have a wife and children."

"We've spoken to the inn and they can accommodate all of you, including your families. However, if you have someplace else you can stay, that's acceptable as long as you inform us of your temporary address."

"My word," Alice said, directing a piercing gaze at Siobhán. "You think one of us is the killer."

"I also have to consider everyone's well-being," Siobhán said carefully. "You're safer in a group. You can watch each other's backs."

"Spy on each other, you mean?" Finnoula asked.

"*Protect* each other," Siobhán said. "In the meantime we'll be working overtime to find the guilty party."

Molly was staring intently at Siobhán, and when Siobhán finally made eye contact, she jerked her head to a nearby table, indicating she wanted to speak with her alone. Siobhán gestured to where Macdara and Aretta sat. Whatever Molly wanted to say, she could say it to them. Molly nodded and headed over.

Eoin cleared his throat. "Dinner is ready whenever you are."

Larry Lorcan patted his belly. "It smells delicious."

Eoin beamed. "A scallop starter followed by roast pork with a cheesy stuffing, topped with a spicy honey glaze, whipped creamy potatoes, carrots steamed in a balsamic bath, golden-crusted biscuits with maple butter, and bacon-wrapped asparagus to start."

To start? It sounded like enough feed for months. Sorrow tugged at her heart. This extravagant menu had been planned for his soft opening, a night of celebration. She was proud of him for making the best of it. "It sounds perfect, Eoin, thank you." Heads nodded as folks added their thanks. Siobhán gestured to the farmhouse tables. "You can sit wherever you'd like, and soon dinner will be on the table." She paused. "Before you leave to go home and gather your things, you'll need to join Detective Sergeant Flannery and Garda Dabiri at their table. You'll be asked to account for your whereabouts for the last few days, especially the last time you saw or spoke to Cassidy Ryan." She nodded to Eoin and he stepped up.

"Dinner will be served communal style, and there are vegetarian or vegan dishes for those with any food restrictions. Each table will also have a bottle of red and a bottle of white, along with sparkling water. If you prefer a pint let us know." He gave a little bow and there was polite applause before they took their seats. Outside, the skies were darkening and a full moon shone its pale light down on the fields. Siobhán took a moment to take it all in before joining Aretta and Macdara.

"What did Molly Murphy have to say?" she asked as she slid onto the bench across from them.

Macdara held up a thumb stick drive. "She filmed them," he said. "She conducted pre-interviews with all of the gardeners. Including Cassidy Ryan."

Chapter 8

After dinner Macdara made the call to wait until the morning to begin investigating the garden tents. Sleep deprivation helped no one. It was his second night on the sofa and although Siobhán could not believe the argument was lasting this long, they'd quickly grown accustomed to keeping their personal lives separate from their professional. Because there was no doubt that this murder probe was going to require all hands in the soil. Bright and early the next morning they sketched out a plan and agreed to tackle Sean Bell's tent first. As far as they knew, he had been the last person to see Cassidy Ryan alive on Thursday afternoon. And, according to him, she'd been snooping in his garden. And now that Siobhán had seen how Cassidy had represented everyone else's garden in her design, she was inclined to believe him. Eoin was the second to last person they knew to have seen someone they thought was Cassidy Ryan; he believed she was at the property in the wee hours of Thursday morning.

"She was ordering her crew around like mad," Eoin said. "But it was down to the wire, so I don't think there was anything unusual about that."

"Did it sound like her voice?" Siobhán asked.

Eoin grimaced. "We were both running around like mad, and all I know was that it sounded like she was giving out to the crew." He scratched his head. "I wish I had been paying more attention, like."

Macdara patted him on the shoulder. "I don't suppose you know who was on her crew?"

Eoin shook his head. "I'm sure the garden committee has that information."

Unfortunately, the garden committee was compromised of their suspects. Siobhán consulted her list as she stood outside the car. "Are we pulling CCTV footage from any security cameras around Sean Bell's flat?"

Macdara slid into the driver's seat, Siobhán hopped into the passenger side, and they buckled up.

"I'm having guards gather CCTV wherever possible," he said, as he started the car and headed out. "They're checking on the location of each tent to see what cameras might be nearby and useful." He sighed. "Unfortunately, most of the tents are situated in areas where there wouldn't be security cameras. And the ones at Sean's property face the car park, not the side field."

Siobhán's phone dinged with a message from Aretta. Larry Lorcan informed her that the tents all had to be finished and "closed up" by 7 P.M. Thursday evening. Given the competition was the very next day, it was logical to assume most of the gardeners would have utilized every moment. Whoever had destroyed all the gardens had done so in the dark of night. It was hard to imagine one person accomplishing all of that without major help.

"I've been thinking about Molly Murphy's interviews," Siobhán said. "She mentioned them when we first met her."

"Did she?"

"Right before she asked you to repeat the test question." Siobhán tried to keep resentment out of her voice. From the grimace on Macdara's face, she'd failed. "My point is—she also mentioned something about Cassidy Ryan writing her some version of a cease and desist letter."

"That rings a bell," Macdara said.

"It might be a good idea to see if Aretta can have a word with her—hopefully she still has the letter."

"Do you mind texting her?" Macdara said. "Probably not a good idea for me to do that and drive."

"Consider it done." Siobhán sent a text to Aretta and received a thumbs-up emoji. "She's on it."

"Molly also thought the reason for Cassidy's paranoia had to do with whatever was in that crate."

Siobhán mulled it over. "Are you thinking this so-called cease and desist letter was written by the killer?"

"It's definitely a thought," Macdara said. "What's your take?"

"It's a distinct possibility. What I know for sure is that Cassidy's garden wouldn't have been complete without some kind of 'showstopper,' as she herself said to Eoin. But it does bring up the question—what was *supposed* to be in that crate, and where is it?"

"Maybe it's wherever she was killed."

Silence filled the rest of the ride as they individually turned it over and over. There were so many sides to this case that Siobhán felt as if she was holding a prism to the sun and every time she turned it slightly, a beam of light focused on something new. She was having trouble forming a cohesive picture. Hopefully by the time they investigated every single garden the picture would start to fill in.

The sun was just starting to rise as they arrived at Sean's flat. It was no surprise to see that several of his neighbors were already standing about in their robes, mugs of coffee or tea clutched in their hands as they gossiped. Siobhán had wanted to bring the black bell from Cassidy's garden to see if they could prove it was Sean's—maybe they could try and place it in the frame from which it fell—but of course entering Cassidy's tent would have to wait. Suited up, Macdara and Siobhán nodded to the guard who had stood watch all evening and dismissed him. In a few hours there would be another here to take his place. "I can take you through everything that occurred on our first visit if you'd like?" Siobhán suggested.

Macdara nodded. "That would be grand."

Siobhán went through the events of the other day, tracing their steps from the first unveiling of the tent to discovering Sean locked in the shed. Footprints covered the grounds from where all the gardeners had trampled. "I should have kept everyone out the minute I saw the vandalism," she said. "I just wasn't thinking."

"You weren't on duty—it's understandable."

He was being polite, which was more aggravating than if he was giving it to her straight. When they were standing in front of the shed, Siobhán pointed to the rake, still lying on the ground, which had been used to barricade Sean inside.

"Maybe we'll get lucky and our killer didn't use gloves," Macdara said as he placed an evidence sticker on the rake. "But I doubt it."

"Especially with all the gardening gloves lying around," Siobhán pointed out. Macdara pulled on the door to the shed and it opened with a creak. Siobhán glanced in. Had Sean really been locked in there overnight?

"There's no odor," Siobhán said. "He couldn't possibly have been in here without nature calling." Now that she thought of it, although he had looked a bit mussed-up and a bit in need of deodorant, it had been nothing extreme.

Macdara nodded. "Lock me in here."

"Seriously?"

"We have to make sure he was telling the truth."

"Not a bother." Normally he would have made a joke, some witty banter about her not leaving him in there for ages.

But today there was silence. He stepped into the shed and pulled the door shut behind him. Siobhán lifted the rake and jammed it into the door the way she had found it. "All set."

Macdara began to shove on the door. His first attempt, it only opened a crack. But on his second attempt, the rake slipped and fell to the ground. Macdara stepped out. "I wasn't even trying that hard," he said. "I thought it would take more."

"He lied," Siobhán said.

Macdara studied the door. "Or I got lucky?"

"That was your second try. Sean said he was locked in there *all night*."

Macdara nodded. "Perfect alibi?"

"I couldn't have done it, I was locked in a shed all night?" Siobhán posited. "He's definitely risen to the top of the suspect list." If Sean hadn't been locked in a shed all night, where did he go and what did he do?

Macdara rubbed his chin. "But if Cassidy's body was delivered in that crate, as we believe, then Sean wouldn't have needed an alibi for Thursday afternoon."

"Maybe the killer wanted to control the narrative. We're not usually home on a weekday morning." They had taken the day off so she could study for the detective sergeant exams. She felt a twist of guilt as she recalled how Macdara insisted he help her study.

"Meaning the killer assumed we would have to wait for the state pathologist to determine the time of death?"

"Correct. We have to wait for that regardless, but until proven otherwise we would have believed our two witnesses who claimed they saw Cassidy Ryan on both Thursday morning and afternoon."

"There's another scenario we should at least consider," Macdara said. "Isn't it possible that Cassidy Ryan's body wasn't in that crate?"

"I suppose. But the delivery lad said it was heavy."

Macdara nodded. "He could have been in on it." From the tone of his voice, this possibility bothered him as much as it did Siobhán.

"If she was not in the crate, then what was?"

"Perhaps nothing. A Trojan horse."

"For what purpose?"

"Again, to control the narrative. We have two witnesses who claimed they saw Cassidy on Thursday. Maybe they did. Maybe the crate was to make us doubt, get us hung up on whether or not she was already dead, whether or not there's an imposter out there."

"If that's the case—his or her evil plan worked." *Infuriating.*

"We'll find that delivery lad." Macdara jotted down a note. "Lock me in the shed again so you can film it," he said. "We can confront Sean Bell with the footage when we conduct our interview."

"Brilliant." And he was. Her detective sergeant husband was brilliant. And handsome. And funny. And terrible at apologizing. They repeated the shed experiment, and this time the rake slid off the first time Macdara attempted to shove it open. Siobhán recorded it all. She couldn't wait to see Sean Bell's reaction—and explanation. Would he pile another lie on top of the first?

They returned to the tent, and systematically began mapping it out, documenting the damage.

"There were koi fish in the water feature," Siobhán said. "Swimming in muck and debris. Guards scooped them into plastic bags for Nessa O'Neill. She said her pond would do nicely."

"I'm glad they're still alive," Macdara said. "I've never asked for an autopsy on a fish."

Siobhán continued to stare at the water. "I wonder. Were they trying to kill the fish? Maybe testing out a poison?"

"If Cassidy was poisoned I'm sure all of these gardeners know which plants kill and in what amount."

Nature, like everything else, had a dark side. "Here's the golden bell," Siobhán said, pointing as she led Macdara to it. "Sean insists his was black—and there's a black bell in Cassidy's garden."

"Replaced with a gold bell," he said. "Interesting."

"And Cassidy herself was spray-painted gold, and there was a golden rose in Teagan's garden."

Macdara's eyes roamed the once-serene Japanese garden. "Is our killer playing up a theme?"

"A gold theme?" She pondered it for a moment. " 'All that glitters is gold' . . . 'pot of gold' . . . 'Midas touch' . . . can you think of any others?"

Macdara grimaced. "Dullahan . . ."

"Dullahan?" Siobhán had missed that one. *The Headless Horseman.* "What made you think of that?"

"Molly Murphy," Macdara said.

"Come again?"

"She mentioned him last night when she approached myself and Aretta at the restaurant," Macdara clarified. "She glanced out the windows as it was getting dark, said something about how eerie it was that Cassidy Ryan had been murdered nearby, and then said that it was the perfect setting for *The Headless Horseman.*" He frowned. "Only that's not exactly what she said. She said *horsewoman.*"

"Horsewoman?" Siobhán echoed. She felt a shiver run up her spine. "Interesting." As far as the setting last night, Molly had a point. With the nearly full moon and green hills rendered black in the darkness, she could picture Dullahan riding up on his horse, holding his head aloft. *Or hers* according to Molly. Dullahan was often depicted as a coachman holding his own head, riding a black horse into the dark of night. Legend had it that if he visited you, it was because you were marked for death. And in the myth, the only thing that had the power to keep him at bay, the only thing that could repel him was gold. "It's no surprise that a writer has an active imagination." Macdara nodded. "True. She is a scribe, after all. And even though I dodged asking for an autopsying on a fish, I'm certainly not going to be the local detective who believes in a mythical horseman, male or female, with or without heads."

Siobhán was only half listening; she was still lost in thought. In some of the renditions of the myth, Dullahan and his headless self rides a black carriage pulled by six black horses. They gallop so fast, fire can be seen coming from their hooves and nostrils. She couldn't help herself, snippets of various renditions of the ghoulish tale played in her mind: *He is evil and relishes taking lives. He only speaks when he arrives at his destination. And then he only speaks a single name. It's the name of the victim whose life is about to be taken.* Siobhán was suddenly grateful they hadn't started this work in the dark of night, for she could hear those hooves galloping; she could imagine the head with no body whispering a single name in the dark: "*Cassidy.*" She'd been feeling more emotional than usual lately, and these thoughts didn't help.

"Siobhán?" Macdara asked, breaking into her daydream. "Everything alright?" His voice was low and husky—she wasn't the only emotional one; was an apology forthcoming?

She waited a moment but none was offered. "I was away with the fairies. We'll have to check for gold at the other locations. But why would the killer be telling the tale of Dullahan?"

"Honestly, I'm reaching here. But Molly's comment was the first thing I thought of when you mentioned gold. After the leprechauns and rainbows, that is." He winked, then froze as if he'd completely forgotten they were in an argument. He cleared his throat and put his business face back on. Siobhán tried not to let her smile show. He was so going to apologize first.

With her gloved hands, Siobhán picked up the golden bell. "It's heavy." She stuck an evidence sticker on it and placed it on the nearby table. But when she looked again at the spot where it lay, she saw a flash of white. She knelt to examine it. It was a receipt, partially buried.

Macdara edged in. "What is that?" It was smeared with dirt, and she could only make out one word: *Raven.*

"A receipt from the charity shop," Siobhán said. "The one on the ground floor of Teagan's flat."

"Interesting," Macdara said.

"I wouldn't mind a little shopping," Siobhán said. "You?"

Macdara nodded. "You took the words right out of me mouth."

Chapter 9

The charity shop was jammers. A one-room operation, its floor-to-ceiling shelves were fully stocked with items. A true place to treasure hunt, if other folk's rubbish was your jam. It seemed everyone in town had gathered in the shop to gossip. Given Teagan Moore's garden was located out back and his flat upstairs, Siobhán wasn't surprised to see the crowd, although the minute she and Macdara stepped in, eyes around them widened and mouths dropped open. They could either clear the shop, which would draw even more suspicion, or they could try and be as subtle as possible whilst asking the salesclerk a few questions. Often the owner was at the counter, sitting in a wooden chair behind the action, watching whoever was working his register—or his customers, but right now the chair was empty. Siobhán knew the young clerk; her name was Emily Dunne and her parents had been frequent visitors to the bistro when Emily was young. She looked about Ann's age now, and as Siobhán and Macdara approached, she seemed on edge. "How ya," she said. "Is there something I can help you with?" She swallowed and nervously tucked a strand of brown hair behind her ear.

"Hi, pet," Siobhán said. Macdara had quietly moved everyone else away from the counter. "I have a receipt from the shop here and I'm wondering if you can tell me anything about it." She slid the evidence bag across the counter.

As Emily bent her head down to examine in, her hair fell in a curtain around her face. It was as if she was trying to hide in plain sight. "Looks like someone paid fifteen euro for . . . a bell?" Her voice wobbled and carried throughout the small shop.

Siobhán placed her index finger to her lip to quiet her down. It took her a few seconds but Emily finally copped on and nodded. Her eyes flitted about the shop as she licked her lips. *Nervous.* Siobhán leaned in and lowered her voice as a way of demonstrating how loud the volume should be. "This bell was purchased ten days ago. By any chance do you remember this transaction?"

Emily shook her head. "I'm only filling in for Ann Doyle. She's on holiday."

"Is there any kind of record book Ann keeps or anything like that?"

"I can contact Mr. Fields if you like. But I haven't been told anything about a record book."

"Not a bother, luv, you're doing great. Is Mr. Fields coming in today?"

"He's out of town."

"I see." Siobhán removed her calling card and slid it across the counter. "This conversation is between us. Yeah?"

Emily gulped. "Of course."

Siobhán joined Macdara by the door and they stepped out onto the footpath. She filled him in on her interaction with Emily while he took notes. "Should we head for the Kilbane Inn to speak with Sean Bell?"

"Before we do that," Macdara said, gesturing down the street, "I think we ought to pop into Turn the Page."

The bookshop. Siobhán raised an eyebrow. "I always love a wander around the shelves, but what are you thinking?"

"I'd be curious if anyone has purchased any mythology lately."

She saw where he was going with this. "You don't think Molly Murphy's comment about *The Headless Horseman* was off the cuff?"

Macdara shrugged. "It probably was. But she has been hanging around all of our gardeners. Maybe someone else started the thread."

"I see," Siobhán said. "A little dull reading perhaps?"

He raised his eyebrow. "If by 'dull' you mean the terrifying legends of Dullahan, then yes. A little Dull reading." He chuckled, then caught himself and his serious face was back on. "Does that sound ridiculous?"

Siobhán shook her head. "Sure, we're right here, aren't we? It couldn't hurt."

Containers of flowers showcasing a rainbow of color were situated in front of Turn the Page bookshop. In the window a sign read: WE ARE PROUD SPONSORS OF KILBANE'S TOP GARDEN CONTEST! Once again Siobhán was reminded of how much a killer had already taken from the town. A life, of course, was the most serious offense of all, but this killer had also stolen joy. Everyone who lived here had been robbed of the joy that the gardening competition brought to their close-knit town every year. "I think downtown should still host the gardening booths," Siobhán said. Every year while the contest was taking place, downtown Sarsfield Street essentially transformed into a gardening convention. Florists, nurseries, musicians, and food tents would populate the small area. Folks could shop, get gardening advice, and enjoy everything from petunias to a petting zoo.

"Excellent idea," Macdara said. "We need something to

keep the town calm and focused." He pulled out his mobile phone and began to text someone. "Aretta will contact all the businesses and oversee the security."

"Brilliant." Mass panic would have helped no one, and now businesses in the area wouldn't have to suffer a complete loss because of this killer. They were piling a lot on Aretta but she was no stranger to delegating and an excellent coordinator.

A bell dinged as they stepped into the bookshop and Siobhán was immediately comforted by the mahogany shelves with colorful spines, cozy walls painted a calming shade of forest green, and soft lighting. The owners, Padraig and Oran McCarthy had brought so much to their little town. Culture, comfort, and escape, not to mention their impeccable eye for design. Siobhán was even starting to read for pleasure, and Oran and Padraig never judged her choices. Given that when they first opened, Oran had decided they would only sell literary books, he'd come a long way. Now in addition to literary endeavors, there was every genre imaginable and this shop had become a haven for many. Siobhán gave a little smile as they passed the claw-foot bathtub in the center; today it was filled with gardening books. A giant vase of flowers from Bloom's Florist sat on the counter next to flyers for the garden tours. Padraig sat behind the counter, his nose in a book. He casually looked up when they entered, then sat up straight when he saw it was them. "Detective Sergeant," he said. "Garda." He placed his finger in the book to keep his spot and smiled as they approached. "Are you looking for another Western?" he asked Macdara.

"Not today," Macdara said. "Why? Do you have one?"

"I've been making a list for ya." He glanced at Siobhán. "I have a few new releases you might like as well." Padraig and Oran were excellent curators. "A little romance, perhaps?" he said to Siobhán.

"I could use some," she deadpanned. She felt Macdara stiffen next to her.

"And I could use a bit of adventure," Macdara said. "Tales of lonesome cowboys without a care in the world."

"Ride on, Cowboy," Siobhán said, without even attempting to hide her sarcasm.

Padraig was beginning to look alarmed, his eyes darting about the shop as if seeking backup. Was this row ever going to end? Should she ask for marriage therapy books? Did they have any on dealing with a stubborn goat of a husband? "May I suggest *Men Are from Mars, Women Are from Venus?*" Padraig said under his breath.

"We'll pop back in when we can and have a look at your suggestions," Macdara said. "But right now, we have a few questions."

"Is this about the murder?" Padraig whispered. Given no one else was in the shop, it wasn't necessary, but Siobhán appreciated the discretion.

"I'm afraid we can't divulge anything of the sort," Macdara said.

Padraig held up his hands, then stared forlornly at his book. He'd lost his place. "I understand completely."

"Has anyone in the past few weeks asked for books on the theme of gold or myths? Specifically *The Headless Horseman?*"

Padraig's eyes widened. "I'm afraid it's Oran you need to speak with. I just returned from a conference." He turned to his computer. "But I can do a quick sales check." Siobhán was sure his mind was racing, wondering what gold or the Headless Horseman had to do with the case. He suddenly stopped and leaned in, frowning. "We did sell a big book of

Irish lore—exactly two weeks ago. I know for a fact there's a section on Dullahan."

Macdara leaned in. "Do you have a copy of the book?"

Padraig sprang up, and holding up his index finger, he went straight to a nearby shelf and soon returned with an enormous book: *Irish Lores and Legends.*

"Light reading," Macdara quipped.

Padraig nodded. "I think every Irish lore under the sun is between these pages."

"Put it on the Gardai's account," Macdara said.

Padraig rang it up, then slipped the book into a bag and held it out. It took Siobhán ages to realize that Macdara was waiting for her to take it. She did so grudgingly. Just when she thought they were easing their way back to normal.

"Do your records indicate who purchased the book?" Macdara asked.

Padraig shook his head. "It was paid in cash. But I'm sure Oran will remember." He glanced at his phone. "I could call him now, but I would be remiss if I didn't mention that Oran is catching up on his sleep, and he said if I disturbed him for any reason, it better be a matter of life or death."

Macdara shook his head and handed him his card. "Just have him give me a bell if he remembers who purchased the book. We might need a look at your security footage as well."

Padraig nodded.

They started to leave, but Siobhán stopped and turned back around. "Did Cassidy Ryan ever come into the shop?"

Padraig nodded. "I wasn't here—again, it was Oran— but he did mention her." His tone and expression conveyed there was more to the story.

"Anything in particular?" Macdara asked.

Padraig gulped. "Oran can be quite excitable so it might be nothing."

They edged in. "Go on, so," Macdara said.

"He said that most of the gardeners have wandered in at one point or another. And of course they all purchased books on gardening, garden design, that kind of thing. But Cassidy?" He leaned in. "She purchased a book on . . . stalkers."

Siobhán felt her heartbeat tick up. "Stalkers," she repeated. She glanced at Macdara. Was Cassidy Ryan being stalked? If so, why hadn't she contacted the guards?

"Stalkers," Macdara repeated. "Give Oran another hour of shut-eye and then wake him up. If he gives out to you, tell him *we* said it's a matter of life and death."

"No word from Dr. Brady?" Macdara asked as they stood just outside the bookshop, pondering their next move.

Siobhán glanced at her phone. "Not yet, but I'm sure she'll be here as soon as she can."

Before they could say another word, they were distracted by a commotion down the street. As Siobhán and Macdara rounded the corner they saw people exiting the charity shop in a wave, as if being rushed out with the sweep of an unseen broom. "Let's go," Macdara said. They hurried in that direction and they drew closer in time to see Emily Dunne turn the sign on the front door to CLOSED, shut off all the lights, and pull the shades tight.

Macdara groaned. "Looks like we hit a nerve."

This was peculiar indeed. What had sweet Emily Dunne gotten involved in? "Shall we go bang on the door?"

Macdara shook his head. "I'm due for a meeting with headquarters." He held up his mobile phone. "I've asked Garda Dabiri to meet you at the Kilbane Inn—show Sean

Bell the video of me *easily* breaking out of his shed and see how he reacts." Macdara took the bag with the big book of lore and gestured to the station down the street. "After my meeting, I have to start on a load of paperwork. I'll try to be done by the time Dr. Brady arrives."

Siobhán gestured to the shop. "And what of Emily Dunne?"

Macdara sighed. "We'll add her to the list, but I don't see her as a top priority."

"Right," Siobhán said. For a moment, they stared at each other. This is normally where he'd be leaning in for a kiss. He stood straight. "Ride on, Cowboy," she said again, as she saluted. He frowned. She tried, and failed, to hide a victorious smile.

By the time Siobhán pulled into the Kilbane Inn, Garda Aretta Dabiri was waiting for her by her garda car. Like Siobhán, she was dressed in her uniform: navy blue trousers with a light blue polo shirt complete with a gold shield just above her heart (and on her sleeve), and the navy cap with gold shield adorning her head. She looked sharp as always. Their uniforms had been revamped a few years ago, and in inclement weather they also wore two-toned yellow and navy waterproof jackets. Aretta flashed a smile and a wave as Siobhán emerged from her vehicle.

The inn was always a spot of cheer, reflected in a series of rooms painted yellow with trim the color of a robin's egg, and arranged in a horseshoe shape in front of the car park. Today there were even more ceramic planters than usual situated by the rooms, bursting with color. A floral scent filled the air, along with the scent of coffee brewing. None of the gardeners were out and about, even though it was nearly noon.

"I've already spoken with the organizing committee for

the garden contest and they were thrilled to hear they can still set up their booths on Sarsfield Street."

A spot of good news. "Well done." Aretta acknowledged the compliment with a smile. "Anything from Molly Murphy on that cease and desist letter from Cassidy Ryan?"

"Molly is searching for it," Aretta said. "She seemed extremely paranoid that it wasn't where she thought it should be."

Siobhán raised an eyebrow. "She thinks someone took it?"

Aretta tilted her head. "She didn't say that in so many words, but that's the feeling I was getting."

"In that case, we'll need to find out who could have access to it."

"Should I ask her to come into the station?"

"We still have to go through all of her videotaped interviews. Probably best to wait until we've done that in case we have additional questions on those as well."

Aretta started typing into her phone. "I'll make a note that you want to follow up with her on that letter. And maybe you'll find a copy in Cassidy Ryan's rental."

"Excellent point." They had filed a search warrant, but they still hadn't made contact with the landlord so there was nothing to do but wait. It had been another point of contention that Cassidy Ryan was no longer a local. She had lived in Kilbane as a child, but she'd left to attend university and she'd never looked back. Her family had moved shortly after, following her to Dublin where she now resided. Or had resided. Cassidy had yet to marry; rumors swirled that she didn't want to give up the attention from all men just to settle for one. Everyone thought she was so successful. But if that was the case, why come back for this contest? Was she secretly broke and she needed that ten thousand euro? Or was she proving a point to the town where she'd grown up? Maybe she hadn't felt welcome here, maybe winning was going to be her revenge. But it was all speculation and Siobhán knew better than to listen to rumors. She needed to stick to the facts.

Siobhán jerked her head to the office, a small house to the left of the inn where owners Emma and Eileen resided. The sisters threw open the door before they could even knock. Dressed in matching floral robes, their blond curls looked a bit mussed up, and they were blinking as if they were being assaulted by the daylight. It seemed everyone was sleeping in this morning; no doubt everyone had been up to the wee hours of the morning chin-wagging about the murder.

"Morning, ladies," Siobhán said.

"Morning, Garda O'Sullivan," they said in unison.

"You as well, Garda Dabiri," the one on the left added, and the other nodded. Siobhán could never tell the twins apart. Aretta nodded back and lifted her hand in greeting.

"We're looking for Sean Bell," Siobhán said straightaway. "We'll eventually be speaking with all the gardeners," she added. "But Sean is first on our list." She didn't need either of them spreading rumors, and as good-natured as they were, gossip was inevitable.

"Ah, yes, poor Sean," the one on the right said, a hint of concern knitting her brows. The other nodded. "Did someone call you?"

"Call me?" Siobhán said.

"Poor Sean?" Aretta repeated.

One of them opened her mouth to speak, but Siobhán held up a hand. "I do apologize, and I know we go through this every time but—"

The one on the left raised her hand. "Emma."

"Eileen," the one on the right said with a grin.

Even if they were messing with her, as they were known to do on occasion, at least Siobhán could call them some-

thing other than "one on the left" and "one on the right."
"Thank you."
Eileen gestured to the inn. "He's in Room 10, but he's not there at the moment."
"How do you know?" Siobhán asked. They weren't exactly the type to spy on their guests.
"He's out in the gazebo," Emma whispered. "He and the missus had a bit of a row last night. We saw him slink out with his pillow and blanket." She gestured to their robes. "Apologies, but it took us ages to get back to sleep."
"How heated did this argument get?" Siobhán said. She would have heard if guards had been called in for a domestic dispute.
"There was a lot of yelling," Eileen said. "Mainly by the missus."
"We were wondering if we should intervene when she booted him out," Emma finished.
Marital problems. Siobhán sighed. It was a club she wanted no part of, and yet today she was a card-carrying member.
"Did you catch any of the argument?" Aretta asked. "Enough to know what the quarrel was about?"
They shook their heads. "The only thing I caught for sure was when she screamed, 'How could you?'" Everyone looked elsewhere as they considered this. It was never fun to poke into someone's marriage.
"We'll head to the gazebo then," Siobhán said. "And I'm not asking you to snoop, however . . ."
Emma was the first to catch on. "We'll keep our eyes and ears open."
"Thank you."
"Would you like coffee or tea to take with you?" Eileen asked.
"No, thank you," Aretta said. She was always so disciplined.

"I'd love a cup of coffee," Siobhán said. The twins stepped back and gestured to the small coffee bar behind them. Siobhán made herself a cup and then fixed an herbal tea for Aretta. Even though she would never ask, Siobhán was getting better at reading her colleague. No coffee or tea for Sean, however. At least until they learned what put him in the doghouse.

The air was brisk but carried a lovely floral scent, and the sounds of chirping birds added to the ambiance. Siobhán's mam could have identified the exact flower filling the air with perfume, be it heather or honeysuckle, but to Siobhán's untrained nose it was simply pleasant. But a gathering of lilacs to her left was the most likely culprit. Overhead, swollen clouds sat low, and in addition to the flowers, Siobhán could smell impending rain. Today should have been the first day of the public touring the gardens, and if the sky delivered on its promise by the afternoon they would have been hurrying in and out of the rain as they explored the garden tents and marveled at the creations. Perhaps if they solved this murder quickly, they could pay homage to Cassidy Ryan with the gardens—have a public memorial in each tent—but given this case seemed anything but simple, Siobhán knew she was battling a case of wishful thinking.

Ahead, a lattice framework beckoned, festooned with climbing yellow roses in a shade that nearly matched the inn. Farther inside the gazebo, they could see Sean Bell pacing the interior, his mobile phone pressed tightly to his ear. Before she could think it through, Siobhán grabbed Aretta's hand and pulled her behind a nearby massive hedge. No doubt if he looked closely enough, he'd be able to spot them, but it was too late now. Aretta parted some of the greenery so they had a clear view of Sean.

"As soon as possible. *Please,*" he said. He seemed to be making an attempt to keep his voice down, but Sean's tone carried an edge of annoyance. Between this and the argument with his wife, it was beginning to emerge that Sean Bell was a man with a temper. "It's a simple request."

Then again, maybe he was talking to his wife and they were simply rehashing their argument.

"Just this, I *swear.* I'll never ask you for another favor as long as I live!" That must have ended the call for he tossed his phone onto the iron bench with a clank. He put his hands on his head and cursed. Siobhán's phone dinged, making both herself and Aretta jump. Sean stilled. "Who's there?" he yelled.

Siobhán popped up, then snatched a piece of the shrubbery. She pulled Aretta up next and handed it to her. "Do you have an evidence bag handy?"

"It's in the car." Aretta was used to Siobhán's improvisations, and she always played along nicely.

"Garda?" Sean Bell was coming down the steps, headed for them.

"I hope we didn't disturb you," Siobhán said. "We were just checking the soil."

Aretta held up the piece of shrubbery. "And the plants."

Sean tilted his head in confusion. "Does that have something to do with the murder?"

"Excellent question," Siobhán said. "But I'm afraid we cannot comment at this time."

"Top secret," Aretta said. "Need-to-know basis."

"Plants have a lot to say," Siobhán said, twirling the green leaves. "If you know how to listen."

"Right," Sean said. "I didn't realize you gardened."

"I didn't either," Aretta chimed in. They both stared at Siobhán.

"I dabble," Siobhán said. "I dabble in gardens."

"She's a part-time garden-dabbler, alright," Aretta added. Her sense of humor was blossoming right along with the flowers.

"My thumb might not be green exactly," Siobhán continued. "But I'd say it's green adjacent." She turned to Aretta. "What do you think?"

Aretta nodded. "Definitely adjacent. One day. One day your thumb shall be green!"

Sean gave his head a shake as if hoping to dislodge the entire conversation. He jogged back up the steps and grabbed his phone. He started down them again and began to head toward the inn.

"Don't forget your pillow and blankie," Siobhán said. "You don't want Emma and Eileen to have to tidy up after you, now do you?"

He reluctantly turned to look at the pile on the bench behind him. "Right," he said. He gestured to the office. "Did they hear us?"

Siobhán sipped on her coffee. "What's that now?" She held eye contact. Sean broke it first.

"Never mind. I'd better let you get back to—the shrubbery." He snatched up the blanket and pillow and hurried away.

Aretta frowned. "I thought you were supposed to show him a video."

"I was," Siobhán said.

Aretta gave it a beat. "And you changed your mind because . . . ?"

"Because he's up to something," Siobhán said. "And I want to know what it is."

"I see," Aretta said.

Siobhán was disobeying a request from Macdara, but he respected her instincts, and her instincts were saying they needed to hold back and find out what he was up to. If she showed him that video right now, he would lie. He would spit out an unlikely explanation and clam up. "Any plans for the day?" Siobhán asked casually.

"Let me guess," Aretta said.

"Follow him," Siobhán said, before Aretta could read her mind. "I want to know where he goes, and what he does."

"On it." Above their heads, a murder of crows lifted off from a nearby tree, startling them with the collective flap of their wings and long and pitiful caws. It sounded ominous. It was as if they could see all the troubles that lay ahead and were banding together, as one, to warn them.

Chapter 10

Dr. Jeanie Brady had her hands full as she approached The Six. She was juggling a large potted plant and a bag from the bakery just outside of town. Given she'd been on a health kick for ages, Siobhán was surprised, but thrilled, to see the bag of treats.

"This is for Eoin," Jeanie said, setting the potted plant down. "For his opening." She gestured to the tent, cordoned off with crime scene tape. "Or what should have been his opening."

The door cracked open and Eoin's head appeared. "Much appreciated, Dr. Brady. A fern, is it?"

"How many times do I have to tell you to call me Jeanie?" She grinned and looked at the plant. "Aye, it's a fern. But he's a lively thing, isn't he?"

"Lovely," Eoin said. "I'll find the right spot for him."

"I'm truly sorry your opening has been delayed, luv."

"That just means you'll have to keep sampling my meals," Eoin said. "Starting this evening?"

"I'll probably need the sustenance," Jeanie said. "I have a feeling it's going to be an all-nighter."

Eoin nodded and picked up the fern. "I'll bring you a menu shortly and you'll have your choice."

"What's in the bag?" Siobhán asked, hoping she didn't sound too eager.

"Sweets from the bakery for yourself and Macdara," Jeanie said. "Is he in there?" Once more she pointed to the tent.

"He's in meetings most of the day," Siobhán said, taking the bag. "I'll make sure to share." *If he apologizes.*

"I had the apple tart meself. It was off the charts."

"You're eating sweets again?"

"In moderation. Life is too short not to indulge now and again."

"I agree. And you look fabulous as always."

Jeanie waved the compliment away as if she didn't welcome the attention, but a smile betrayed her. "I drove through town. I see they're still setting up tents on Sarsfield Street for the garden competition."

Siobhán nodded. "Everyone agreed that folks needed something to distract them. Too much time and money went into this. It's awful business, altogether." They were at the opening of the tent now. Siobhán hadn't said a word to Jeanie about the body being presented as a golden statue. She wasn't trying to be coy, but this case hinged on the bizarre nature and presentation of the body, and the only way to truly understand that was to experience the shock for oneself.

Jeanie laid her bag down on a nearby table that had been set up for evidence, and Siobhán placed the treats next to it. As much as she wanted to dig in, they would be even better for torturing Macdara into an apology. The pair of them donned protective suits, booties, and gloves.

"Ready?" Siobhán stood poised near the opening of the tent.

"Ready," Jeanie said.

Siobhán pulled the tassel and once more the flap of the tent fell open. Jeanie gasped. "Remarkable," she said as she took in the garden installation. It was truly a work of art. An explosion of color and design. Jeanie gravitated toward a row of foxglove, standing tall with their bell-shaped heads, their colors blending from purple to white. "Digitalis purpurea," she exclaimed. She turned to Siobhán. "Do you know what happens after foxglove blooms?" Siobhán shook her head. "It dies." Siobhán grimaced and Jeanie shrugged. "It's nature's way."

Siobhán couldn't help but think of poor Cassidy Ryan. She too had been in the height of her bloom, but her death wasn't nature's way. It had been the way of one evil man, or one evil woman. Then again, with this case, it was possible they were searching for a team of depraved killers.

Jeanie had moved on to the native to Ireland section that was an obvious rip-off of Nessa O'Neill's garden. "Bells of Ireland," she said, bending down to examine the green calyxes in the shape of tiny cups. Next to it, bright yellow heads of fuchsia swayed in the slight breeze. "Fuchsias are my favorite. This one is known as 'Tom Thumb.' " She took a moment to inhale, then immediately turned to the statue and scanned it from head to toe. "Right, let's see what we have then."

"You knew?" Siobhán was slightly disappointed.

"Unless you buried the body in a patch of shamrock, I don't see any other option." She began to circle the statue. "Gold spray paint," she murmured. "We have ourselves a showman."

"That's what I was thinking."

Jeanie nodded. "It's going to complicate things. I'll need to remove the paint carefully."

"I know she's covered in it, but I can't see any obvious

signs of trauma, or cuts, or ligature marks—do you think that's all due to the paint?"

Jeanie didn't answer right away; she continued to examine the body. "I'll need to do a full autopsy, but it doesn't appear as if she succumbed to blunt force trauma—there are no obvious wounds. Given all the deadly plants and flowers that exist—are we thinking poison?"

Siobhán shrugged. "It's a strong possibility. But I'll leave that determination in your capable hands." She gestured to a group of hedges lining the back of the tent. "Gold is developing as a theme," she said. "Let me show you something."

Jeanie followed her to the hedge. Siobhán knelt and pointed to the small opening that had been carved in the bottom. Jeanie reached in and pulled out the miniature golden statue. "My word."

"I think gold is the killer's calling card," Siobhán said. "So far we've also found a golden bell in Sean Bell's garden—he claimed his original was black. And a golden rose—which presumably had been meant for the winner—was found in Teagan Moore's desecrated rose garden."

"A bell for a bell, a statue for a statue, and a rose for a rose," Jeanie said. "Interesting."

"We haven't examined the remaining gardens yet, but I'm assuming we'll find similar items."

Jeanie turned the statue around, examined the bottom. "I don't think this is anything old or valuable."

"Fool's gold?" Siobhán said.

"Look here." Jeanie pointed to scratch marks on the bottom. "Someone didn't want us to know where this came from."

"We'd definitely like to trace its origins," Siobhán said. "I didn't know if you wanted it first in case it was used as the murder weapon."

"I will have to examine our victim's skull, which right now is obscured by her long hair—but once I determine it *wasn't* blunt force trauma, I will make sure you get this back straightaway. In the meantime, do you have photos of these objects?"

Siobhán nodded. "We do."

They gravitated back to the golden body that was Cassidy Ryan. "The Midas touch, is it?"

"Macdara and I have been pondering that. Given the eerie nature of finding gold amidst such chaos and violence . . . I don't know why exactly, but our intrepid reporter said something to Macdara about Dullahan. Only she changed horseman to horsewoman."

Jeanie's mouth dropped slightly open. "That's a creative interpretation."

"She's young and definitely ambitious. Apart from her creative goals, there's no doubt she likes stirring the pot when it comes to these gardeners. It's apparent she wants to spice up her articles."

Jeanie lifted an eyebrow. "Is she a suspect?"

"At this juncture everyone is equally suspicious." Siobhán paused. "But if it's not her, and we find golden objects in the remaining gardens, someone might just be pointing their green thumb her way."

"A carousel of suspects," Jeanie mused. She patted Siobhán on the shoulder. "And people wonder how I can work so closely with the dead." She shuddered. "It's the living I fear." She headed for her satchel. "Looks like we both have our work cut out for us. *The Headless Horseman.* I never would have imagined."

"Along those lines we stopped in at the bookshop. Someone did recently purchase a big book of Irish lore, but the customer paid in cash and we're waiting to see if Oran remembers who it was." Given the garden competition drew crowds from neighboring towns, even well before the event officially opened, it might have been a stranger. Either way Oran should have called by now. Maybe he left a message with the station.

Jeanie returned to staring at Cassidy Ryan's body. "I suppose we'll find our answers under the layers," she said. She glanced at the ground. Gravel had been spread in between the flower beds. "Too many footprints, I suppose, but none that point to our killer."

"Maddening," Siobhán said. "And with all the gardening gloves lying about, I have my doubts that we'll find DNA." She filled Jeanie in on what they knew so far—Sean's lie about being trapped in a shed, the destruction to the other gardens, the animosity many of them felt toward Cassidy Ryan for being a professional landscape designer while the rest of them were amateurs.

"It sounds like it's a jungle out there," Jeanie mused as she studied the base of the statue where water collected in an old trough. "Quite deep for a garden installation," she mused aloud, half to herself and half to Siobhán. She leaned closer. "Did you see this?"

Siobhán stared at the dark water, the white of the tent reflecting on the surface. It took her a moment to see it, but then it was obvious. Gold flecks of paint glittered on the surface. "You think the killer braced her to the trellis and painted her here?" *Right here? Under their very noses?*

Jeanie shook her head. "From the trace amount of flakes I'd say it was a touch-up." She gestured to Siobhán's notebook and Siobhán jotted it down. "Do any of the other gardens have a water feature?"

"Every single one of them," Siobhán said. "It was mandatory this year."

A magnificent butterfly landed on a vibrant peony in front of them, and as it balanced, it slowly unfolded its colorful wings. It had no inkling of the tragedy that had occurred within this idyllic world, a thought that brought both comfort and sadness. Amidst all this beauty, there had been violence. While those closest to Cassidy Ryan would grieve, life would march on, with its rhythms, its pace, its sorrows and joys. To someone out there, the killer, or killers, Cassidy's death had been a solution to a serious problem. A cause for celebration. The looming question, one that would surely keep Siobhán awake (along with thoughts of the Headless Horseman galloping, galloping, galloping), was: Who benefited the most from Cassidy Ryan's death? Who was silently celebrating her murder? And what secrets would Dr. Jeanie Brady find underneath the layers of the poor woman's golden facade?

Chapter 11

Siobhán was due to meet Macdara soon but found herself with an hour to kill. She spent it in town wandering through the labyrinth of gardening booths. After receiving the news that the show could partially go on, volunteers and booth owners had wasted no time setting up. A kaleidoscope of flowers in every direction vied for attention, while gardeners competed for space and attention from the vendors. The Garden Advice booth had the longest line. Conversation swirled around her, their voices mingling with the sound of wind chimes. Lorcan Nursery's booth loomed ahead, showcasing a display of exotic orchids. Siobhán couldn't help but think about Nero Wolfe, and wished the fictional detective was here to help them solve the case. Siobhán found Larry Lorcan huddled behind shelves of gardening equipment, as if a handful of skinny rakes would be enough to hide his large frame.

"How ya?" Siobhán said. Larry nearly jumped out of his skin. That's when she noticed he was scarfing down a massive burger. "Sorry to disturb your lunch."

He set the burger down on a nearby table, wiped his

mouth with a napkin, and shrugged. "Garda O'Sullivan. What a nice surprise." A bit of sauce clung to his chin. Siobhán gestured to it, and he snatched up the napkin and dabbed it, which only served to distribute more sauce all over his face. "Now. How's that?" he asked.

"Perfect."

He grinned, looked around secretively, then leaned in with onion-scented breath. "Don't let the plant lovers see me eating meat."

"If they're plant lovers, tell them you're *saving* the plants by eating meat instead of them."

Larry stared at her for a moment, his brows knitted in confusion. When the joke finally registered, he leaned his head back and roared with laughter. "I'm going to remember that one, I am." He wagged his finger at her. "Now. Are you here on business or thinking of getting into a bit of gardening yourself?"

"I was curious about something—I take it you carry garden accessories in the nursery?"

He gave a hearty nod and pointed to a section in the booth. "We have a few on display. The solar light turtle is me favorite—the family of rabbits are our bestseller. We have solar lights, and wind chimes, and an entire selection of fairies and fairy houses back at the nursery."

Siobhán turned to take in the ceramic turtle. "Lovely." She cleared her throat. "I like a bit of sparkle—do you know if you have any items in gold?" She laughed before he could answer. "I don't mean real gold, of course." At least she didn't think so. "But imitation gold?"

Larry frowned. "I can't think of anything off the top of me head. We might have a bauble or two back at the nursery. Would you like me to give you a bell after I check the inventory?"

"That would be grand." Siobhán handed him the card. "Am I the first to make such a request?" She didn't want him to know this was part of her investigation. Larry didn't seem like the type who could keep a secret.

"You'd be surprised," he said. "People ask us all sorts of things."

Was he being evasive or just making casual conversation? "How are you holding up?" Siobhán asked.

"Me?" He seemed startled.

"Not singling you out by any means. Murder has a way of rattling everyone."

"Right, right," he said. He eyed his burger.

"I'll let you finish. But I will be seeing you soon."

"I must seem heartless," he said. "It is horrific what's happened to that beautiful woman. I tend to eat when I'm stressed."

"I completely understand. We'll be doing a round of interviews soon—speaking to everyone in the competition—until then—try and write down anything you can remember about your dealings with Cassidy Ryan—or anyone else that might have mentioned her."

"I don't want to cast suspicion on anyone. . . ."

"All I want is the truth."

Larry gulped. "Even if it makes someone look bad?"

"Even if it makes someone look bad." She gazed around as if the conversation meant nothing. "Did you have anyone in particular in mind?"

Larry licked his lips. "I'll be telling you more about it in our official interview, like," he said. "But Cassidy did come to me a few days ago and said that one of the gardeners was harassing her."

Siobhán thought of the book on stalking she'd purchased at the bookshop. She edged in closer. "Did she say who?"

"That was the thing. She didn't know." He stopped talking and began to blink rapidly.

"She didn't know?" Siobhán repeated.

He nodded. "She felt like she was being followed—and

then she said there was an item in her garden that didn't belong." He shrugged. "She thought someone put it there—was messing with her mind."

The golden statue? "Did she say what it was?"

He shook his head. "But she did say *who* she thought it was."

He was enjoying dragging this out. "And who was that, Mr. Lorcan?"

"You don't want me to wait for my official interview?"

"No time like the present."

He swallowed hard. "Alice McCarthy."

Alice in Wonderland. Siobhán didn't know much about her yet. She was intrigued. "Why did she think Alice was messing with her?"

Larry couldn't wait to spill the tea. "Have you seen Alice's husband?" Siobhán shook her head. "Women say he's a real heartbreaker. *Handsome,*" he added in case Siobhán wasn't following his drift. "And apparently Alice caught Mr. Handsome and Cassidy Ryan flirting outrageously in public. Can you imagine?" He leaned in. "Touching and everything. In front of everyone, like!"

"Do you know when and where this took place?"

He frowned. "A restaurant I believe. Or was it a pub? Maybe a chipper?"

She sighed. *Grain of salt.* "Thank you," Siobhán said. "You've been very helpful." *Not.* She would have to do some digging. Maybe she was a gardener after all.

Larry's eyes gleamed. "I'm like an amateur sleuth, am I?"

"Absolutely," Siobhán said. "As amateur as one can possibly be."

Siobhán drifted near a cluster of food booths where the scent of veggie burgers and curried chips mingled. One could find every variety of cuisines here, but many stalls boasted plant-based offerings. She was debating whether or not she wanted to eat, while snippets of conversation drifted past.

"Dead in her tent! But they won't say how . . ."

"They think one of the gardeners is the killer. Can you imagine?"

"It's not Finnoula Connor. She's too tiny."

"Not too tiny if Cassidy was shot . . ."

"Or stabbed."

"And don't underestimate Finnoula. She might be tiny, but she's as hardheaded as bristles on a scrub brush."

"Cassidy Ryan was gorgeous. It didn't do her any favors." They spoke about such darkness while holding tulips, and roses, and peonies.

"Earwigging?" a female voice from behind said. Siobhán turned to find Aretta cupping her ear as if straining to hear nearby conversation.

"Any chance I can get," Siobhán replied. "The gossip is fierce." She gestured to the food booths. "Lunch?"

Aretta shook her head. "Do you have time for a catch-up?"

Siobhán nodded. "I'm just waiting on Macdara."

Aretta's expression was serious. "I do have a bit of news regarding Sean Bell."

Siobhán felt a shot of adrenaline. "There are some lunch tables set up down the way. I'll just order a few things so we can sit and chat." She gazed at the menu in front of the chipper stand. "You know. Support the cause."

"Absolutely," Aretta deadpanned. "One must always support the cause."

"Sean Bell's wife gave him the official boot," Aretta said, her voice low. "She tossed his luggage bags outside the door to their room. He ended up renting another from the twins." Siobhán's gob was full of curried chips so she nodded for Aretta to continue. "He was only in his room long enough to stow his luggage bags. Next thing you know I was tailing him as he took a drive."

"Where did he go?"

"Butler's."

Butler's Undertaker, Lounge, and Pub. It was just down the street. "Day drinking?" Siobhán raised an eyebrow.

"Clandestine meeting." Aretta's energy shifted into high gear as she pulled out her mobile phone, swiped through the screen, and showed Siobhán a grainy image. Despite huddling in a dark corner, Siobhán recognized the woman sitting across from Sean. And the last time she'd seen her, she'd closed the charity shop as soon as Siobhán and Macdara had left.

"Emily Dunne," Siobhán mused. Did this have anything to do with her closing the shop in such a hurry? They had found the receipt to Raven's in Sean's tent. But if he was the one who had purchased the golden bell, why did he claim otherwise? It would mark the second lie out of the gardener's mouth. Was he a killer trying to cover his tracks? How had he roped poor Emily into it?

"Do you know her well?" Aretta asked.

Siobhán nodded. "She works at Raven. The charity shop. This morning we paid her a visit—asking after that receipt we found in Sean Bell's garden. And—minutes later she closed down the shop." Siobhán studied the photo. "Apparently something came up."

"Interesting," Aretta said.

Siobhán nodded. "Isn't it?" Now they were going to have to pay a visit to Butler's. Hopefully the owner, John, could shed some light on what Sean and Emily were whispering about in that dark corner of the pub. Because even though they often faded into the background, publicans usually had stellar hearing. Unfortunately, they also often had a "no talking out of school" conviction—*what happens in pubs stays in pubs*—so they were going to have to do their best to get him to spill the beans.

"I can forward you the photo—shall I send it to Macdara as well?"

"You shall," a male voice said from behind. Macdara slipped into a chair opposite Siobhán, and Aretta began to fill him in on the recent events. Siobhán made a point of looking attentive, but her heart squeezed with pain. His blue eyes, his messy hair, that lopsided grin. Why was he dragging this argument out so long? She hated this. She wanted them back to normal. She wanted her husband back. He suddenly made eye contact and they stared at each other.

"Consider it done," Aretta said, breaking into the moment. If she thought it was odd that Macdara sat next to her she didn't let it show.

Siobhán felt a wave of nausea. "Are you alright?" Macdara asked, his voice low and husky. She must have looked a fright for him to break through his armor.

"I shouldn't eat food out of a booth," she said. She pushed the curried chips away. "Help yourself."

"Trying to give me food poisoning, are ya?" His tone was jovial, but Siobhán had a feeling that was for Aretta's benefit. "Only messing," he said when Siobhán didn't reply. "Do you want to go home and have a lie-down? I can ask another guard to accompany me to the next garden."

"I'm available," Aretta said.

"I was hoping you could start going through CCTV footage," Macdara said. "I know it's tedious, but we have a lot to get through."

"I don't mind at all," Aretta said.

"And I'm not going home," Siobhán said. "I can deal with an upset tummy."

Macdara squinted as if trying to suss her out, and then shrugged. The armor was back.

Siobhán nodded to Aretta. "Can you recap your afternoon of tailing Sean Bell for Sergeant Flannery?" Macdara's sigh was the loudest she'd ever heard. This time Siobhán could see a reaction from Aretta, a slight raise of an eyebrow and a glance at Macdara. Although the pair was known for their banter, it was obvious that Aretta could tell something was off, but she was too professional to mention it.

"Absolutely." Aretta filled him in on the afternoon.

"That lines up," Macdara said when she was finished.

Siobhán hadn't expected that. "Emily? Sweet little Emily Dunne at the Raven? That lines up?"

Macdara shook his head. "Not that bit. But the problems with the wife." An awkward silence followed. Macdara finally cleared his throat. "I have a bit of a recap of me own." Siobhán and Aretta leaned in. "The guards who searched Sean Bell's house found divorce papers from a few months ago shoved in a drawer." He cleared his throat again, as if the topic was getting too close for comfort. "His wife signed the papers, but he hasn't."

"That is interesting," Siobhán said.

"It gets better." Macdara pulled out his mobile phone. "The newspaper clipping is in the evidence room at the station, but you should be able to see well enough." He turned the phone. Siobhán took it and brought it close to herself and Aretta. It was a newspaper article Molly had published after the gardeners were first selected for the Top Garden Competition. Securing a spot was no simple task, every year at least a hundred gardeners applied. But that wasn't the interesting bit. One of the gardeners was "missing" from the photo. Where there should have been a head, there was a blank spot. Someone had cut Cassidy Ryan out of the photo in the newspaper. Was Sean Bell her "stalker"? Or had Sean's wife picked up a pair of scissors in a jealous rage? Did she suspect Sean and Cassidy of having an affair? "This was found in Sean Bell's house?"

Macdara nodded. "In the same drawer as the divorce papers he hasn't signed."

"One of the gardeners, Nessa O'Neill, made a joke about Sean and Cassidy knocking boots. Maybe she was onto something." And if Cassidy was being stalked—by Sean, or Sean's wife, or someone else—why hadn't she reported it to the guards? Siobhán continued to chew on it. "We're going to have to speak to the wife."

Macdara nodded. "Let's add that to our ever-expanding to-do list."

"Now I'm eager to get to that CCTV footage," Aretta said as she stood and collected the food cartons.

"Thank you," Siobhán said. "Will you be at The Six later?" For a moment Aretta looked stricken. How long was she and Eoin going to keep up this charade? Everyone knew they were in love. Siobhán wanted to celebrate the fact, but she was taking her cues from them. "Eoin is serving all the meals he'd prepared for the opening," she added. "He needs all the mouths he can get." She felt Macdara staring at her, and she wondered how difficult it was for him not to turn her off-the-cuff comment into a bawdy joke.

"As Siobhán O'Sullivan would say," Aretta began, " 'I'll be there with bells on.' " She set off with a grin.

They were alone again. Silence filled the space between them. "He needs all the mouths he can get, does he?" Macdara finally said.

Siobhán couldn't help a grin from escaping. "I wish they'd just get over themselves and announce to the world they're in love."

Macdara stared at her, his expression masked. Was this it? Was he finally going to apologize? Her stomach rolled. Maybe it hadn't been the curried chips giving her problems at all. Maybe it was their marriage. Macdara stood. "If you're ready, let's head to the next garden."

Siobhán struggled to her feet, as a wave of dizziness hit. "No!" She hadn't meant to say it out loud; she'd been giving herself a command. She could not get sick. He hurried to her side, as if she was in danger of keeling over. "I'm fine," she said. "Let's go."

"Siobhán," he said, his voice thick with concern. "This case will still be here tomorrow. You can rest."

"Not on your life. Who's next on the list?"

Macdara sighed. "The front-runner," he said.

Finnoula Connor. Siobhán was going to have to put her poker face on, no matter what her stomach did to her. She was not going to let go of this case. "Lead the way."

"First stop, the chemist," Macdara said. "I need some tablets. Just in case *my* stomach starts to bother me."

Siobhán wasn't going to argue; some stomach tablets might do her good. And even though it wasn't an apology, she felt a little glow inside, competing with the nausea. He still loved her. He might be browned off, but her handsome, stubborn, sometimes rude-goat-of-a-husband wasn't going anywhere.

Chapter 12

As if adding insult to injury, rain began to fall as Siobhán's and Macdara's boots sunk into the soggy remnants of Finnoula Connor's once-pristine garden. The wind beat at the flaps of the tent as if outraged by their presence. Four gold trophies, symbols of Finnoula Connor's former glory, lay submerged in the mushy ground. Guards had suctioned as much water out as they could, but it was still a mess.

"Four first-place trophies," Macdara said. "Gold trophies I might add."

"Wait," Siobhán said. "I was at the opening ceremonies, and I believe Larry Lorcan said that Finnoula has won the past *three* years in a row."

Macdara scanned the ground. "And yet there are four."

With gloved hands, Siobhán lifted one. 1ST PLACE KILBANE'S TOP GARDEN CONTEST. The second one was exactly the same. But the third one she lifted had another message: BEST WEEDS. The fourth was another 1st Place trophy. "Best weeds," Siobhán said. "I'd say we found our odd man out."

"Someone could have had this trophy specially made," Macdara said. "Maybe if we can figure out where it was made, it will lead to the *who*."

"It looks like one of those jokey things you can buy on Amazon."

Macdara nodded, then shrugged. "Someone either had a grudge against all of these gardeners, or they want us to *think* they did." Although once more they weren't dealing with real gold, but the trophies were heavy. They marked them as evidence and set them on a nearby table that had been set up by the guards. They continued to investigate the garden.

Even if she knew the names of all the plants and flowers, they were indistinguishable now, mushed and drowned, and flattened. "I just cannot see Finnoula Connor, let alone any of these gardeners, doing this to his or her own garden."

Macdara raised an eyebrow. "Even to get away with murder?"

"Now," Siobhán said, "there's that." Desperate times and desperate measures. Was Finnoula Connor their killer? Had her jealousy so enraged her that she murdered Cassidy? "A ten thousand euro prize and another trophy on her mantel just doesn't seem like a strong enough motive for one of them to destroy his or her own garden, let alone murder."

"Maybe there's more to it."

"Excuse me!" A male voice called out. Siobhán and Macdara whirled around to find a tall man standing at the entrance of the tent, a determined expression stamped on his face.

"Do not take another step," Macdara said. "Did you not see the tape? This is a crime scene."

The man glanced down, nodded at the tape, then took a giant step backward. "Better?"

Macdara grunted. "What can we do for you?"

"My name is Collin Cunningham. I was on Finnoula Connor's work crew." Macdara and Siobhán stepped forward and introduced themselves. He tipped his hat. "I know you have more important things on your mind, like, and I don't want to seem disrespectful to the dead, but I was wondering if you could help myself and the crew with a spot of bother."

"And what spot of bother would that be?" Macdara crossed his arms and used his sternest voice.

"We were supposed to be paid, like. The day before the competition. And Ms. Connor refused." He took out a cigarette and struggled to light it against the wind.

"No smoking at my crime scene," Macdara said.

The man sighed, nodded, and put the lighter away. The cigarette dangled from his lips, drooping as the rain soaked it.

"She's probably just been caught up with the trauma," Siobhán said. "Have you tried speaking to her?"

"Course I have! And it's not like that. She refuses to pay because she let us all go. Gave the entire crew of four the boot on the Tuesday before the competition." He shook his head. "It's not *our* fault. We were ready and willing to work."

Siobhán tensed and she could feel Macdara do the same. Collin spit his cigarette out, but after clocking Macdara's expression, quickly retrieved it from the wet ground and stuck it in his pocket. "Out of the blue, she told us we were 'useless' and 'no longer needed.' Bollocks! That's four days of work we're owed!" This time he simply spat on the ground. "It's not even *her* money, it comes from the Top Garden Committee. And wouldn't ye know it, it turns out she's *on* the garden committee. For all I know, she spearheads the whole thing. And if she doesn't sign off on it? We don't get paid." The passion was evident in his voice. Or was it anger?

"You're absolutely right," Siobhán said. "We will speak with her."

"Thanks a million," he said. "From meself and the crew."

He pulled out his mobile phone. "Can ye take down me digits?"

"Here." Macdara took the phone, poked at it, and handed it back. "That's my personal mobile number. Call me in a few days. We'll sort it out for ye."

"What did this garden look like when you left it?" Siobhán asked.

"Gorgeous," he said. "We did every single build she asked for—she had a *waterfall*." He opened his mobile phone, swiped through it, and handed it back to her. Macdara huddled next to her as she scanned through them. She could smell his cologne, and although it wasn't the worst in the world, it turned her stomach. *She was getting sick. She couldn't get sick. Not in the middle of this murder probe. Concentrate.* The photos showed the progression of a meticulous garden plan complete with a waterfall.

"Is there any chance the waterfall malfunctioned?" Siobhán said. "Could that be the cause of the flooding?"

"Malfunctioned?" He squinted and shook his head. "Someone must have removed the plumbing mechanism that recycled the water instead of allowing it to overflow."

Siobhán nodded. "Would this have required a great deal of expertise?"

"I wouldn't say a great deal of expertise. Some. But one could always look it up on YouTube." He shook his head as if the very thought saddened him.

Macdara handed back the phone. "Would you mind texting me every photo of the garden that you have?"

Collin nodded. "Give me your number and I'll text it straightaway."

Macdara gave it a beat. "I've already programmed me number into your phone." He grinned. "You watched me do it."

Collin's face reddened. "Right, so. I was only messing. I'll be sending them." He waved his phone in lieu of a goodbye and trudged off.

Finnoula Connor had been the first to grant them permission to search her home and they headed there before she could change her mind. The door opened with a creak. They stepped in and closed it behind them. Sitting in front of them, on an entryway table, was a statue of a black horse rearing back.

"Does that remind you of anything?" Macdara asked.

Siobhán studied it. As far as an artistic piece was concerned, it was magnificent. Siobhán could feel the energy of the horse, the movement, the passion. "There's no headless man atop him," she said. But she'd be lying if she said it didn't conjur up images of Dullahan. "Speaking of which—have we received a call back from Oran?"

Macdara nodded. "We're playing phone tag. I believe I'm it."

Siobhán sighed. "We certainly do have our hands full with this one."

"I received a message this morning from one of the guards watching over this property," Macdara said. "Guess who tried to get into her home after she was already escorted in by the guards, and after we made it clear they were off-limits?"

Finnoula. Was there incriminating evidence she'd wanted to get her hands on? Siobhán snapped a photo of the horse. "You're just telling me this now?"

"It truly slipped me mind until just now."

She couldn't fault him for that; this case was bombarding them from multiple angles. "You don't honestly think she was going to secret away this horse sculpture?"

"Doubtful," Macdara admitted. "But there must be something in here she doesn't want us to see."

"Let's keep looking then." They continued into the sitting area where a sofa and two comfy armchairs huddled near a fireplace. If one were to imaginee a gardener's cottage, this would be it. It had a French vibe as well. The wood planks on the floor had been painted white, matching all the walls. Vases of flowers, plants, and prints with botanical themes cheered up the simple space. Beyond the sitting area was a small but tidy kitchen, and down a short hallway to the left were two bedrooms and a bathroom. One of the bedrooms had a desk piled with books. Siobhán wandered over. The first several on top were books on gardens. Magnificent displays. Slipped in between them was not just a newspaper clipping, but the entire paper of the same photo Macdara had found in Sean Bell's flat. But unlike Sean's photo, Cassidy Ryan was fully visible in this one, head and all. Siobhán studied it further and then gasped.

"What is it?" Macdara asked, as his hand flew to his chest.

"Sorry, sorry," Siobhán said. "Look." She showed him the photo.

Macdara nodded. "The same as I found in Sean's." He waited. "What about it?"

"I just hadn't made the connection before—but in Sean's photo—"

"She's headless," Macdara said. His eyes widened. "Just like the Headless Horseman."

"Horse*woman*," Siobhán clarified. "I never thought you'd be right about the Dullahan angle."

"Be still me heart." The jovial Macdara was back, but not to his full capacity. But Siobhán couldn't worry about their squabbles right now; she needed to focus. Siobhán turned away from the desk. "That one," Macdara said, pointing toward the pile of books. "Second from the bottom."

Siobhán turned back around and immediately saw the

thick book. She dug it out of the pile: *The Big Book of Irish Lores.* "Finnoula, Finnoula, Finnoula," she said. "What are you playing at?"

Macdara gently took the book from Siobhán. "Once we get confirmation from the bookshop that it was indeed Finnoula who purchased this book . . . ? Between that and dismissing her garden crew—she's going to have a lot of explaining to do."

Chapter 13

Siobhán and Macdara took in the remnants of Alice Mc-
Carthy's *Alice in Wonderland* oasis, and Siobhán's heart
couldn't help but ache for the poor woman. The once-
whimsical installation, which had been designed as a playful homage to the classic tale, had now gone as sideways as
the fictional Alice's adventures. The tea party had literally
been upended: table and chairs heartlessly overturned, their
surfaces strewn with torn petals, biscuit crumbs, and shattered cups. A tea-stained tablecloth was wrapped around
the neck of the Mad Hatter, and his hat lay smooshed beneath a nearby hawthorn bush, its jaunty feather broken in
defeat.

The characters from the classic tale had all been skillfully
crafted out of papiermâché, and even with them torn apart
and half drowned, Siobhán could see they certainly could
have bumped Alice's garden entry into the top spot. At the
center of the devastation stood a figure of the White Rabbit,
frozen in a stance of shock, his painted eyes wide and mouth
agape. He towered over a prone replica of Alice, who had
been unceremoniously dumped into the small pond that served
as the garden's water feature. Her once neat blue dress was

ripped and sodden; several layers of paper had peeled away and were now floating atop the surface of the water. A gold pocket watch swung from the White Rabbit's paw, swinging like a pendulum over Alice's pale, dead face, the accusing rhythm a reprimand, as if he were hypnotizing poor Alice into a waterlogged state of eternal woe.

"Our golden item," Siobhán said, staring at the pocket watch. "We'll have to check to see whether or not it's original to the garden."

Macdara nodded. "It would be fitting for the rabbit to have a pocket watch, would it not?"

"It would. But it might not be Alice's original watch." She didn't see any other golden items. *Bell, rose, statue, trophy, pocket watch* . . . What did they all mean? "The White Rabbit looks almost identical to the one we found in Cassidy's garden." Had Cassidy stolen Alice's White Rabbit, thus forcing her to make it again? Something like that would have been enough to enrage her. But if she felt Cassidy had been stealing from her garden, why hadn't she reported to the guards?

Nearby, the sardonic grin of a Cheshire cat startled Siobhán. She nearly missed it, but now she wondered how, for it seemed to be staring directly at her. It was crouched beside a Bells of Ireland plant, whose funnel-shaped-flowers had caved in and were bowing to the ground. The cat's eerie smile seemed to be the only thing in the entire garden left intact. She couldn't help but shiver, and try as she might to look away, her gaze was continuously drawn back to those exposed teeth. Macdara gently stepped in front of her, blocking the view.

"We're dealing with a lunatic," he said. "A killer as mad as the Mad Hatter."

"And as crafty," Siobhán replied. This was no mere vandalism; it was a statement—a story of its own, written through the medium of destruction. "And I believe when we check with Alice McCarthy, she'll tell us she did not intend *that*." She pointed to nearby hedges in which someone had ferociously carved out: EAT ME.

"I just cannot believe that one person did this much damage to four gardens in one evening without being seen or heard."

It did seem impossible to believe. A tale as fantastical as the Headless Horseman. "We need to gather all of the garden crews and see if any of them can shed some light on the last week of the competition," Siobhán said.

"I believe a group interview is being set up," Macdara said. "But now I'm wondering if we should speak to them one on one."

Siobhán nodded. "Earlier today, I overheard some gossip about Alice McCarthy." Siobhán felt guilty spreading it, but every little bit could help them nail this creative killer.

"I'm all ears." Macdara glanced at the March Hare in the distance. "No pun intended."

Despite her best efforts to keep it in, Siobhán let out a laugh. and she could see a flush of satisfaction come over Macdara. She had to ignore the flip of her stomach and focus on the tale at hand. "Apparently she and the husband recently had a big public row over Cassidy Ryan."

"Let me guess," Macdara said. "Our supposed femme-fatale struck again."

"Flirting and touching in public, that sort of thing. And of course there are rumors of an affair."

"If her husband was having an affair with our victim and she knew it—that's motive," Macdara said. "Looks like in addition to Sean Bell's wife, we need to speak with Alice McCarthy's husband."

"The more we look into this case, the bigger it gets." Just then, Siobhán caught a shape out of her peripheral vision—a figure in black, moving erratically in the distance. It almost appeared headless as it dipped and weaved between a line of hedgerows bordering a farmer's field. "Dara," Siobhán called out, already breaking into a run. He was at her side in an instant, their footsteps in sync as they pursued the enigmatic figure. Ahead they watched him leap a fence and weave around a curious herd of cows before disappearing from sight. Macdara took off, leaving Siobhán behind. She felt a wave of dizziness as she tried to push harder, once again ignoring the little voice inside her warning that she was coming down with something.

Macdara easily mounted and dismounted the fence and soon he too had disappeared. It took Siobhán more of an effort to get over it, and when she landed she felt an unmistakable squish as her boot sunk down. She looked down and confirmed her fear. *Cow dung.* That pretty much summed up how she felt. By the time she cleaned the bottom of her boot on a nearby rock, and then pushed through the cows, she could see Macdara had cornered the figure by an old stone wall. Panting, she reached them just as Macdara yanked the hood from their quarry. She stopped and stared at the terrified baby face that blinked back at them. It was none other than the delivery lad. The one who had shown up at their property, then most likely dropped off, in a crate, the corpse of Cassidy Ryan.

"Owen Sheedy," Macdara said, drawing the lad's name out so that he had sufficient time to work up a sweat. Garda Dabiri had joined himself and Siobhán at the station and they were now camped out in Interview Room 1. The walls, a sterile shade of cream, seemed to absorb the tension in the air rather than reflect it.

Owen swallowed and nodded. "Yes, sir. *Detective Sergeant.*" Now that his dark cloak had been removed, and he wasn't in the tan uniform that had fooled Siobhán and Macdara into believing he was a true delivery person, Siobhán took in his University of Limerick jersey and buzz cut and prayed she wasn't staring at a baby-faced killer. Most juries would want to send him home to his mammy. He could have been Ciarán.

"I was told it was a statue," he said before they could even ask. "I wouldn't have delivered it had I known. He gulped and the sound echoed throughout the small room. "I *swear* on me mam and da's life." With each utterance, his voice rose a notch. He cracked his knuckles as another look crossed his face, one of horror. "You won't tell me mam and da, will ye?" He shook his head. "There'd be war. I swear I didn't know. I swear." He dropped his chin as sobs overtook his lanky body.

Siobhán's heart squeezed. "Look at me, pet," she said.

It took a moment, but after much sniffing and wiping of the eyes, he looked at her. "I *swear* on my life, on anyone's life." He stopped talking, his mouth dropped open. "I didn't know." He threw a desperate look at Macdara. "I had to shower a dozen times and I still don't feel clean. Someone set me up!"

Macdara groaned beside her, Siobhán knew he had wanted to play bad cop, but there was nothing they could now say or do to this lad that he wasn't already saying or doing to himself.

"Tell us exactly how you came to pick up and deliver that crate," Macdara said. "Leave nothing out." They had already sussed out some facts about him before the interview and now they wanted to see if his answers would match up.

He gulped and nodded. "I was on Cassidy Ryan's garden crew."

"And yet you pretended to be a delivery lad," Macdara said.

He threw a look of desperation to Siobhán, who simply stared back. He tried Aretta, and only when he realized they were presenting a united front did his gaze return to Macdara. "The uniform was with the crate. The night before

Cassidy left me a voicemail. The instructions were to pick up the crate from Raven—the charity shop—at half-nine. When I arrived, I was met by the clerk—Emily Dunne. She was already out by the footpath, the crate next to her, and to be honest, she looked a bit nervous. Kept looking up and down the street like she didn't want anyone to see us. She had five hundred euro in cash for me but only if I wore the uniform." He stared at their faces as if trying to ascertain if they were buying what he was selling. At this very moment, guards were searching for Emily, and as soon as she was brought in, she would be next in the hot seat.

"And you didn't think that was odd?" Macdara asked. "That you were being paid five hundred euro in cash *and* you had to pretend you were a delivery lad?"

"Honestly?" He shook his head. "Not when it came to Cassidy. She's a bit out there, like. I thought it was part of the competition."

"Did you save this voicemail?" Macdara asked.

He stared without blinking, then his head sunk to the table once more. "She instructed me to erase it."

"How did she instruct you?" Aretta asked.

"Emily told me. She even said she had to *watch* me do it."

"And you didn't think *that* was odd either?" Macdara was losing patience, and Siobhán could tell he wasn't quite buying the innocent act. And normally she would have forged a strong opinion, but she was vacillating between believing him and thinking she was watching an Oscar-worthy performance. She also couldn't shake the disbelief that somehow sweet Emily Dunne was somehow mixed up in all of this.

"Everything about it was a bit, odd, alright? *Showman-ship*." He gulped. "To be honest, the oddest bit was that she was paying me five hundred euro. Like you said, Detective Sergeant, it was odd. But I mean five hundred euro is a lot for a lad like me."

"In cash?" Siobhán clarified.

He nodded, then threw up his hands. "I know, I know. But even if I did think something funny was going on, I was thinking—somehow she was cheating, ya know? I didn't think she was dead and stuffed in that crate." He shivered, and then the tears started again. "She was a bit of a diva, alright, but I liked her. Who would do something like that? Was she really painted gold?"

Of course the rumors had leaked; something as sensational as Cassidy Ryan being turned into a golden statue was bound to spread like wildfire, but nevertheless it was going to hinder the investigation.

"Given what we know now, we must assume it *wasn't* Cassidy who left you that voicemail. Can you think of who else it might have been?"

Owen shook his head. "I assumed it was her, but like she was usually yelling at the crew, so I don't really know her normal voice well enough."

Macdara crossed his arms and put on his stern face. "Why were you lurking about Alice McCarthy's today— and why were you dressed in a long black cloak?"

"I was incognito, like, I didn't want anyone to know it was me," he added, in case they hadn't understood the word. "And I heard the guards were going to be examining Alice's tent today." He gulped. "I wanted to listen to ye talk. I heard you were looking for me and I was afraid you were going to arrest me for murder." Additional tears streamed down his face. Siobhán had no doubt that when he told this story, years later, of the time he was interrogated by the guards, the fact that he cried a river would be conveniently cut out of the story. She was starting to think he'd been nothing more than the perfect scapegoat.

"When is the last time you saw or spoke to Cassidy Ryan in person?" Siobhán asked.

He gulped. "It was another phone call Thursday morning. She said she was off to check on her centerpiece. She told us it was a real showstopper. That's why I didn't think the crate was odd—maybe a bit clandestine—but something was going to go in the middle of that garden. And you know—somewhere there has to be the real statue she intended to be the showstopper."

"Did Cassidy often call you?"

Owen frowned, then shook his head. "Those were the only two times."

Interesting. What if neither call had been from Cassidy Ryan? And his point was a good one. No doubt Cassidy had planned something to be set up in the middle of the garden. The question now wasn't just what it was, but *where* was it? If they could find out where Cassidy's real showstopper was hidden—whatever it may be—would the location lead to the killer?

"What else?" Macdara demanded.

He gulped. "You mean . . ." He leaned in. "Do you mean all the rumors?"

"Yes," Siobhán said. "Tell us about all the rumors."

He shook his head. "It didn't happen to me, like. Unless you count the crate. But I've heard from other crew members that the last week they were told the game had changed."

Goose bumps rose on Siobhán's arms.

"What do you mean 'the game had changed'?" Macdara asked.

"Some crew members were instructed to sneak into gardens at night—to like mess around with them."

"You know this for a fact?" Macdara said.

"No!" Owen held up his hands. "That's why it's called a rumor, like."

"And who did you hear spreading this rumor?"

"I've heard more than one crew member say they heard one or two of them were asked to do things, like. But I never heard any names mentioned."

Great. They were going to have to speak to the crew members sooner rather than later.

"Can I go?" Owen pleaded.

"You can go," Macdara said. He threw down his biro and crossed his arms.

Owen paused at the door and turned back. "If I was you—and I'm not telling you how to do your job, like, but if I was you, I'd want to have a talk with Emily Dunne."

"And if I were *you*," Macdara said, "I'd stay out of the delivery business."

Chapter 14

The glow of the laptop screen cast a pale light across Siobhán's and Macdara's faces as they leaned in, the hum of the video buffering through the quiet of their cozy sitting room. Despite the fact that it had been another long day, they had decided to watch a couple of Molly's interview videos, and what better place to start than with the victim?

Cassidy Ryan flickered to life as she stood in Kilbane's town square, framed by the underpass of King John's Castle. Her outfit was breezy but stylish, her long blond hair flowed down her back, and her posture was impeccable. A floppy hat and large sunglasses completed the picture. Behind her, a wall-sized banner adorned with vibrant hand-painted flowers announced the Kilbane Top Garden Competition.

"Thank you for meeting me here," Cassidy said, beaming at the camera. She spread open her arms. "I find this village square so charming, don't you?"

Molly Murphy glanced at the camera and nodded thoughtfully, her gaze sweeping over the square. "Those of us who live here like it," she replied. "We have King John's Castle, a bookshop, and a garda station. That's history, entertainment, and protection, all in one square."

"Molly isn't holding a selfie stick as per usual," Siobhán commented.

"I actually remember that day," Macdara said with a nod. "She set her smart phone up on a stand."

"Fancy that."

Cassidy seemed to be studying Molly with an appreciative eye. "You have strong journalistic instincts for such a young woman. I have a feeling big things are in store for you."

"Thank you," Molly said, beaming from the compliment.

Cassidy shrugged. "That is, if you ever get out of Kilbane."

Molly visibly flinched. "And yet here *you* are," she retorted.

Macdara raised an eyebrow. "She can really lob it back, can't she?"

"She's holding her own."

"You *just* said Kilbane was charming," Molly continued. "Or was that a little white lie?"

A laugh escaped Cassidy's lips, but the sound was more practiced than joyful. "Darling. One wants to visit charming, not live there. Unless of course we're discussing a prince." She crossed her arms and looked around the square. "Do you think I'd be the success I am if I had stayed in this suffocating village me entire life?"

"Are you saying, for the record, that you find Kilbane *suffocating?*"

Cassidy laughed. "I see what you're trying to do. Discredit me. I think Kilbane is a lovely village. To visit. Especially for the garden competition." She looked directly at the camera and grinned. "I'm a big fan."

"You have a reputation of a flirt," Molly said.

"Do I?" Cassidy sounded pleased.

"Is there a prince in your life?"

Cassidy tilted her head. "Every man can be turned into a prince when you need him to be." She leaned in with a knowing smile as if privy to a secret recipe for romance. "But when you're done with them? They always revert back to frogs."

"Ouch," Macdara said.

Siobhán would have normally made a snarky comment, but it would no doubt lead to playful banter and she was withholding that until he apologized. *Profusely.* On the other hand, she'd refrained herself from looking at him and saying "Ribbit." She mentally patted herself on the back.

Cassidy gestured to the engagement ring on Molly's finger. "That little bling right there, darling? Unless he's ready to move to the city, where all true journalists reside, you're the one who's going to be tied to this place forever."

Molly stared at her ring for a moment, a frown creasing her forehead. Then she lifted her chin in defiance. "Journalism isn't bound to a desk anymore. Ever heard of the Internet? Everyone works from home, wherever that may be."

"Perhaps, but look at what you're covering. A village garden competition. Is that really what you dreamed of as a little girl?"

"I dreamed of winged horses too, like," Molly said. "I grew past it."

"I can only dispense wisdom; I can't force one to take it. But back to your question about a prince. I'm much too busy to settle down with one man. I have clients all over the world. I'm in high demand."

Molly's nod was subtle, her eyes not leaving Cassidy as she scribbled notes. "You don't look like a gardener, if I may say so."

Cassidy's eyes gleamed with mischief. "Is that a compliment?"

Molly shrugged. "Just an observation. Take the other

competitors for example. When you see them you can imag-ine them getting down and dirty in the soil. You, on the other hand, look as if you've never had so much as a speck of dust underneath your fingernails."

"She's not wrong," Siobhán said.

Cassidy lifted her chin to match Molly's. "I'm a landscape designer. We design. I let other people do my dirty work."

"Some people would say that true joy comes from getting your hands deep into the earth. Becoming one with nature."

"Some people lead very small lives." Around them, the rhythm of village life pulsed—a dog barking in the distance, the murmur of conversations from passersby, the gentle chime of the bookshop's doorbell. "I have a particular motto I live by." Cassidy leaned forward, as if it was just her and the camera. "If you've got it, flaunt it." There was a theatricality to her posture, an unspoken invitation to the audience to witness not just an interview, but a perfor-mance. "And believe me. For this competition? I'm so going to flaunt it."

"I see," Molly said in a tone that conveyed disapproval. "I'm sure you're aware that you are the only contestant that doesn't live in Kilbane, not to mention the only professional landscape designer in the competition."

"Throw down," Macdara said.

Cassidy held Molly's gaze, her expression a masterclass in composure. "Is there a question in there, or do I need to borrow a shovel so I can dig for it?"

"You mean have someone *else* dig for it," Molly said.

Cassidy laughed. "You catch on quick."

"Do you think your participation is fair to the other gar-deners?"

Cassidy brushed a strand of hair from her cheek. "The other gardeners? Did you know *they* make up the gardening committee?"

"Your point?"

"The gardening committee makes the rules. The rules do not state that you must be a current resident of Kilbane and they do not state that you must be an *amateur*."

"It doesn't even bother you that you've ruffled some feathers?"

Cassidy seemed to consider this for a moment, her eyes narrowing slightly. "Exactly whose feathers have I ruffled?"

Molly shook her head. "A reporter never reveals her sources."

"Well, then," Cassidy said after a moment, the corner of her mouth turning up, "I guess we're at a stalemate. But in general, I would say this. A competition is just that. A competition. If any of the gardeners feel inferior, why should that be my problem?"

They were expecting the interview to end there, but Molly was relentless. "I guess I'm wondering, with all your worldly clients and talent, why did you even bother to enter a competition in a small village with a purse prize of ten thousand euro? I mean . . . if business is going as well as you say?"

"She has a point," Macdara mused. "What was she doing here?"

"Given I'm just a small-town journalist, I suppose you won't mind if I do a little digging myself? Find out why you're really here."

Cassidy's composure buckled. "You village wench. You belong here after all." Eyes alight with fury, she closed the distance between herself and the camera.

"Hey!" Molly could be heard yelling. "Don't touch my property."

Cassidy smothered the recording device with her palm and the feed was cut.

Nonetheless, Siobhán and Macdara continued to stare. "She certainly hit a nerve," Macdara said.

"Indeed." She didn't have to be speaking to him to know

what he was thinking, what they were both thinking. Cassidy Ryan had entered this competition with ulterior motives, and if they wanted to find her killer they were going to have to suss those out. But the more pressing question in Siobhán's mind was: Given her nose for a story, had Molly Murphy beat them to it? And if so, why had she not said a word about it?

The next video was marked: *Interview with Sean Bell.* This time Molly Murphy was perched on an upturned crate near Sean Bell's garden. Before her stood the man himself, his hands deep in the pockets of his tweed jacket.

"Sean, tell us about your decision to design a Japanese garden for the competition," Molly prompted, notebook in hand, her tone both curious and inviting.

"Ah, well, it's all about finding tranquility, isn't it?" Sean began, his voice the pace of someone who had spent too many hours contemplating the rustle of bamboo leaves. "The Japanese garden represents harmony and balance. I wanted to create a place where one could escape from the world, even if just for a moment." His gaze returned to the space where the border of his garden was delineated. "Imagine by the time the garden tour opens, who knows what mysteries you'll find within? Maybe a sacred temple, or a tea ceremony. Ever since I've immersed myself in this culture, I've become quite the fan of green tea."

"And what about the prize money?" Molly leaned in, her eyes reflecting a hunger for something juicier than green tea and sacred temples. "Ten thousand euro is quite the sum. Any plans?"

Sean's gaze drifted to the distance. "I reckon I'd reinvest it into my passion," he said, a smile touching the corners of his mouth. "Gardening isn't just a hobby—it's a way of life. That money would mean more beauty brought into the world." He broke out into a grin. "But don't tell me wife that, she was counting on a holiday in Ibiza."

Molly nodded, jotting down notes before she glanced back up. "Let's talk about the competition. How do you feel about Cassidy Ryan, a professional landscape designer, being allowed to compete amongst amateurs?" She squinted. "Such as yourself."

"Stirring the pot," Siobhán muttered. "Always stirring the pot."

"I suppose that's part of her job," Macdara said. "Not unlike ours."

"Competition is the essence of growth," Sean mused, brushing a fallen petal from his sleeve. "Anyone who's worried about Cassidy Ryan's involvement has probably got their own insecurities to deal with." He paused, his eyes narrowing slightly. "Finnoula Connor comes to mind."

"Are you suggesting Finnoula might be threatened by Cassidy's presence?" Molly's voice thrummed with excitement.

"She's trying to turn a garden competition into a drama," Siobhán said.

Macdara laughed. "She's young. Driven. We used to be like that."

"We must have been obnoxious."

Macdara laughed again. "Think of it this way—if she wasn't aiming for the Pulitzer Prize in journalism here, we wouldn't have all this footage from before the murder."

"Cheers to overzealous youth," Siobhán said. Were they bantering? It was getting harder to maintain their argument, she was no longer irritated with her husband, and he seemed to feel the same. So where was her apology?

"Let's just say . . . it's Cassidy who should be looking over her shoulder," Sean was saying on the video. Macdara and Siobhán snapped to attention and leaned closer to the screen.

"That sounded ominous," Molly said.

"It is a competition," Sean replied with a wink.

"Are you saying that Cassidy isn't the real competition—you are?"

Sean laughed. "If I don't say it—who will?"

"Is there any meat on that bone, or are you just chest pounding?"

Siobhán laughed. "She's got spirit. I'll give her that."

"I personally don't think being a professional designer is going to do Cassidy Ryan any favors. She spends so much time bending her talents to suit her clients' demands that she might've lost her own vision along the way. Do you think that scares me? Boring! Creativity needs to breathe, to be unfettered. Stifle that, and well, it can be downright dangerous." His gaze fastened on the camera and then the video shut off.

"There seems to be more feed," Macdara said. "I suppose this is a commercial." He chuckled and stretched, then glanced at the sofa across from them, as if dreading another night on it.

"She's back," Siobhán said as an image flickered to life on the screen. Molly Murphy was suddenly inside a house, presumably Sean Bell's. Her camera swept across the cluttered confines of an office. "Is she snooping?"

"If she is, we're witnessing a crime," Macdara replied. They both leaned in.

"Sorry about the mess." The voice was none other than Sean Bell's. Molly had been invited. Siobhán and Macdara let out a sigh at the same time, then looked at each other.

"Jinx," Macdara said. "You owe me a Coke."

"You know they used to use that stuff to clean ship decks," Siobhán said.

"I did not know that," Macdara said. "Imagine that. Tastes amazing and doubles as a cleaner!" He roared with laughter as Siobhán shook her head before turning back to the video.

After panning stacks of gardening books and haphazard

piles of paperwork, Molly's camera zoomed in on the back wall. On it hung a publicity photograph of all the gardeners. They stood in a line, smiling awkwardly for the camera. Cassidy Ryan still had her head. Siobhán pointed this out. Macdara nodded. "If Sean and Cassidy did become entangled, I bet it ignited after the competition began."

"Then his wife could have discovered it and . . . initiated her revenge with a pair of scissors." Siobhán's voice trailed off as she absorbed the thought, her eyes not leaving the photograph.

"It would definitely help to know which one of them decided 'Off with her head.' "

"How long have you been holding that one in?"

Macdara grinned. "Ages."

The footage turned to snow. Siobhán leaned back against the cushions, her brow furrowed in thought. Her stomach was still off. She prayed she'd be right as rain tomorrow. It had to be the stress of knowing she and Macdara were arguing. Should *she* apologize? For the sake of her tummy? Even though it was definitely him that should apologize, maybe she should take one for the team. Then again, if she apologized now, it would set a horrible precedent for all their arguments to come. Macdara had just reached to turn off the video feed when Molly's image popped back on screen.

"Sorry for the abrupt return," Molly began, her voice betraying a tremor. "I'm recording this just in case it ever amounts to anything. It's not on camera but I just went back into the Bells' house to retrieve my mobile phone—I didn't knock because Sean said there was no need." On the screen, Molly shifted, the camera angle catching her biting her lip. Siobhán leaned forward. "But his wife was talking to someone—now I think it's a solicitor—and I caught the tail end . . ."

"Spit it out," Macdara yelled at the screen.

"I very clearly heard Mrs. Bell say 'I have to make sure he's faulted in the divorce . . .' " Molly stared at the camera, eyes wide. "I dashed out, but she probably heard me leaving." She bit her lip again. "I don't know what to do. Do I tell him?"

"The note," Macdara said. "Molly gave me this along with the USB and said it would make sense after I watched Sean's video." He reached into his pocket and pulled out a folded piece of paper. He opened it and showed Siobhán: *I did not tell him. This may not mean anything. But I'll let you be the judge.* The camera went off, and on again. Molly was in an entirely new outfit, and she was standing just outside Sean Bell's tent. Crime scene tape was visible in the background.

"Detective Sergeant, Garda," she said to the camera. "Don't worry, I'm standing way beyond the tape and your guards are doing a good job guarding the perimeter." She panned the camera showing the guards. "Obviously, I'm filming this after Cassidy Ryan's murder. And I swear to ye, I've told no one else what I overheard Mrs. Bell say. But now I'm truly worried. What if she killed Cassidy Ryan and is trying to frame her husband?"

"I told you," Siobhán said. "She's playing amateur detective."

"I remember a certain someone who once did the very same thing," Macdara said. "Turned out pretty good for her." If times were normal, Siobhán would have given him a little shove. He was right. She hated when he was right.

Molly's face softened, an apology etched into her features. "I swear I'm not sharing my wild theories with anyone else—and apologies if I'm overstepping—but there is something remarkable that happens when a girl with a camera enters a scene. The girl tends to disappear, and the scene is wide open. It's amazing what one can pick up." She winked and then the video shut off for good.

"I hope she doesn't continue to snoop," Siobhán said. "For her own safety."

Macdara nodded. "We'll have a word with her."

"Tomorrow," Siobhán said, determination hardening her voice like the ancient stones that made up their village. "We'll talk to Sean's wife."

"Tomorrow," Macdara echoed, his nod slow and deliberate. "And we keep our eyes peeled for scissors."

Chapter 15

A crisp breeze carried the scent of freshly turned soil as Siobhán and Macdara finished their examination of what was once Teagan Moore's rose garden. The sun was blessing them this morning, and Siobhán took a moment to bathe in it. They took the tiled path to Sarsfield Street and stood in front of the charity shop, which apparently hadn't reopened since Emily Dunne had run out. It was too early for the garden festivities to begin, but there were people milling about, biding their time. When they tried to set up an interview with Emily, her parents stated they were getting a solicitor and he would be in touch. She was making herself look even more suspicious, but perhaps it was all due to her parents being overprotective. Murder had a way of rattling everyone to their bones. Either that, or somehow she had played a role in this horrific murder. The only thing of interest they'd discovered in Teagan's garden was that the golden rose had initials etched into it: FC. Was it Finnoula Connor's winning rose from years past? It was one more thing they needed to press her on. But for now they were headed to Butler's Undertaker, Lounge, and Pub, where hopefully the proprietor, John Butler, would know something about

Sean Bell and Emily Dunne's clandestine meeting from the day before.

As they made their way toward the pub (and undertakers), Macdara's phone rang. He spoke briefly and then met Siobhán's questioning look. "Oran just came into the station from the bookshop. He confirmed Finnoula Connor purchased *The Big Book of Irish Lores.*"

"Interesting," Siobhán said. "Why now? With this gardening competition, I can't see her having time to read."

"The timing is odd. We need answers," Macdara said. "We should speak with Finnoula right this minute."

Siobhán held up her hand. They needed to think this through. "If we ask her directly about the book, it's going to set off rumors," Siobhán said. The last thing they needed was mass panic—and a flood of calls to the station with sightings of the Headless Horseman. "On the other hand, we also need to find out why she fired her crew when there were still four days to go."

"Right," Macdara agreed. "And we can't forget about Sean Bell's little act of deception. Claiming he was locked in his shed when he was clearly elsewhere."

"Indeed." Siobhán chewed on her lower lip, thinking. "We need to get them *all* talking, preferably off guard. How about we ask Molly Murphy to do a laid-back piece on the gardeners? With the contest called off and a murder overshadowing it, she could state that she wants to see how they're holding up."

"Teaming up with the enemy?" Macdara said in a playful tone.

"If annoying me were a crime, there'd be no room left in the local jails," Siobhán said.

Macdara's lips twisted into a half smile. "Let's recap. We need to get all of our suspects together, somewhere casual, in the hopes that they loosen their tongues. Lorcan's Nursery would be ideal for that."

"I think we should have a nose around the nursery first," Siobhán said. "Just in case."

"Point taken. I agree."

"Let's have Aretta arrange some kind of a meet-up, but we'll let our gardeners know the exact date is TBD," Siobhán suggested.

"I concur."

He was doing an awful lot of agreeing, which was maddening for someone who couldn't apologize. "And don't forget to schedule Sean Bell's wife for an interview."

"Will do." Macdara's expression turned serious once more. "And we've got the green light to search Cassidy's house."

"We're sucking diesel now," Siobhán joked. "Too bad our list of things to do is longer than hours in the day."

The door of Butler's Undertaker, Lounge, and Pub creaked open, and as Siobhán and Macdara stepped through, they paused at the threshold to allow their eyes to adjust to the dim interior. They passed through the front sitting room and once they were through a red velvet curtain, the place transformed from funeral home to pub. John Butler was behind the bar, polishing a glass and staring into the abyss. He turned when he saw them and set the glass down, picked it up again, brought it close to his face as if it needed a second inspection, then plunked it down again. He was dressed, as per usual, in what looked like a theatrical costume. A stiff white shirt with long puffy sleeves, a black bowtie, and black trousers. John Butler was a longstanding member of the Kilbane Theatre, and it seemed he often brought his "characters" to work.

"I see the town's finest has come to grace my humble stage," John declared, gesturing for them to take a seat at the bar.

"Only the finest for us, John," Macdara quipped, pulling out a stool for Siobhán before plopping himself down. He'd spent the night in bed, and although they were no longer arguing, the strain of politely treating each other like nothing more than coworkers was wearing on Siobhán. If they weren't on duty she'd ply an apology out of him with pints of Guinness.

"We're hoping you could shed some light on a conversation you might've overheard," Siobhán said, as he delivered two glasses of sparkling water.

"Sean Bell and Emily Dunne?" The man didn't miss a trick. John leaned forward, a twinkle in his eye. "I recall only snippets—but from the tone of Sean's voice, things were mighty tense. A bell was at the heart of it, it seemed, and I don't mean his surname." John's brows knitted together as he strove to remember. "Then something about moles . . . I'm uncertain."

"Moles?" Macdara asked.

John nodded. "Moles."

"We don't have moles in Ireland," Siobhán said. At least not the critter kind.

John Butler looked at Siobhán and shrugged. "They only each had a mineral, no alcohol, no food." He took a rag and began polishing another glass. "A bell and a mole. That's all I have for ye."

"We'll take it," Macdara said. "Thank you." They each took a few polite sips of water, and Macdara set ten euro on the bar before they ambled out.

"Big spender," Siobhán said once they were outside.

Macdara laughed. "Guilty. However, by the looks of his wardrobe, he could use a little boost."

"Moles," Siobhán repeated as they strolled away from the pub. "Do you think they were referring to a saboteur?"

Macdara rubbed his chin. "That's as good a guess as any. The only non-human saboteurs are the goats as far as I'm aware."

Siobhán sighed. "Speaking of goats—Nessa O'Neill's gar-

den is next on the agenda. Let's hope we learn something."
She was eager to see what the next golden object would be.
Laughter and voices spilled out from the gardening tents on
Sarsfield Street along with tantalizing smells from the food
booths.

"How's the stomach?" Macdara asked. "Are you getting
hungry?"

"It's grand," she lied. "But let's eat later. I want to get to
Nessa's garden while the sun is still shining."

Chapter 16

Siobhán stepped over a marauding line of ants, and kept her eyes peeled for other creatures as she navigated Nessa O'Neill's chaotic garden. The natural world had been invited in and left to its own devices here. Wildflowers jostled for space among the herbs, and Irish moss weaved around a line of bramble. It was an Irish garden in its truest sense— untamed, free-spirited, with tufts of clover and wild thyme creeping along a trodden path that wound through the tent.

Everywhere there were signs of the goats' impromptu feast: nibbled leaves, trampled flower beds, and, much to Siobhán's consternation, little pellets everywhere she looked— no doubt the poor things' digestive systems were punishing them for their wild binge. They were lucky that none of them had been seriously harmed. Siobhán had yet to spot anything shiny let alone anything gold. Why had this garden been skipped?

Macdara gestured to the barn in the distance. "Miss O'Neill is here today seeing to her naughty goats. Shall we have a word with her?"

"Absolutely. But let's not mention we were panning for gold." So far, despite Sean Bell announcing that his bell had been black, and Teagan Moore insisting he hadn't stolen the prized golden rose, she'd not heard any gossip of a gold connection, and she wanted to keep it that way. This killer would either be upset that his or her story wasn't being told, and therefore maybe try and get it started, or he, she, or they were gloating, thinking they had gotten away with it. In either scenario, this was something only the guards and the killer knew. And when it came to murder probes, secrets were often the keys that could spring a case wide open. But like Macdara, Siobhán had no clue how they all fit, and what story they were weaving. And now, to find a garden without a golden token? *Maddening.*

Nessa must have sensed their presence for she lifted her head and stared at them long before they approached. She was standing in a fenced-in pen connected to her barn. Her goats roamed around, munching on grass, or in the case of one fella, staring off into the distance as if recalling his glory days. *Remember that time we broke into your one's tent and ate everything in sight? Those were the days.* Siobhán was often grateful no one could read her mind, and this was one of those times. It looked as if it had been a raucous party and Siobhán was inclined to think the murder had not happened here. The goats would have been too much of a distraction. Although far from eliminating Nessa O'Neill as the killer, it made Siobhán think twice. The killer would have been smart to murder Cassidy Ryan far away from his or her own garden.

"Detective Sergeant Flannery, Garda O'Sullivan," Nessa greeted them, lifting a shovel. "Tell me you've caught the evil you-know-who." She gave them a look like a mother would give when she didn't want to curse around her children. These goats were her babies.

"It's a slow process," Macdara said with a half smile. "But we're doing everything we can to find the culprit."

"How are they doing?" Siobhán asked.

Nessa leaned the shovel against the pen and clasped her hands. "I'm eternally grateful. Clancy there has a tummy ache, but the vet said it will pass." She pointed to the goat who was staring off into space. "The rest are back to normal." She touched the shovel. "But this was much needed in the aftermath if you catch my drift."

"Drift caught," Macdara said, wrinkling his nose at the smell emanating from her barn. "Literally."

Nessa laughed. "I'm so used to it, I don't even smell it anymore."

"It's a gift," Macdara deadpanned.

Siobhán wandered over to the gate that corralled the goats. It was now latched with chains and a padlock. Siobhán pointed it out. "I take it this is a new addition?"

"'Tis," Nessa said. "There was a simple hook and latch before this." She shook her head. "What is the world coming to that I now have to chain me goats in?"

"Any chance the goats broke out on their own?" Macdara asked.

Nessa laughed, and gestured to them. "Do they look eager to break out?"

They did not. In fact, most of them were huddled around the entrance to the barn. "In all my years with them, they've never tried to open the gate," Nessa said. "Furthermore . . ." She held up a finger and joined Siobhán at the gate. Macdara was holding an empty evidence bag underneath his nose, trying to block the smell. If they weren't already in an argument, Siobhán would have teased him mercilessly about it, perhaps even borrowed someone's goat to bring home. She would have announced it was their new pet, or told him that Eoin was going to start raising goats for milk and cheese for his restaurant. She needed this argument put to bed so they could go back to torturing each other. "Ready for the kicker?" Nessa said, interrupting Siobhán's daydream.

"Ready," Siobhán said.

"When I came home and saw them trampling through me tent, I of course came straight to this gate. It was *closed* and the latch secured. My sweeties are clever, but not clever enough to close the gate and latch it behind them."

An extra touch from a creative killer. One who wanted them to know it was them. A blatant taunt: *Catch me if you can.* If only these goats could talk.

"Here, take a look at this." Nessa reached into her pocket and pulled out a small object. Between her thumb and forefinger was an antique pen nib, ornate and gold-plated, with intricate scrollwork etched into its surface—a tool of a bygone era. The tip was stained with ink, long dried.

"Found it in Clancy's mouth, poor thing. He'll chew on anything that sparkles."

Macdara had made his way over and leaned in to peer at the curious relic. "A *gold* vintage pen nib," he mused aloud.

"He picked this up from the tent?" Siobhán asked.

Nessa nodded. "Curious, isn't it?"

"It's probably nothing," Siobhán said, snatching the evidence bag from Macdara. "But you never know." Before Nessa could close her hand around the object, Siobhán took it and dropped it into the evidence bag. Relief settled over her. Every garden had indeed had a golden object. Now they just needed to figure out why, and what those objects were trying to say.

"We'll get out of your hair," Macdara said. He gestured to the goats. "Or their hair."

They started to walk away. "Have you spoken with Teagan Moore yet?" Nessa called after them.

Siobhán stopped and turned back to Nessa. "Why do you ask?"

Nessa chewed on her bottom lip. "Perhaps I shouldn't have said anything."

"And yet you did," Macdara said.

"He said something odd to me the other day, that's all."
She shrugged and turned her back on them.

"What did he say?" Macdara asked in a voice that commanded attention.

Nessa slowly turned back around. "He asked me if I knew anything about a mole."

Siobhán and Macdara exchanged a glance. "What do you mean?" Macdara said. "There are no moles in Ireland that I'm aware."

Nessa laughed. "Not an actual mole," she said. "A human mole."

Siobhán felt the hairs behind her neck stand up. "Say more."

Nessa shrugged. "You should speak with Teagan. I thought he was being paranoid, but something convinced him that the garden committee had gone rogue this year and one of the contestants had secretly been told to gather intel on the gardens. I wouldn't have believed it except"—she stared out toward her tent—"Larry Lorcan is a spy-novel enthusiast. I could see him doing something nefarious like that."

"In a garden competition?" Macdara's disbelief was evident in his voice.

"Like I said, I wouldn't have believed it. . . . But then again, I wouldn't have believed Cassidy Ryan would have been murdered, a pen nib was in me goat's gob, and there would be crime scene tape wrapped around me tent, now would I?"

When Siobhán and Macdara pushed open the doors to the garda station they found Garda Dabiri waiting, papers clutched in her hand. The room smelled faintly of brewed coffee, which to Siobhán, made her feel like she was back at her family bistro. She realized she'd missed it, and she could not wait for Eoin's restaurant to open. And unlike the bistro, in which they had been renting the building, this time, they owned it all. What a blessing. The sooner they solved this case, the better for everyone. At this stage of the game, every second counted.

"Emily Dunne is waiting in interrogation Room 1."

"With a solicitor?" Siobhán asked.

Aretta shook her head. "I believe she's escaped her parents' grasp and come on her own."

"Good girl," Siobhán said.

"I should warn you—she's been hysterical ever since she arrived." Aretta glanced toward the hall that led to the interrogation rooms. "Nonstop crying."

"Poor pet," Siobhán said. "Let's hope she can clear up her involvement in this mess."

"I've been going through CCTV footage, and there's something related to Emily that you should see."

"Do you have it cued up?" Macdara asked.

Aretta nodded. "In the viewing room."

They followed her to the viewing room, which had only been officially set up last year. It was a small space with a large computer monitor and all the bells and whistles needed to view CCTV footage. They all stood in front of the monitor as Aretta pushed Play. It only took a second to see that the camera was positioned with a view of Sarsfield Street in front of the charity shop. Soon, a man came into view. He had a cap on, head down, but he was dressed in the outfits designated for the garden crew. They all wore green pants and a T-shirt with KILBANE TOP GARDEN COMPETITION, along with a wind jacket and cap of the same color and the logo: KTGC accompanied by a shovel and a flower. Siobhán knew it well, for her brother Eoin had designed it. She'd been thrilled that he was slipping in some art time— he was an excellent artist, and she knew it would be a good distraction from his restaurant stress.

"We can't see his face," Macdara said.

"Here's the second clip. Three days later." It was a repeat

of the first, the only difference being the date. There were four more visits after it. "I checked, and every visit was on Emily Dunne's shift."

"Unless she's dating whoever that is—something is obviously going down," Siobhán said.

"We've also spoken with a dozen crew members so far," Aretta said. "They were each given two sets of the uniform. And over three of them so far have reported losing one set."

"Losing?" Macdara said.

"I suppose it didn't occur to them to say *stolen*—for who would steal the uniform of a garden crew?"

"Someone who didn't want to be recognized," Macdara said.

Aretta nodded. "Make that three someones?"

"That clocks. One person could not have damaged all these gardens solo." Siobhán studied the figure on the screen, now frozen. "This person may not be a member of the crew at all."

"The killer or killers could have come and gone from the gardens posing as a crew member," Macdara said. They were all thinking out loud, processing the implications.

"Three missing uniforms?" Siobhán asked.

Aretta nodded. "And we've only interviewed about half the crew, so it's possible more will report theirs were snatched."

Macdara crossed his arms. "Maybe this person hid a uniform at each garden site so that he or she could come and leave as himself, but while there could hide amongst the crew by donning the uniform?"

"It does seem as if multiple scenarios are possible," Aretta said.

Siobhán jotted down a few notes. "Maybe Emily can shed some light on this."

Macdara turned to Aretta. "Good work." She nodded, a smile appearing and then fading as she acknowledged the compliment. He glanced at Siobhán. "Given Emily's state of mind, perhaps we should go slow. Why don't you and Aretta conduct the interview?" He glanced at Aretta.

"Of course," Aretta said.

"Not a bother," Macdara said.

Siobhán pointed to the evidence bag still in Macdara's hands. "Don't forget to log that."

Aretta glanced at the golden yoke. "Find something?"

Macdara handed it to her. "Straight from the goat's mouth." He shook his head. "I hope I never hear meself saying those words again."

"An antique pen nib," Siobhán said as Aretta brought the bag close to her eyes.

Aretta examined it closer. "Do you think the killer dropped it?"

Siobhán shrugged. "I don't think Cassidy Ryan was killed by this object or anything like that. But we believe that for some reason our killer is leaving golden objects in each garden."

"We believe it might be a nod to Dullahan," Macdara added.

Aretta arched an eyebrow. "Dullahan?"

"*The Headless Horseman*," Siobhán said. "I know it sounds a bit outrageous, but when I have a moment I'll go over all the breadcrumbs that led us to that conclusion."

"Molly's a reporter," Macdara said. "Maybe she can shed some light on the antique pen."

"Maybe it's her pen," Aretta suggested.

"Her pre-interviews did take place at the homes of our gardeners," Siobhán said. "It is possible she dropped it." She shrugged. "I'm more interested in whether or not she's found the so-called cease and desist letter from Cassidy Ryan."

"They were kind of contentious in their first interview,"

Siobhán said. "Maybe that's why she didn't want to do another?"

Macdara shrugged. "She seemed to be enjoying the battle."

"True. And it's hard to imagine her declining the spotlight for any reason."

Aretta was studying Siobhán. "Sometimes I think you're part witch."

Siobhán's head snapped to Macdara and she stared at him, daring him to comment. He looked to the ceiling, and was doing a poor job of trying not to laugh.

"I'm sure we know my husband's interpretation, but whatever are you on about?"

Aretta handed the sheet of paper in her hand to Siobhán. *Cease and Desist* was centered at the top. It was the letter from Cassidy Ryan to Molly Murphy. "She found it?" Siobhán asked.

Aretta shook her head. "That's the other odd bit. The guards found it when they searched Teagan Moore's flat."

"Teagan's flat?" This case was starting to feel like a con man's game of shells. "Evidence keeps cropping up in the oddest places," Siobhán mused.

"Odd, indeed," Macdara said, turning to Aretta. "Have you spoken to Teagan about it?"

Aretta shook her head. "I thought you two might like to do the honors."

"Absolutely," Macdara said. "Who knew gardeners could be so duplicitous?"

Siobhán started to read the letter while Macdara looked over her shoulder:

> *Dear Ms. Murphy,*
>   *I cannot comply with your request for an interview, I am in the weeds, as they say. And furthermore, I know what you're really after is*

*gossip, and you had better watch what you
say. This assignment isn't for a tabloid. Why
don't you pen something meaningful? Believe
me—I will expose you and you will not come
up smelling like a rose. You're young, but that
does not excuse you. My advice? Put your
head down and mind your business. Only then
can you stand up tall. When you finally grow
up and wish to apologize, give me a bell.
Maybe you can photograph me holding the
winning trophy, but until then—stay away
from me and my garden!*
Yours truly,
Cassidy Ryan

"That's a bit odd," Macdara said. "Did Molly write any
salacious gossip about her?"

Aretta shook her head. "I scoured all of her interviews.
None of them are disparaging."

"This is a typewritten letter to boot," Siobhán said. "And
despite using the words *cease* and *desist*, it's far from being
a legal document. I hate to keep repeating myself but odd,
odd, odd."

"Cassidy Ryan was known to be dramatic though, wasn't
she?" Macdara asked.

"Yes," Siobhán said. "But she was also a diva. Why would
she turn down a simple interview? Molly writes for the
Kilbane Times, not the *Irish Times*. And Molly was hired
by the garden committee, not a tabloid. It doesn't make
sense."

"Unless this letter wasn't written by Cassidy Ryan," Aretta
said.

Siobhán wasn't sure where to go with it. "We are going
to have to get to the bottom of it. I hate to think Teagan

Moore wrote this—but if he didn't, why on earth was it in his flat?"

"Maybe Molly showed it to him?" Macdara asked. "Wanted to get his take on it?"

"I feel as if we have a list of never-ending questions." Siobhán sighed. "When we gain access to Cassidy's rental we'll have to see if we can find a draft of this letter on her laptop, or any other sign of the original."

"The same goes for Teagan's flat," Macdara said. "I'll have to review the list of items the guards found."

They had been tackling things in order of urgency. Until now Teagan Moore had been low on their radar. His outpouring of grief over the destruction of his rose garden had been raw, and if Siobhán was a betting woman—genuine. But if Cassidy was somehow involved in destroying their gardens—could she see him retaliating by killing her? Defending his roses? Your average person would do no such thing. But Teagan's connection to his roses were that of a parent to a child.

"We'll have to keep watching Molly's interviews with the gardeners," Macdara said. "Maybe something will stand out."

"I'm overwhelmed just thinking of everything we have to do," Siobhán said. "We need more hours in the day." Macdara and Aretta murmured their agreement. Siobhán read over the letter again. "Someone could have put a bug in Cassidy's ear about Molly Murphy," Siobhán said. "And maybe she was paranoid about whatever her showstopper was going to be. But denying the spotlight when you're trying to win a competition? I just can't see it." Her sixth sense was kicking in, and she'd learned to listen to it, but she'd also learned that until she was one hundred percent certain it was best to keep her piehole shut.

As Siobhán headed toward the interview rooms, Macdara's phone rang. Siobhán waited; one never knew when a single call could change the course of an investigation. He stepped away to answer it, and a few moments later returned. "I believe we've summoned the gods," he said. "Search warrant for Cassidy Ryan's flat just came through."

"Finally," Siobhán said. "Let's have our chat with Emily Dunne and Finnoula Connor, then head straight over."

Chapter 17

Emily Dunne sat hunched over, her sobs reduced to sniffles, yet her distress remained palpable. Siobhán set a glass of water and box of tissues in front of her before taking a seat.

"Thank you." Emily grabbed a tissue and gripped it tightly.

"The last I heard, your parents did not want me questioning you without a solicitor present."

Emily shrugged. "They were trying to protect me. But I'm an adult now. I want to tell you everything. I want to help."

Siobhán started the recording device, went through the disclaimers, and had Emily state that she was willingly being questioned without a solicitor.

"I didn't know," Emily said, as soon as they'd taken care of the housekeeping. "I thought it was part of the competition." She made eye contact with Siobhán, eyelashes wet from tears, pupils dilated.

"You were acting as a mole?" It was a stab in the dark, but Siobhán couldn't think of any other reason why Emily and Sean would be hunkered down in a dim pub in the middle of the day discussing moles.

Emily's eyes widened as she nodded. "Did someone tell you? Am I in the clear?"

"Why don't you start from the beginning, pet?"

"It all started when Sean Bell asked me to procure a bell for his garden." She hicupped. Siobhán gestured to the water. Emily nodded, grabbed the cup with both hands, and drank the entire thing in one go.

"Better?" Emily nodded. "Now."

"I wanted to make sure that locating a bell for Sean's garden wasn't against the rules so I called Lorcan Nursery to speak to the judge."

"Mr. Larry Lorcan was it?"

She nodded again as if thrilled they were speaking the same language. "He didn't know either. He said he had to speak to the garden committee and get back to me." She stopped talking and looked thoughtful. "Do you think they should be here for this?"

"We talk to folks one on one. You're doing great. Did the garden committee come to a decision?"

"That's the thing! I thought they had. Because a woman called me three days later. She said she was the president of the garden committee."

"Was it Finnoula Connor?" Siobhán had no idea whether or not there was such a position.

"It was just a phone call, she didn't give her name—I didn't even think to ask."

"Alright, not a bother. Go on."

Emily sniffed and grabbed a tissue. "She said that yes, of course, I could procure any item requested by any of the gardeners, and then she asked if I wanted to become even more involved."

"You're sure it was a woman?"

"If it was a man, he was speaking in a woman's voice, like."

"Right." Siobhán had to remind herself that if it was one

of their male gardeners, they could have convinced a woman to make the call for him. Either that or he was able to mimic a woman's voice. She had to keep all possibilities open, including that this wasn't a call from the killer, and including her least favorite option—Emily Dunne could be an excellent liar. But if Emily was to be believed, it was a woman on the phone. Yet in the CCTV footage, the visitor in the garden contest uniform was a man. Had two of their gardeners paired up to sabotage the competition this year? And was Cassidy killed because she copped onto their plan? Is that why she was snooping on the other gardens?

Emily leaned forward. "Turns out—there is no president." Betrayal, guilt, and fear played out on Emily's face.

"I see." Siobhán thought as much. Emily was a little late coming out with that little tidbit, but this was why one had to be patient when interviewing subjects. And if Emily Dunne was innocent, she had already paid quite a price. Currency? Anxiety. This was what happened in life. One started out pure and innocent. And then little by little, other people chipped away at one's composure.

"Why me?" Emily wailed, the waterworks starting anew. "Why did someone so evil drag me into this?"

"Are you positive that you didn't recognize the voice?"

"I keep going over and over it in me mind, trying to see could I figure out the identity of the caller. But it was a bad reception, like. Noise in the background. She sounded quite a bit older than me. But not old old. You know?" She suddenly tilted her head and stared at Siobhán. "Your age, like."

Fantastic. Siobhán supposed it was good she was not yet old old. She mulled over Emily's statement, approaching it from the perspective that Emily was telling the truth. At some point she'd consider the alternative, but right now she believed her. Perhaps the background noise had been meant to disguise the caller's voice. In that case, it was someone

Emily knew. Then again, in a town like Kilbane, strangers did not stay strangers for long. "What else did this woman say to you?"

"She said that if I was willing to be a participant that I had to be undercover." She held the tissue under her nose. "At first I was excited. She made it sound like it was meant to be something fun."

"When exactly were you contacted?"

Emily nodded as if she had been expecting the question. She pulled out a sheet of paper covered with notes. "It was Tuesday morning. Only three days before the official unveiling."

"You're sure?"

Emily nodded. "I started taking notes as she spoke. Three days was such a short timeline. I was excited to be a part of it but . . . I guess there was a part of me that knew it sounded off. I should have come to the guards. Do you think Cassidy Ryan would still be alive if I had come to the guards?" Tears filled her eyes. Siobhán resisted the urge to reach out and hold her hand. "I didn't enter *any* of the gardens. I swear. I was just a middleman for pickups. Like the crate." She hung her head. "I heard her body was in it. I feel sick. I can't sleep thinking about it."

"Who dropped the crate off at the charity shop and when?"

"It was dropped off very early Thursday morning. I arrived at eight and it was already on the footpath. All I had to do was keep an eye on it until a delivery lad picked it up. I should have known better. But as far as who dropped it off? I haven't a clue."

"Did you see any lorries parked on the street?"

"There were several. A butcher's truck, the tent-delivery folks, table and chair setup, the works."

"Right." For the garden competition. Of course by Thursday morning setup had been in full swing.

Emily reached for another tissue even though the tears had stopped for now. "I should have come to the station and checked that what I was doing was okay."

"You're coming forward now. That's what matters." Siobhán hesitated. She did not want to cause further alarm, but Emily had to cop on. "Listen to me very carefully. You should not speak of this to *anyone* else. Not until this case is solved. Do you understand?" Emily bit her lip and nodded. "You've already spoken to someone, haven't you?"

Tears began to fall down her cheeks. "Molly and Owen. They're my friends. And Owen was used too."

"Owen Sheedy, the lad who delivered the crate?" Emily nodded again. "Was Molly also manipulated by this person?"

Emily emphatically shook her head. "No. She was shocked when I told her. But . . ."

"Go on, so."

"I think she's investigating it, like. Using her training."

"I see." Molly Murphy needed to be careful. Unless she was the killer, in which case Emily Dunne needed to be careful. "I'm going to ask you not to say another word to either Owen Sheedy or Molly Murphy, including what we spoke about in here."

Emily nodded emphatically. "I swear."

Three days before the official opening someone decided to sabotage the gardens. Was someone simply trying to win the competition, or was there another reason? Cassidy Ryan was the only one whose garden was intact. Some might think that indicated that she was the culprit. And although here were plenty of dumb criminals, Cassidy Ryan had been a bright woman. And seemingly confident. It did not make sense that she would feel so threatened by these amateur gardeners that she would concoct such a plan. But if she did—how dumb did you have to be to leave your own garden untouched? But supposing for whatever reasons it was her . . . maybe one of the other gardeners—Sean Bell came to mind—discovered her plot and decided to put an end to it . . . *permanently.*

Siobhán felt a ripple of anger. This killer had used this young girl, manipulated her. "What did she ask you to do?"

"She asked me if I watched any of those competition shows on Netflix. There's a load of them. Baking, glass blowing, cooking—there's one called *The Traitors* . . . Have you seen it?" Siobhán shook her head. "It's gas. It takes place at a castle in Scotland." She waited for a reply. Siobhán just stared at her. "There's also one called *The Mole.* I hadn't seen that one. But I watched it that night, right after she asked me if *I* would like to be one of the moles."

One of the moles. This killer needed help to destroy all of the gardens, and he or she knew it. How many moles were there? If there were others, they must have realized they'd been played and were tunneling themselves underground. "What did she ask you to do?"

"She said that during the next three days, members of the garden crew, who were also moles, would come in to get instructions. She would call me every morning with those instructions."

Maybe that was why multiple garden outfits were missing. Unless some of the real crew members had taken place in the sabotaging efforts. "Did more than one person in the garden crew come in at a time?"

Emily shook her head. "One at a time, but several times a day, like over the next three days." She frowned. "They all covered their faces though. A black face mask, large sunglasses, and their caps pulled low. I would stand outside the shop, as if I was getting ready to either open or close it, the person would simply walk by, and I would hand them the note with the name written on it."

"Men and women?"

She shrugged. "Their uniforms were often baggy—and

they never spoke. The transactions were so quick, it was impossible to tell."

"They never spoke?"

She shook her head. "They just passed by and took the slip of paper with the name."

"These instructions did not specifically say what these gardeners should do?"

Emily shook her head again. "I had no idea they were going to actually destroy the gardens. I swear."

Once again, if Emily were to be believed, she was simply a messenger. Why couldn't this mastermind have gone directly to the garden crew and given her instructions? Or a direct text or call? Three days meant they were down to the wire. Why had someone developed such an elaborate, and let's face it, strange, way of communicating? "Let me make sure I have this correct. Every day this woman would call you and give you the name of one of the gardeners. You would simply write down the name and someone else would come in and pick up the name?"

"Yes, that's exactly it. Once before I opened the shop, and once before I closed."

Maddening. And very odd. "But the crew members were in disguise and none of them actually spoke with you?"

"That's right. I would simply hand them the name."

"Was there ever anyone else in the shop when this occurred?"

Emily bit her lip. "It was only before the shop opened, or on my breaks. The person would only approach me if I was on the footpath in front of the shop and the sign was turned to CLOSED."

Someone had gone to great lengths not to be associated with these messages. No phone calls, no eyewitnesses. "And were any of these phone calls to your mobile phone?"

"No. Always the shop phone."

Traditional phone lines were being phased out in Ireland, but many shops still used them. Phone records, if requested directly after this interview, which of course, Siobhán would do, would take ages to come in. And even then, if the caller had already created this complicated method of communicating, chances are they'd used a burner phone. "Was every single gardener's name mentioned during these exchanges?"

"Yes. There were two calls a day. Looking back on it now, it was so creepy. I mean the only thing the caller ever did was whisper a single name."

Like Dullahan. Riding to his victim's house, uttering nothing but the name of the doomed person . . . "Do you remember the order the names were mentioned?" Siobhán had no idea if this information would be helpful or not, but thus was the nature of investigations. You had to collect every piece of data you could, and then sift through them for meaning.

"I wrote them down." Emily consulted her notes. "The first day the names were Sean Bell and Alice McCarthy. The second day Nessa O'Neill and Finnoula Connor. The third day, Teagan Moore and Cassidy Ryan." Aretta and Siobhán made eye contact, and Siobhán could see that Aretta was equally perplexed. Emily hung her head. "I'm such an eejit. I should have known it was all a lie. I mean these gardeners are *old*. Most of them. They've probably never even watched these shows."

Siobhán bit her tongue. Emily had been extremely naïve, but that wasn't a crime. "When was the last call and the last visit?"

Emily gulped. "Thursday—the penultimate day of the garden designs."

Something had happened early in that week that triggered all of this. Would they ever find out what? "Cassidy Ryan. Did she ever come into the shop?"

Emily shook her head. "I was hoping she would come in. She was class. And gorgeous. I wasn't surprised though. I figured she only wanted fancy items for her garden." She swallowed hard. "I can't be an accessory to murder because I swear on my grave I didn't know anything about a murder. Am I going to jail for the rest of me life?"

"Let's repeat this for clarity. Did you know they were planning on murdering one of the gardeners?"

"Oh, my word. No. Of course not. I swear on me life. On me mammy and daddy and granny's life. I swear. I swear. I swear, I swear." She dropped her head to the table. "Everyone's going to know. Me life is ruined. It's ruined!" The sobbing started in earnest.

"Listen to me," Siobhán said. "If what you're saying is true, and you thought it was part of the game, we're not going after you for that. And I'm not here to spread town gossip. But we are going to check out your story. Fair?"

"Fair," Emily wailed.

"And after the murder . . . why did you meet with Sean Bell at Butler's?"

Emily lifted her head. "He wanted to confirm that he bought a black bell from the shop—which he did. And he wanted to know if I knew anything about the golden bell."

"What did you tell him?"

"I told him I knew nothing about it."

"Did anyone else ever specifically ask you about sourcing a gold item for them?"

"No." She tilted her head. "Why? Did every garden have something gold?" Emily's voice no longer sounded innocent and pure; instead, she seemed hungry for information. Was she still playing a game? Was she playing Siobhán? If so— what in the world was her motive?

"I only ask questions," Siobhán said, using her sternest voice. "I don't answer them." As the investigation went forward, they were going to have to keep an eye on Emily Dunne.

"Of course, of course," Emily said, her tone reverting to that of a meek and shy young woman.

"What did you get in exchange for all of this, Emily?"

Emily's head snapped up in surprise. "What do you mean?"

"Did she pay you? Did she say she would pay you?"

Emily frowned. "No, no, nothing like that. She said it was an honor just to be a part of the game."

"I see." Someone had paid Owen Sheedy five hundred euro to deliver one crate. Granted, it probably had the body of their victim in it—but was it possible they didn't pay Emily Dunne so much as a pound? *No.* And that was how Siobhán ended the interview with their young, weepy subject: with a bold-faced lie.

Chapter 18

Twilight crept over the village, coating the skies with reds and oranges, and bringing the day to a close for many, but inside The Six the evening was just getting started. Not only were they expecting Dr. Jeanie Brady to join them, Aretta Dabiri was here in an unofficial capacity, along with Ciarán and Ann, the youngest members of the O'Sullivan Six. They were excitedly roaming about the restaurant with Eoin, who was giving them a tour of the "finished product" with the pride of a new father.

Aretta, who had not seen Ciarán or Ann in a while, was eager to hear news of their lives. "I hear you're excelling on your camogie team," she said to Ann.

Ann, arguably the most modest of the six, blushed. "My wrist work has gotten fierce," she said with a smile.

"She's not messing," Ciarán chimed in. "I've seen her wield that stick better than most lads."

Ann looped her arm around her brother. "And this one has gone and joined a trad band."

"He's done what now?" Siobhán said from across the room. She was over to Ciarán in a flash. "You've done what?"

Ciarán gave Ann an *I told ya so* look before facing Siobhán. "They're a brilliant group, but their fiddler dropped out, and they've asked me to take his place. I said yes."

"Well done," Macdara said.

"Is it?" Siobhán said, turning to him. "You're familiar with them, are ya?" Macdara shrugged and exchanged a look with Ciarán. *I tried.* "What does this mean exactly?" Siobhán said to Ciarán. "How many are in the band? Who are their parents? You get paid? Where do they play?"

Ciarán was already shaking his head. "Don't be weird."

"I can get even weirder. Answer the questions."

"Yes, we get tips, and a cover from the pub—and we're going on tour. There are four lads, and one colleen. I have no clue who their parents are and you shouldn't either. But we're definitely hitting the road. America, here I come."

He was tall, his voice was deep, and he was standing up to her with ease. They were all grown up. Every one of them was leaving her. Would Eoin move his restaurant to a new location as soon as he was able?

"Brilliant," Eoin said, joining the Brutus Team and patting Ciarán on the back. "You're flying it." Ciarán beamed. Siobhán's stomach did a somersault.

"Stop fussing," Ciarán said. "We don't leave for another month." With that he moved to the other end of the restaurant, no doubt to avoid a deeper inquisition. Siobhán tried to put it out of her mind and headed for Jeanie Brady who was standing by the windows looking out at Cassidy Ryan's tent. They had decided on dinner first and autopsy results after, but she needed a distraction and Eoin had announced it would be at least thirty minutes before dinner was served.

Jeanie turned as Siobhán approached. "I know that look," she said. "You want to talk shop."

"I know we said we'd wait—"

Jeanie waved her hand. "We have time to kill—no time like the present."

"My thoughts exactly."

"Will Aretta and Macdara be joining us?"

"We will," Macdara said. Apparently they had seen the freight train that was Siobhán O'Sullivan barreling toward Jeanie Brady, and had decided to tag along.

"Let's take this outside, shall we?" Jeanie glanced over at Eoin, Ann, and Ciarán who were laughing in the corner. "I wouldn't want to ruin their evening."

After calling to Eoin to give a holler when dinner was ready, they stepped outside. It was a dark, still night, and overhead stars glistened. Siobhán took a moment to bathe in them.

"I dare say, I found the autopsy results surprising," Jeanie began as soon as they were some distance from the restaurant. "Cassidy Ryan was drowned."

"Drowned?" the three of them replied in chorus.

Siobhán was rarely shocked, but this one had her mind spinning. "Are you sure?"

Jeanie nodded. "Unmistakable. Water in her lungs, a small gash on her temple and bruising on the back of her neck. From the look of the wound I believe she hit her head when she either fell, or most likely, was pushed into a body of water. Did any of the gardens have large rocks in their water feature?"

"I'm sure some of them did," Siobhán said. "Every garden was required to have a water feature this year."

Macdara nodded. "Off the top of me head—Sean Bell's garden had plenty of rocks. Nessa's bathtub didn't, but she could have hit her head on the side of the tub. Alice and Teagan had fountains—but as Jeanie pointed out she could have drowned in a small amount of water. And then there's Finnoula Connor. We'll never know what her garden looked like, the entire garden was flooded."

"Maybe it was flooded on purpose. Maybe she wanted to hide that a murder took place there?" Aretta offered.

"Maybe," Siobhán said, still fixated on the cause of death.

"I know that look too," Jeanie said, wagging her finger. "You're off with the fairies, are ya, Siobhán?"

"Right, right," Siobhán said, realizing she had no idea what Jeanie just said. *Drowned?* These gardeners might technically be amateurs, but they knew their way around plants. They would not only know which ones were poisonous to humans, no doubt they also would have plenty of them within reach. Did this mean it wasn't a gardener who murdered Cassidy? Had she enraged a crew member?

"Could it have been an accidental drowning?" Macdara asked.

Jeanie shook her head. "Given the bruising on the back of her neck, I believe once she was facedown in the water, someone held her under." Jeanie took a deep breath. "What's most curious about this situation is that most drownings are actually quite hard to prove. For example. They could have drugged her, placed her in water, and most likely we would have assumed it was an accident. Not that many people take a bath in the middle of a garden—but stage a few empty alcohol or pill bottles next to her—it could have looked like a suicide."

"Or they could have staged it to make it appear that she tripped and fell," Macdara said.

"I was just thinking along the same lines," Siobhán said. "Any of the gardeners could have poisoned her, and we might never know she was murdered."

"In summary," Macdara said, "anything short of spray-painting Cassidy and propping her up in her own garden, and we might never have opened a murder probe in the first place."

"It's bold," Siobhán agreed. "Our killer was filled with rage."

"Does this eliminate the gardeners as suspects?" Aretta's voice was measured. "At least in our minds?"

Siobhán didn't want them to come to that conclusion this

soon. "Maybe that's exactly what someone *wants* us to do. Eliminate the gardeners, conclude they couldn't possibly be so blatant. Assume they would have poisoned her. Assume they would have staged her death to look like an accident. Having us do gymnastics trying to figure it out might be their exact goal. And it's nearly working."

They'd reached the tent now, and Macdara turned on the portable lights. Together, they stood amidst the beauty of the garden, a stark contrast to the ugliness of the crime they were piecing together. The absence of an installation in the center of the garden stuck out like two missing front teeth. Beauty and destruction vying for space. *Drowned.*

Siobhán felt a cold shiver trace her spine, and it wasn't from the slight chill in the air. Love her or hate her, Cassidy Ryan had been a force of nature. It was incomprehensible that she had been extinguished by such a cruel and intimate act. Downright chilling. "Whoever did this was driven by fury," Siobhán said. "And a need to humiliate."

"Rage can be a powerful motivator," Macdara added. "And a dangerous one."

"I don't believe she was killed here," Siobhán said. "There's not much of a water feature to speak of." The fountain was deep, but not wide. There would have been signs of a struggle. Not to mention the fact that her body had literally been delivered in a crate.

Siobhán began to pace in front of the tent. "We cannot close any doors at this point. Take our conversation with Emily Dunne. I never would have imagined someone went to such complicated lengths to communicate with the persons picking up the messages. This killer's motivation is not yet clear, but I do believe they were making decisions out of necessity. We just don't have the whole picture yet."

"Or," Macdara said, "as Aretta pointed out, it might not be one of our gardeners."

"All possibilities exist." Siobhán's mind raced, connecting dots that formed an increasingly sinister picture. "We should consider areas other than the gardens," Siobhán said. "There's the river by the abbey, of course. And Lorcan's Nursery boasts a lily pond inside the greenhouse."

"That's right," Macdara said. "And we've never declared it a crime scene."

Siobhán felt like this case was drowning all of them.

"A lily pond is definitely a place to search," Jeanie conceded, her brows knitting together in concern. "If you search the scene and have any suspicions whatsoever, I can come down and get a sample of the water. Then I can compare it with the water found in Cassidy's lungs. That should nail it down."

"Should we try to get water samples from each garden as well?" Aretta suggested. "I can organize that."

"I'd much appreciate that," Jeanie said.

Macdara gave Aretta the go-ahead and turned to Jeanie. "We'll set up a visit to the nursery straightaway and keep you posted."

"I don't envy you lot," Jeanie said. "You're busier than me with this one." A collective sigh was heard.

"Tonight, we should watch at least one more of Molly's interviews," Siobhán resolved. "Tomorrow morning, we search Cassidy's flat and pay a visit to Lorcan's Nursery."

"Right," Macdara agreed. "We'll assign guards to revisit all the gardens. Aretta, while they're collecting water samples, make sure they look for traces of Cassidy's hair in the water feature or specks of gold spray paint."

"Absolutely," Aretta said.

Jeanie nodded. "Pay particular attention to objects such as large rocks in the water, and/or any signs of blood."

"Good work, Dr. Brady," Macdara said.

"I feel old whenever anyone calls me Dr. Brady," Jeanie said, waving it away with her hand. "And don't thank me yet. There's more."

The three of them stared expectantly. "Your report mentions several folks claimed to have seen Cassidy Ryan on Thursday afternoon."

"That's correct," Siobhán said. "Including Eoin." She and Macdara stared at Jeanie intently. "But that's not possible if she was delivered in that crate Thursday morning."

Jeanie smirked. "Trying to take over me job, are ye?" She laughed before proceeding. "You are correct. I don't know who they saw, but it wasn't Cassidy Ryan." Jeanie paused. "I put her time of death to be three days earlier. Either late into the evening on Monday, or more likely the wee hours of Tuesday morning."

In the dark of night. Siobhán's mind conjured up the carriage driven by the Headless Horseman. "That's why someone needed to change the rules of the game with only a few days before the competition opened. That's why they needed to drag Emily Dunne and Owen Sheedy into it. Not to mention whoever the people were that showed up at Raven's to get 'instructions.' "

"You haven't picked up anything on the security cameras?" Jeanie asked.

"It's a slog," Aretta said. "With so many gardens there is a lot to get through."

"Let's prioritize the ones on Sarsfield Street," Macdara said.

Aretta nodded. "Will do."

"Let's not get our hopes up," Siobhán interjected. "Emily said every person who stopped by went to great lengths to disguise themselves. The garden uniforms, hats pulled low, sunglasses. They also didn't speak to her. If she didn't recognize them up close, I'm not counting on us recognizing them in grainy footage."

Everyone paused to take this in.

Aretta put away her notes as she gazed off into the distance. "Why would Cassidy Ryan be hanging around a water feature in the middle of the night?"

"We have so many unanswered questions. And now that we know Sean Bell and Eoin did not see Cassidy Ryan on Thursday, I'd like to see if Eoin remembers anything else about the encounter." Siobhán glanced up at the restaurant; from out here it appeared to be glowing.

"Let him enjoy this evening," Macdara said. "We can speak with him in the morning."

"Anything else you need us to know?" Macdara asked Jeanie as they headed back to The Six.

"There was less decay in the body than I would have expected to see," Jeanie said. "If she was murdered in the lily pond, I would expect a greenhouse to have the opposite effect. Hot air can reduce a body to bones in a matter of weeks."

"Maybe that's why she was placed in some kind of freezer," Siobhán said, turning to Macdara. "Have we discovered a freezer at any of the locations so far?"

"No," Macdara said. "We have not."

"Don't get me wrong. She wasn't frozen solid. She was just cold enough for the paint to stick."

"Nessa O'Neill has several outbuildings on her property," Siobhán pointed out. "Maybe there's a freezer hidden in one of them. We'll have to go back over all of our crime scenes."

"I know it goes without saying that we need to keep this new time of death to ourselves," Macdara said. "The killer's plan seems to hinge on us believing she was alive up until that Thursday."

"Supper is almost on the table," Eoin's voice rang out into the night air. Overhead a full moon glowed.

"We'll be right there," Siobhán called out. She started to head for the restaurant with Jeanie and Aretta.

"Siobhán?" Macdara said. "Can I have a moment?"

"We'll save you a seat," Jeanie said with a wink, and she and Aretta continued on their way.

Siobhán turned to Macdara, her eyes welling up. Life was way more stressful when they were arguing. Macdara took Siobhán's hand, his fingers intertwining with hers.

"Dara—"

"Me first," Macdara said. He got down on one knee. Siobhán's hand flew to her mouth. She was going to lose it. "Siobhán O'Sullivan. Your husband has been a stubborn, rude old goat, and I shouldn't have let this drag on so long. From the bottom of my heart. I am truly sorry." His voice caught, and she couldn't take it any longer. She helped him to his feet. "Forgive me?" he said, his eyes locking on hers.

"There's nothing to forgive. I'm sorry. I've been so wound up, so emotional lately. And maybe a tad stubborn to boot."

Macdara threw his head back and laughed. "Let's get Molly Murphy here to share that breaking news." He pulled her into his arms and she let him hold some of her weight.

"I thought I was getting better, but between Ciarán joining a gang."

"Trad band—"

"—And this awful news . . . my stomach is still in knots." She glanced toward the restaurant. Lit from within, it seemed to glow, and she was comforted at the sight of the people within, people she loved fiercely.

"That's it," Macdara said. "We're calling Dr. Brennan in the morning."

"Only if I can squeeze it in," Siobhán said. "I'm not backing away from this case."

"I wouldn't want you to back away. In *any* shape or form." He went in for a kiss, and just like that her world was in balance again. She let the kiss take her away, take *them* away.

"I never want to argue again," she said when they came up for air. "Life is too short."

"Good," he said. "Because these past few days definitely shaved a bit of mine off." He stretched. "And we need to replace that sofa—it's a nightmare on me back."

"Then we're never replacing it," Siobhán said. "That way you'll never sleep there again."

Holding hands, they made their way back to the buzz of the restaurant. As they reentered, they saw everyone huddled together, and familiar voices rang out. Gráinne and James. "They're right here," Eoin said to the familiar figures on his iPad as he turned it to face Siobhán and Macdara. "They were all alone out there in the dark."

"Siobhán and Macdara sitting in a tree," Gráinne sang from the iPad. "*K-i-s-s-i-n-g.*"

"We're still waiting for the baby in the baby carriage," James added.

"Ah, stop, will ya?" Siobhán said, her face heating up. "I wish the two of you were here so I could give out to ye properly."

"Careful what you wish for," Gráinne said. "That's why we called."

"We'll be there for the opening of the restaurant," James said. "Now that the opening has been delayed, we were able to work out our schedules."

"That means a lot." Eoin's voice was thick with emotion, and Siobhán was on the verge of bawling. They might be living separate lives, but they were still a unit. A family. Their binds might stretch but they would never break.

"And we'll get to attend one of Ann's camogie practices, and we can't wait to hear Ciarán and his new band," Gráinne added.

"Can we also come to the inn?" Ann asked. "I miss Lahinch." In the short time they'd been there, Ann, ever the athelete, had taken up surfing.

"There's always a room for ya," Gráinne said. "But I'll have to put you to work." She groaned. "Don't get me started on the repairs."

As they ended the video call, with more than a few good-byes, and took their seats for dinner, Siobhán found solace in the familiar. No matter what lay ahead, she would find strength in their union, the roots that held them together. She had this land, she had this tribe, and she had a chef-prepared plate of steak with a peppercorn sauce, veg, and roasted potato in front of her. And she knew, as well as she knew her own shadow, that she could never fight the darkness of the world without this home, without this love, without this light.

Chapter 19

"Let's just watch one interview," Siobhán said, holding up her index finger. Macdara sighed. It was late, they had ended the evening on a happy note, and her husband wanted them to get to sleep. And given they had just made up after a big fight, he may have had other things in mind as well. But Siobhán couldn't shake the feeling that they were getting behind on this case, despite spending every waking minute working on it.

Macdara frowned. "If this is anything like—'I'm off to the pub but just for one—' "

"One means one," Siobhán said. "I swear." Seconds later they were seated at the kitchen table under a dim light, the laptop in front of them. Molly Murphy's image filled the frame, and before any interview began, she flashed her engagement ring. A man with an easy smile slid into view; he pressed his lips to hers in a fleeting kiss, before exiting the frame.

"Her fiancé, I presume," Siobhán said. She checked her notes. "Brandon."

"Ah, young love," Macdara replied.

"What does that make us?" Siobhán asked. "Old love?"

"I see you two have patched things up," a voice on the tape said. For a second Siobhán was thrown; it was as if the person on the video was speaking directly to them. The camera switched directions, and sitting before them was Alice McCarthy. The smirk on her face said it all. She was inside her home at a desk next to a pile of books.

"We're engaged," Molly said with a touch of sheepishness.

"I'm aware. I think everyone in town is aware," Alice said.

Molly stared at her, and from her facial expression, she had taken the comment as a dig. "Don't worry. I won't be asking *you* for marriage advice."

"We fought in front of her too," Siobhán said. "I'm surprised she hasn't called the whole thing off."

Alice's face soured instantly, her eyes narrowing into angry slits that seemed to pierce through the screen. "I know exactly what you're insinuating." Her voice was sharp, each word clipped with barely contained fury. "Are you going to spread that filth in your little blog post?"

"I had no ideas these gardeners were so on edge," Siobhán said. She knew from experience that anger was a form of poison.

"It's not a blog post," Molly said. "It's an official article, like. For the *Kilbane Times*."

"Is it now?" Alice retorted, her voice laced with disdain. "And here I was thinking you were reporting on some Pulitzer Prize-winning book."

Siobhán and Macdara exchanged glances. The tension between the two women, even on video, was thick enough to slice. And yet, since the discovery of Cassidy Ryan's murder, neither of them had said anything about how vitriolic this interview had played out.

Siobhán gestured to Macdara and he paused it once more. "Alice must think Molly is going to write about the public row with her husband," Siobhán said. They still hadn't spoken with him. If only there were more hours in a day.

"It's probably a wise suspicion," Macdara said. "Molly seems intent on digging up gossip."

"Do you really think Ms. Murphy would go that far astray?"

Macdara tilted his head as he mulled it over. "You said it yourself. She seems to enjoy stirring the pot."

"I guess she wants to make a name for herself. Whatever it takes."

With a click, they returned to the browned-off faces on the video.

"I understand your garden will showcase an *Alice in Wonderland* theme," Molly said, her voice smooth and professional. "Tell me why."

"Smart," Macdara said. "An open-ended question."

"My husband is not having an affair with Cassidy Ryan," Alice volunteered, her tone defiant.

"She can't let go," Siobhán said. "I've never seen this side of her."

"But he is the friendly sort, especially after a few pints," Alice continued, "and I might have lost me temper and given out to him in public—but it's Cassidy that was draping herself all over him."

"Noted." Molly's pen hovered above her notebook. "Off the record, that is. Honestly, I was just making polite conversation before the interview. Your marriage or your feud with Cassidy Ryan is not the subject of my article."

"My feud?" Alice's laugh was short, devoid of humor. "I don't have a feud. I have a grudge." Her hands wrapped around a cuppa, knuckles whitening as though she were anchoring herself against an onslaught.

"She should have had a *Snow White* theme," Siobhán said. "She looks the part."

"She's less attractive the more she speaks," Macdara said. Siobhán took his hand and squeezed. "What's that for?"

"You're a good egg," Siobhán said.

"Cracked and scrambled," Macdara replied.

Siobhán laughed. "And once in a while over easy." She returned her attention to the video before Macdara could give out to her for being over hard.

Molly's gaze was firmly on Alice. "Please. Tell me about your plans for your garden." Her voice was soft but insistent, no doubt an attempt to steer them back to safer waters.

Alice's grip on her cup relaxed, her shoulders eased down from their defensive posture. A flicker of pride lit up her features, momentarily softening the lines of consternation. "I've always been enthralled with *Alice in Wonderland*. It might have started because she's another Alice, but then I truly fell in love with the story. The madness, the unpredictability, adventure—it's a lot like gardening."

"This year there certainly promises to be a little madness," Molly said cheerfully.

"See?" Siobhán said. "Just when Alice is finally letting her guard down, Molly is stirring the pot!"

"She could just be engaging in a bit of humor," Macdara said.

"Have you heard the rumor about Cassidy Ryan?" Molly continued.

Alice snapped to attention. "No. Tell me."

"Despite the fact that I'm only reporting for a village newspaper, I've done me research. Cassidy Ryan is only in this competition because it's a requirement for the *other* garden competition she's enrolled in, an international one with a prize pot of a million euro."

"What?" Siobhán said to Molly as if she could respond.

"The hole deepens," Macdara said.

Molly's eyes glimmered with anticipation as she awaited Alice's reaction.

Siobhán paused it and stared at her husband. "You're right, you're right. You're right, wifey," he said. "She's stirring the pot."

"Right? Every single time!"

Macdara stared at the screen as if trying to read the minds of the women caught in a frozen moment. "Have you heard anything about this other competition?"

"Not a word. Not a single word." And in this town that was downright suspicious. If any part of this salacious gossip was true, there was zero chance that Alice McCarthy hadn't shared it with the other gardeners, not to mention Molly herself. In fact, a tidbit like that would have gone off like a rocket. "Perhaps they don't want to speak ill of the dead," Siobhán said. *Or they had a guilty conscience.*

"They're afraid if they bring it up—not only do they sound petty—"

"—They put a spotlight on themselves as a murder suspect."

"A million euro?" Macdara said. "Would a garden competition actually pay a million euro?"

"Let's keep watching." Siobhán pushed Play.

"A million euro?" Alice echoed.

Macdara paused the video once more. "I would say that's a million reasons to kill," he said.

Siobhán nodded. "But even if it's true, Cassidy didn't actually have the million euro, and even if she did—how would killing them help any of our gardeners get his or her hands on it?"

"We need to find out if it's even true. Maybe Molly isn't just stirring the pot, maybe she's making up the ingredients."

"I wouldn't put it past her," Siobhán said. "But this is the kind of information one can easily verify." If it wasn't so late, she'd be on the phone with Molly Murphy right this minute, seeking clarification. "Hold on." She opened a new screen on the laptop.

Macdara groaned and glanced at the kitchen clock. "We're going to be sitting here until sunrise."

"Who could sleep after this?" Siobhán said. She glanced at her husband. "Besides you." She brought up another screen and began a search. "Garden contests, million euro prize pots," she narrated. She scanned the results and then let out a little gasp. "Here it is. The contest is being run by an international online gardening store . . . purveyor of luxury sculptures and exotic plants . . . hosting a contest with landscape designers from around the globe." Siobhán continued to read, her lips moving. "Here! This contest is nearly like a treasure hunt."

"Treasure hunt?"

"The contestants have a list of requirements they have to fill, and one of them is to win a local garden competition."

"And of all the villages in all of Ireland, she picks ours." He shook his head and pushed Play.

"I have no idea about any other competition," Alice was saying.

"Google it," Siobhán and Macdara yelled at the screen in stereo. Then they looked at each other, laughed, and fist-bumped. It felt so good to be back to their old selves. She never wanted to argue with him again.

"One of the requirements of this million-euro-prize-pot is to win a local gardening competition," Molly said. "That's the only reason Cassidy Ryan is here."

"That's why she's invaded our competition?" Alice said. Her hands, which had been resting on top of her desk, clenched into fists. Molly had done more than stir the pot, she'd taken an electric beater to it and whipped it into a frenzy.

"I plan on nabbing her for a second interview," Molly

stated. "I will make sure to ask her about it." Alice had risen and was now pacing back and forth behind her desk. "What else would you like folks to know about your garden?" Molly said in an upbeat tone that didn't match the current vibe.

Alice whirled around and collided with her desk, jostling her stack of books. One slid to the floor, landing with a thud.

"Is that *Alice in Wonderland?*" Molly inquired, as Alice bent to retrieve it.

"No," Alice replied curtly, turning the book to the screen. The cover, sans jacket, was black, and the first thing Siobhán noticed was both the title and image were embossed in gold. The image: A horse rearing back, with the man sitting atop him, holding the reins. At least she assumed it was a man. But how was she to know? He or she were missing their head.

"*The Headless Horseman?*" Molly said, turning the book over in her hands. "Not what I was expecting."

"Nor me," Siobhán said. The mention of the Headless Horseman caused her to spring to her feet. She placed her palms on the kitchen table and hovered over the laptop. "Does every single one of them have a copy of that tale?"

Macdara groaned. "Right," he said as he stood to stretch. "Coffee?"

Siobhán chewed on her lip and placed her hand on her stomach. "My tummy hasn't forgiven me yet," she said. "I'd better not."

"I'm taking you to the doctor *tomorrow*," Macdara said.

On the screen, Alice caressed the cover of her book. "The tale of Dullahan has always terrified me. As a child it gave me such nightmares. The thought of a man, riding around, holding his own head in his hands?" She seemed to shiver. "Terrifying."

Suddenly the video shut off, but there was still audio. "What's the story?" Molly said. "This wasn't in your first interview." There was a click and then the sound was cut as well.

Siobhán arched an eyebrow. "First interview? I thought this was the first interview?"

Macdara thunked a coffee cup down, opened another cupboard, and brought out a bottle of whiskey. "My stomach is just fine," he said before Siobhán could lecture him. "It's me head that's suddenly hurting."

"Have one for me," Siobhán said. "I hope Molly Murphy is getting a good night's sleep. Because she's not going to rest again until I get a few answers."

Chapter 20

Siobhán and Macdara were deep in conversation when they neared the cottage rented by Cassidy Ryan. They'd reached Molly Murphy by phone and she'd seemed taken aback that she'd been caught on audio mentioning that her interview with Alice wasn't the first one. She'd told them that on Wednesday before the official opening of the garden tour, Alice McCarthy had asked for a do-over. Apparently she'd just learned that Molly planned to play clips on social media over the weekend and she wanted something a little more exciting. "Out of curiosity," Siobhán had asked Molly, "I believe I heard you commenting that she didn't mention *The Headless Horseman* during the first interview. Is that correct?"

"Yes," Molly said, with an inquisitive look. "That just came up because she knocked the book off her table. It is odd though."

"Why is it odd?"

A long moment of silence followed. "Yes," Molly said slightly louder, her tone sounding forced. "I'm here on Sarsfield Street chatting with the gardeners as we speak."

She couldn't talk. "We'll let you go for now, but we need to set up an official chat. Garda Dabiri will be contacting you to schedule one."

"Not a bother." Molly hung up first.

By the time they pulled in front of the rental cottage, Siobhán's mind had been so preoccupied that the sight before her was impossible to comprehend. Violent flames danced in front of them, engulfing the cottage, spewing ash and smoke.

"Fire!" Macdara yelled, pulling out his mobile phone and jumping out of the car. Siobhán quickly exited the vehicle after him and was immediately struck by the heat even though she was a fair distance away. The fire crackled like some kind of creature, gorging on its prey. Siobhán knew that smell. Acrid, like burning plastic, and it brought her right back to the time her dairy barn had been set on fire by a killer. And although this time she was standing outside the house, far enough away that she wasn't inhaling that vile smoke, the memory of that terrifying day was with her in an instant. Macdara must have been thinking about it too, for he suddenly ran back to her, put his arm around her, and drew her close. "Firemen are on their way."

Despite the heat, Siobhán shivered. "If we hadn't interrupted our morning for my doctor's appointment, we could have been trapped inside."

"I don't even want to think about it," Macdara said, his voice deep and protective. The news that the doctor had given them was not something they could even begin to process until this case was behind them. She had scheduled a follow-up appointment in a few weeks, and they would take it from there. Meanwhile, they made a pact not to discuss it until then. The air around them had taken on a dirty-orange hue, and a crowd was starting to gather on the road. Soon the sound of firetrucks blared and minutes later two large trucks arrived. Firemen sprang out, unfurling their hoses. Siobhán had never been so happy to see water arc into the sky. They battled the flames until the last flicker of orange surrendered to the water, leaving the cottage and front garden buried in ashes, looking like a scene out of the apocalypse.

"No one was inside," Macdara said. "At least there's that."

"Someone knew we were coming," Siobhán said. "There was something they didn't want us to find." It was maddening that the answers they sought were once so close, and yet now so very far away. Anger rose within her, fueled by a sense of helplessness.

"Breaking a window to crawl in and fetch whatever it was they were after would have been easier," Macdara said. "Why set the whole place ablaze?"

"Maybe they knew what they were looking for, but they didn't know exactly where to find it. And the longer they hung around . . ."

"The higher the likelihood that we would nab him."

"Or her." *Or them.* This case was confounding. If only they had arrived sooner. What if something in that cottage had pointed directly to the killer? This case could have been over right now. They could have been celebrating. *If only . . .* Siobhán shook off the thought. It was a waste of time. "Maybe it was something like her laptop. Even if they had taken it, once we did our search and found it missing, its very absence would have been a clue."

"Someone is desperate," Macdara agreed.

"One is always desperate when trying to get away with murder."

The cottage, now a skeletal frame, had burned its secrets to the ground. Macdara stepped away to speak with the firemen. Now they had one more crime scene, what was left of it, and Siobhán didn't know how much more they could take. She was buoyed by the arrival of Aretta who approached Siobhán with an expression that was both grim and calm.

"Are you alright?" Aretta asked straightaway. Siobhán nodded, as tears welled in her eyes. It was all the stress, the memories, and the fury that a killer had done this minutes, maybe even seconds, before they arrived. The cottage was surrounded by fields, the nearest house a speck in the distance. But the road in front of it was a busy one; it was the road leading out of town, and if one had a sweet tooth, it was a straight path to the old flour mill that housed one of the best bakeries around. It explained the long line of cars that seemed to grow longer by the second as people stopped to gawk at the destruction. "I'm giving you a hug," Aretta said, and then she did.

"Thank you. I'm not usually so emotional."

"You could have been in there. You wouldn't be human if you weren't emotional." Aretta reached into the pocket of her uniform and brought out a chocolate bar. "It was the best I could do on short notice."

Siobhán bit her lip as this brought on more of the waterworks. She nodded her head as she gratefully took the chocolate bar. Aretta nodded back and patted her arm.

"I don't look forward to ringing the owner with this news," Aretta said.

"I'm sure Dara could do that."

Aretta was already shaking her head. "I'm learning that part of this job is doing things you'd rather not be doing."

"Part of it?" Siobhán said, breaking the gloomy moment with a laugh. "I'd say it's 99 percent."

Aretta raised an eyebrow. "What's the one percent?"

"This." Siobhán raised the chocolate bar. Aretta laughed. "Maybe we'll find something in the rubble," Siobhán said, mostly trying to convince herself.

"One can hope," Aretta said. "But from the looks of it, it's going to be a long process."

A sudden sound cut through the morning stillness—a horse whinnying, followed by the unmistakable rhythm of galloping hooves. Aretta and Siobhán locked eyes. "What in the world?" Siobhán said. The distressed horse sounded as if it came from the charred remains of the cottage itself. Soon every person nearby drew closer, their faces reflecting a variety of puzzled reactions. If there weren't others around, reacting to the same thing, Siobhán would have worried that the vile smoke had gone to her poor head and she was hallucinating. And then she wished she was. As they all stared at the house, a male voice rose out of the ashes and pierced the silence with a stage whisper: "Cassidy."

Chapter 21

Mist sprayed at the verdant fronds arching above the entrance to the greenhouse. Siobhán and Macdara stepped into its humid embrace, cocooned in nature. Every surface in Larry Lorcan's nursery was bursting with life, from the classical roses to the exotic orchids that stretched their spotted petals towards the glass panes above. They passed by beds of marigolds, their orange heads bobbing gently in the humid air, trellises adorned with climbing ivy, and clematis that created lush green walls. Brightly colored butterflies danced among the flowers like living confetti, adding to the enchantment of the place.

They were headed to the lily pond, which glimmered just beneath a small wooden bridge. The structure arched up above the water, and looked as if it was being remodeled, for the left side had ancient banisters with peeling paint, whereas the right side had been replaced with new wood and new paint. It would make sense that Larry was sprucing things up for the crowds, but why hadn't they finished the job? She pointed it out to Macdara, then jotted down a note, and took a photo.

"It's odd that he only had one side repaired, but he is known to be a bit tight in the wallet."

"True," Siobhán said. "And this should have been finished long before we discovered Cassidy Ryan's body."

"Unless . . ." Macdara said.

"Unless he knew she was dead before we knew it." As difficult as it was to imagine Larry Lorcan murdering Cassidy Ryan, Siobhán had to make room for the possibility. She'd learned early on that murderers could just as easily be the lad or lassie next door, or the grandfatherly or grandmotherly figure down the block. If only they came with some kind of warning: KILLER written on their foreheads or some such.

She turned to stare into the water, taking in the white and pink blooms spreading across the reflective surface, mirroring leaves, flowers, and the sky. If they weren't here on such a serious matter it would have been peaceful and romantic. Smaller red blossoms floated amongst the lilies, standing out like splotches of blood. "Are those rose petals?" Siobhán asked.

"I'm not an expert," Macdara said. "But if I had to place a bet, I'd say you were spot on. I'm afraid I was too busy thinking of something far more grim."

"The pond is large enough to drown in," Siobhán said.

Macdara nodded. "And had she been murdered here, the heat in this greenhouse would have dried out her body rather quickly," he added. "We need to search this place top to bottom for a freezer." These grim observations and realities were the nature of the job, but it felt sacrilegious in such a serene environment. *Drowned. Dried. Frozen.*

"And yet, murdering her here would have been incredibly risky," Siobhán said. "How could anything have happened without multiple witnesses?" The nursery employed half a dozen people and had security cameras. They had already requested them early on and Larry must have fully complied or Aretta would have mentioned it. On the other hand, she also would have mentioned it if something alarming had been caught on the security tapes. Perhaps the guards hadn't gone through them yet, which was understandable. Security tapes had been pulled from every crime scene, downtown, and the nursery. There were only so many guards to go around. They needed to speak with Larry Lorcan straightaway.

As if they had summoned him with their thoughts, a large shadow fell upon the pond, and they turned to find Larry Lorcan himself standing behind them. "Thank you for waiting." His brow creased as he approached. "I heard about the fire at Cassidy Ryan's cottage. Terrible business, altogether. I pray no one was inside?"

"It's been locked up as a crime scene since her murder," Macdara said. "No one was inside."

"Thank goodness for that." He took a deep breath. "I don't suppose you've caught the you-know-what who did it?"

"We'll be sifting through the ashes," Siobhán said. If he was trying to get the dirt, he wasn't going to get it. They began to walk, and every now and again Larry would stop to point something out. First, they were introduced to a display of dahlias, their intricate petals unfolding in a riot of colors, and next, their attention was drawn to a line of snapdragons standing like soldiers on-the-ready. Bees hummed lazily around speckled foxgloves, dipping in and out of the bell-shaped flowers in the age-old dance of nature. Above them, birds chirped from their unseen perches.

"What can I do for you?" Larry finally asked, stopping beside a bed of lavender that filled the air with a sense of calm. *The calm before the storm.*

"When was the last time you saw Cassidy Ryan?" Siobhán inquired, her gaze steady.

Larry removed a sheet of paper from his pocket. "I kept

a schedule of the gardeners' visits, and I knew you'd be asking so I've already looked it up." He handed the paper to Macdara. "Monday morning," he said, his voice low. "Five days before the official unveiling."

Siobhán and Macdara exchanged a glance. This fit with Jeanie Brady's time of death. Monday would have been her last full day on earth. Had Cassidy Ryan been murdered here? Would the security footage show her entering the premises but never leaving?

"Tell us about that encounter," Siobhán said, hoping her voice gave nothing away.

He dropped his gaze to his fingernails. "She was very excited," he said. "Her showstopper had come in."

Showstopper. Goose bumps rose on Siobhán's arms. "Go on," Macdara said.

"As you know, the garden contestants could choose any type of flowers or plants for their installations, even ones out of season. Cassidy was curating hers at her rental cottage. She was planning to deliver everything to her garden spot at the last minute, on that Friday I believe, and this particular specimen was the most cherished of all her orders, the pièce de résistance!"

"I'm anxious to see it," Macdara said.

Siobhán thought of the garden in front of the cottage, now buried in ash. Had they been plants that Cassidy had been waiting to transport to her tent? The thought of them never making it there filled her with a profound sadness. She swallowed hard, hoping she could keep her emotions in check. She was just about to ask what this showstopper was when her brain finally registered the implications of what Larry Lorcan had just said. "Wait. She was curating her garden at the rental cottage?"

Larry nodded, not missing a beat. "She didn't trust the other gardeners not to peek," he confided. "At the time, I thought she was being paranoid, but now . . ." He shook his head. "You hear about people who have premonitions of their own deaths. I can't help but wonder . . ."

Siobhán shivered despite the warm air. "Did anyone else know this was her plan?"

Larry Lorcan frowned; the alarm in her voice had registered with him. "Myself. A few of my employees, who knew better than to gossip about it, and of course, her crew."

"The last time you saw her, did she seem distraught in any way?" Macdara asked.

"Quite the contrary," Larry said, gesturing toward the back of the greenhouse. They followed as he continued to speak. "She was over the moon about her acquisition. If you'll follow me, you'll soon see why."

"Did she mention anything about being involved in *another* garden competition?" Siobhán asked as they ventured farther into the dome.

"The million euro one?" Larry called out without turning around. Siobhán watched the back of his head as it nodded. "It was all she could talk about." Larry stopped suddenly, and whirled around, causing Siobhán and Macdara to step back. His hands found each other, twining nervously. "But I warned her, I did. Told her not to say anything in front of the other gardeners. Plants may stay buried in this town, but secrets? They're always unearthed." A look of worry flittered across his face. "Keeping mum about the contest wasn't the only thing I warned her about. Her acquisition concerned me as well, like. Something this rare, this valuable? I *pleaded* with her." He crossed himself. "May she rest in peace." Instinctively, Siobhán and Macdara did the same, and then they were walking again.

"What is so rare and valuable?" Macdara asked.

"I'm getting to it," Larry said. "Literally."

As their conversation waned and the sound of their footsteps echoed, the greenhouse seemed to swell, punctuated only by the occasional chirp or rustle of leaves. "Here we are," Larry said, stopping at the very last section of the greenhouse. In the corner, a single privacy fence was set up, blocking something from view. "In the end, she'd left her showstopper here. She was supposed to return on Thursday evening to pick it up. She said this was the one piece she'd be placing into the installation herself, right in the middle of the garden."

In the middle of the garden. Where instead they found her body . . .

Siobhán's skin prickled once more. Was Larry Lorcan about to reveal the true statue Cassidy Ryan had envisioned as the garden's centerpiece? But instead of moving the privacy fence aside, he turned to an easel next to it, also covered with a black sheet. Siobhán hadn't even noticed it. That certainly didn't bode well for her detective skills. He whipped off the covering and they found themselves staring at a poster-sized photograph of a pale white orchid. The top petals spread out like a star, but beneath it the petals took on the shape of a person dancing a jig—at least it looked like that to Siobhán. It took her a moment to realize it had no leaves.

"Dendrophylax lindenii," Larry said, wiping sweat off his brow. "The rarest orchid of them all. Endangered. Wild. Found only in the Everglades of Florida, Cuba, and the Dominican Republic. Now, before I show you Cassidy Ryan's miraculous showpiece, let me assure you, this was not plucked from a faraway snake-infested swamp. Nor did anyone plunder the black market of orchids. I'm sure you've heard of the film, *The Orchid Thief?*" He studied their faces eagerly.

"I'll add it to me Netflix queue," Macdara said. "For now, why don't you cut to the chase?"

Lorcan pouted for a second and then shrugged. He pointed to the orchid in the photograph. "This beauty was the exact one the main character was chasing after, determined to clone. When Cassidy first told me she'd been in contact with a botanist who has been cultivating this artificially, for *years*, mind you, why I thought she was mad. And even though it was delivered here, that is my only part in whatever voodoo she used to source this. I was willing to be the orchid keeper, because, well, my hands are clean. And to be honest, when she told me, I just had to see it for myself. Ghostlike. Fairylike. Dancing. She said this botanist used pollen from all three locations to create a Frankenstein Flower if you will. Detective Sergeant, Garda . . ." He turned to the hidden display and gestured with a flourish. "I present to you—Cassidy Ryan's pièce de résistance, the Ghost Orchid."

He moved the privacy screen to the side and they all stared. Sitting atop a pedestal was an enormous display box. An enormous, *empty* display box. For a moment no one spoke.

Macdara was the first to break the silence. "I see why they call it the Ghost Orchid."

Siobhán felt a swoosh of air, and startled, turned to see how Larry was coping. He had fainted dead away.

Larry sat in the back of the ambulance, drinking water but refusing to be taken to the hospital. "I don't understand," he said over and over again. "I don't understand."

"When was the last time you saw the Ghost Orchid?" Siobhán asked.

"When I showed it to Cassidy," Larry said. "On that Monday." He held the bottle of water up to his forehead. "It was safely ensconced in its case, tucked behind that privacy screen." He pointed to it as if proving his point.

Macdara lifted an eyebrow, and Siobhán knew he was holding back a sarcastic retort on Larry's conviction that a privacy screen and a display case should have been enough to secure one of the rarest orchids in the world.

"She would have killed me," Larry said. "If Cassidy Ryan were alive and she knew that someone snatched it under me nose? She would have killed me."

What if she had discovered the theft? She could have accused Larry, threatened him even, maybe they tussled near the bridge.

"Have you turned all your security tapes into the garda station?" Siobhán asked. As distraught as Larry seemed, she had to remember it was possible that he had stolen it himself.

Larry nodded. "Every single one of them."

"We'll get a team watching them today."

"You have to understand. My nursery closed to the public after Cassidy's orchid was delivered. Only my employees, the gardeners, and their crew had access."

"I know you're in distress," Siobhán said. "But I must ask—why did you not lock it up?"

"Because a nursery isn't a jail, Garda. Where would I have locked it up?"

"Did Cassidy mention she was worried about whether or not it was secure?" Macdara asked.

An expression flitted over Larry Lorcan's face, one of outright terror, but he soon wrestled it down. "No," he said. "Not at all."

Something told Siobhán he was lying. Not only were they going to have to look at all the security footage, they were going to have to question every single person who was in the nursery that week. Her stomach flipped. It must have shown on her face, for Macdara instantly shot her a look. He turned and placed his hand on hers. She squeezed it back. She was grand. And she was not going to step down from this case. "Pardon me, Mr. Lorcan," she said. "But I'm going to need to use your restroom."

Larry looked off to the distance and waved over an employee. A young man hurried over. "Would you please escort Garda O'Sullivan to the private restroom?"

The employee nodded. "Certainly. Follow me."

The same lad was waiting for Siobhán when she finished in the restroom. "Have you been working here all week?" she asked as he began to escort her outside.

"Mostly," he said. "But everything has been hush-hush, so there were days the employees weren't allowed in. I never knew gardeners could be so secretive."

"Are you saying there were days the gardeners were here but the employees were not?"

He nodded. "Mostly in the evenings. Larry was allowing the committee to hold their meetings here. I was worried they would go around touching all the plants. Gardeners can be handsy, you know?" He was talking so fast she figured it was a rhetorical question. "Most people know the etiquette. I mean, do museum guides have to tell the public not to touch the paintings?"

"They certainly do," Siobhán said. "All the time."

"Then why is it okay to paw the petals?" He plowed on as if she hadn't negated his statement.

He stopped talking and she let him take a breath. "Anyone in particular come to mind?"

"Nessa O'Neill for one," he said straightaway. "And when I told her she could not keep touching the plants, she said they *liked* it. She made it sound like they were asking for it. Sounds like an abuser to me."

"Speaking of abuse," Siobhán said, "I noticed a portion of the bridge across the lily pond looks as if it's recently been repaired."

"Right?" he said. "Sean Bell did it for free."

"Oh? That was nice of him—what happened?"

"One of them must have leaned on it, even though they

all denied it. I think it was Mr. Moore. Someone threw rose petals into the pond and I'd say the most likely person to have done that was Mr. Roses himself."

"I can see how you reached that conclusion."

"I'd make a good detective, wouldn't I?"

Not with that motor mouth. "Absolutely. You'd be brilliant."

"Thanks." He beamed.

"I thought I saw rose petals in the pond," Siobhán mused.

The lad groaned. "I thought I fished them all out."

She pulled out her notebook. "When exactly did all of this take place?"

He suddenly stopped and stared at her. "This isn't, like— an official inquisition, is it?"

"We're just having a chat."

He nearly crumpled with relief. "When I locked up Sunday night, everything was pristine. I'm off on Mondays. But when I came in Tuesday, Sean Bell was fixing the bridge and I had to use a net to pluck petals out of the pond." He glanced at her notepad and a look of worry crossed his face. "I had assumed it all went down on one of their committee meetings. Monday evening most likely."

"Do you still have that net?"

He frowned. "Somewhere."

"Have you used it since?"

"No."

If Cassidy had been in that pond, it was possible there could be strands of hair clinging to that net. She tried to sound calm. "I'm going to need you to get it and bring it to myself and the detective."

"Now?" He was starting to regret chatting with her; it was written all over his face.

"In a moment. Just a few more questions. Do you know if Cassidy Ryan attended the committee meetings?"

"You better believe it. She told me that if she didn't watch them like hawks they were going to do something to get her chucked out of the competition."

"I see." She would most likely have more questions after the security footage was reviewed.

He gulped. "Should I have said something, like? Am I in trouble?"

"Not at all. If you don't mind fetching that net, I'll be right outside."

"Can I ask?" He scratched his head. "What does the net have to do with anything?"

"You can ask but I'm afraid I cannot answer. And I expect I can trust you not to say a word about it to anyone."

"Absolutely." He mimed locking his lips and throwing away the key.

"Now. Do you mind retrieving it?"

"Straightaway." He turned and jogged off.

As she exited the nursery and waited for the lad, she stewed on everything she'd just learned. Was it possible? Had Cassidy Ryan drowned in the lily pond? And whereas Nessa might have been fondling the plants, which one of the gardeners got handsy with Cassidy Ryan? Had she been pushed over the wooden guardrails of that little bridge? Was Sean Bell just being a good egg or was he fixing it out of guilt? If her death took place here, common sense would say that it had to have been after the committee meeting. Monday evening. That tracked with Jeanie Brady's time of death.

She was interrupted by the lad returning, a net in his hand. She slipped a pair of gloves out of her pocket, donned them, took the net, and thanked him. "Don't forget. This is between us, yeah?"

He saluted. "Mum's the word." He grinned. "See what I did there? Mums? Like the flowers?"

"I caught your drift," Siobhán said. "Good one." He was grinning when he strolled away. Hopefully there would be an evidence bag in the squad car. And even though the net had been submerged in water, as she drew it closer, she observed something blond hanging onto the net. Siobhán knew it in her bones—Cassidy Ryan had died in that pond. Larry Lorcan wasn't going to be thrilled that his entire greenhouse was now a crime scene. Macdara was still deep in conversation with Larry; even from a distance she could see they were having a pleasant chat. Siobhán hung back. She'd rather give Macdara the news in private—and she also didn't want to see Larry faint twice in one day. She took the opportunity to run the net over to the squad car, and was happy to find a few evidence bags in the boot. She secured the net and locked it up. As she headed back to the car park, she found herself turning over everything she'd just learned.

The garden committee consisted of the gardeners involved in the contest, which meant most of their suspects had been at the nursery around the time Cassidy was killed. Although Cassidy was not on the committee, she had arrived that evening to check on the other gardeners, not to mention her orchid. But what if one of the other gardeners had beaten her to it? Had she caught one of them trying to steal her rare orchid, her showstopper? From the sounds of it, it had to be worth a healthy sum of money. If Cassidy had caught someone in the act of stealing it, maybe when she confronted him or her—things escalated. She could have been pushed over the side of the bridge, thus breaking the guardrails, and landing in the pond. But this killer didn't stop there.

He or she rushed down to the pond while she was probably flailing to get out, and then, he or she crossed the morality line forever, and held her under. Given the amount of water in her lungs—*if* she fell from the bridge, it was possible that in a matter of seconds the incident had gone from an accident to an act of evil. Or perhaps she was deliberately pushed. Did someone toss those rose petals into the lily pond as an act of remembrance? *Teagan Moore?* Were they looking at a killer with a conscience? Or was this crafty killer trying to throw shade on Teagan? And where was the Ghost Orchid? Was it with the killer? Siobhán sighed, feeling as if she was watching a shell game play out, and never sure which cup to keep her eye on. On the bright side, they may have just answered a crucial question—*where* was she killed—but the *who* and *why* remained as opaque and elusive as their missing orchid.

Chapter 22

Siobhán O'Sullivan stood at the rear of Lorcan Nursery as employees exited the building, trudging past guards who were cordoning off the greenhouse with crime scene tape, their faces etched with confusion and concern. Each one was stopped by a pair of guards standing just inside the back storage room who studied the personal contents they carried with a meticulous eye. Anything related to gardening—gloves, spades, and in one case, a small fern—was confiscated, and even their personal belongings were examined.

"I could have never imagined a case with this many crime scenes," Macdara said, coming up behind Siobhán and watching the proceedings. "*Guinness World Records* might have to start a new category just for us."

Larry Lorcan was pacing like a penned animal near the entrance of the greenhouse, his hands gesturing wildly as his voice reached a feverish pitch. "But who will tend to the begonias? They need watering twice a day! And the humidity levels for the orchids—"

Macdara and Siobhán exchanged a glance. "He has a point," she said as Larry continued railing against the shutdown. "They are living things."

Macdara groaned. "Tell him we'll see to it. Have him make a list of how to care for everything inside."

"Good man," Siobhán said. "Mr. Lorcan," Siobhán called as she approached. "We cannot risk anyone tampering with potential evidence. The integrity of the investigation must come first."

Lorcan's expression contorted with dismay. "This cannot be a crime scene," he insisted. "I turned over all my security tapes. Did you *see* anyone murder Cassidy Ryan?"

Siobhán had just been briefed on the security tapes. "Your cameras do not cover the greenhouse," she said. "Neither do they cover the back exit."

Larry opened his mouth then shut it several times. "It was never necessary," he said.

"Write down a detailed list of the kind of care your plants need," Siobhán said. "You have my word; we'll mind them."

Relief softened Larry's stern features. "There is a delicate balance of light and shadow needed for the foliage," he began, "and precise measurements of water for each species, not to mention a soothing voice and the tender touch required for the seedlings in the propagation area." He stopped and wiped his brow. "And there are a few more delicate souls who only thrive if you sing to them. 'Danny Boy' is a favorite."

"I'm not singing 'Danny Boy' to plants," Macdara yelled from a distance. Her husband had excellent hearing.

Larry sighed and gave Siobhán a look. "They'll also tolerate 'Whiskey in the Jar.' "

"I know you're under duress, but I can't memorize all of this. You need to write down the instructions."

Larry continued as if she hadn't spoken. "Too much water and you'll drown them; too little and they'll wither and die." Larry's voice rang with a fervor that bordered on the religious. Relief swept over Siobhán as Garda Dabiri edged her way in and handed Larry a notepad and biro.

"Come sit in the shade," she said, taking his arm. "I can get you some water."

"It's not just about keeping them alive," Larry yelled as she dragged him away. "They need to *thrive*."

"Much like us," Siobhán murmured. It was beginning to feel like all their suspects were delicate flowers on the verge of wilting.

"Some of them have birthdays coming up!" he wailed from a distance. The sound of a vehicle pulling in caught Siobhán's attention. Jeanie Brady was here. She exited her car and approached with a somber expression. She was already wearing her protective suit, booties, and gloves, and carrying a satchel. Macdara joined Siobhán at the entrance to the greenhouse, and by the time Jeanie reached them, they were suited up as well.

"Wearing the same outfits to the party again, I see," Jeanie said. "I suppose it's too late to go home and change." They all smiled at the joke, but the prospect of what lay ahead was too grim for genuine merriment. "I hear you've found Cassidy Ryan's final resting place."

"We believe so," Siobhán said. "Follow us." This time the trek through the greenhouse was anything but relaxing. The hot still air felt stifling, and even the plants seemed to be watching and whispering. When they came to the lily pond, Jeanie's eyes landed on the bridge. Macdara pointed out that one section had been recently repaired. Jeanie approached, taking in the bridge and the pond below.

"We'll need to drain the pond," she said. Siobhán nodded her agreement but she couldn't help picturing the disruption to the carefully curated ecosystem. "It will take some time to get the necessary equipment. In the meantime, we can speak to Mr. Lorcan about ways to preserve what life we can."

"If only lilies and koi could talk," Siobhán said.

"Are those rose petals?" Jeanie asked.

"They are," Siobhán said. "We're going to be speaking to Teagan Moore as soon as things are set here."

"Blond hairs caught in the net," Jeanie murmured. "A broken bridge, and the right environment to dry out a body as quickly as possible before sticking her in some type of a freezer and spray-painting her gold." She surveyed the greenhouse then turned back. "Any sign of a freezer anywhere in the nursery?"

"Not a one," Siobhán said. "I've searched everywhere."

Jeanie nodded. "I suppose if there was a freezer here someone hauled it out as fast as possible."

"We also have a missing Ghost Orchid," Macdara chimed in.

"Unfortunately, nearly *all* our suspects were gathered here on Monday evening, and Sean Bell repaired the bridge on Tuesday morning," Siobhán said.

"And there are no security cameras in the greenhouse," Macdara added.

"Sounds like draining the pond will be the easiest chore of them all," Jeanie said. "We also need to see if we can identify which areas in the greenhouse would be advantageous to prepare the body."

Make her into a statue. Siobhán shivered despite the heat. "Recycling bins," she said. "We need to check the recycling bins."

The recycling, three large dumpsters, were lined up against a back fence. Siobhán lifted the lid on one and peered inside. There were the usual suspects on top: empty plant containers, bottles, and cardboard.

"Siobhán," Macdara said. "We have plenty of guards here. It's time you learned to delegate." Siobhán continued to dig. He was right. The bins were deep, and one of them would be bad enough, but three of them would take a team effort. She backed off and Macdara chose a couple of guards to suit up for the sifting. By the time they returned to the greenhouse, a truck hauling machinery was pulling into the car park. The pump for the pond had arrived. The guards searching the bins approached, both carrying large evidence bags.

"Found something?" Macdara asked.

The guard held up the bag. Siobhán had to stare at it for a while before she recognized what the items were. First, a pair of gloves thick with golden paint, and then a gardening apron, also glittering with golden specks, along with several pieces of cardboard, coated with gold.

"No spray paint cans, or any kind of paint?" Siobhán asked.

"You're not allowed to discard them in bins," one of the guards said.

"Well, then," Siobhán replied. "Looks like we have a rule-following killer." The guard's cheeks flushed red. "But you have a good point. The killer wouldn't have wanted anyone to kick up a fuss if they saw paint cans in the recycling bins."

The guard perked up and nodded.

"We need to search the entire grounds, nursery, and greenhouse for gold paint," Macdara said. "Most likely spray paint."

"Mining for gold," Siobhán heard another guard say under his breath. "Yay."

The hum of a water pump soon filled the air, the mechanical heartbeat quickening as the water level in the pond started to fall. While they had waited for the pumps, employees had been escorted in to transfer the koi and the lilies to a nursery in the next town. Draining the water was a slow process, each inch revealing more of the darkened silt below. "I only need to find one more hair," Jeanie said, making her way carefully down to the drained pond. "I can already see several rocks on which she could have hit her head."

Watching her sift through the soggy remains was torture. Jeanie didn't need an audience, so Siobhán headed outside to speak with Larry. She found him leaning against the back of an old lorry. The writing on the side was faded but she could make out the word: MEAT. "I finished the caretaking list," he said. "I've given it to Garda Dabiri."

"Excellent," she said. "I need to ask you what service you use to pick up empty cans or gallons of paint."

"Paint?" A flicker of panic came over his face, and for an instant, he seemed to teeter on the edge of confession.

"Mr. Lorcan?"

"Paint," he said again in the tone of someone stalling for time.

"I don't have to remind you that this is a murder probe, do I?"

He sighed. "No, Garda, you do not."

"The name of the service?"

He crossed his arms and looked anywhere but at Siobhán.

"Is there something about paint and our gardeners that rang a bell for ya?"

"No," he said. But the sweat pouring out of him said otherwise.

"If you know something—no matter how small—you must tell me."

He sighed, righted himself from the van, and turned around. He pulled his key out, unlocked the back, and opened the door. A gob of spray paint cans rolled out at once, somersaulting all around the car park. She didn't need to pick one up to know they all sprayed gold. But that wasn't the only thing that had Siobhán rooted to the spot. She felt a blast of cold air coming from the lorry. It was refrigerated. "Macdara?" she called out. "Detective Sergeant Flannery?" she quickly corrected.

"I'll fetch him," a nearby guard said.

"Finnoula Connor," Larry said, his eyes darting toward the nursery with fear.

"These were her paint cans?"

He nodded. "She asked me the same question you just did—she wanted to know how we disposed of paint." He sighed as he eyed the cans, as if the thought of picking them up was too much to bear.

"Don't worry, they'll all be retrieved by us and marked as evidence." She eyed him. "What were you doing with them?"

"There's a recycling center that gives me a few bob back for them. I planned on returning them soon."

"You didn't think it was odd that she had gone through this many paint cans?"

He shrugged. "I thought maybe it was something for her garden installment. I'm not an answer man. I'm a nursery man!"

Macdara soon joined Siobhán by the van. He took in the paint cans, then stepped toward the lorry. "It's refrigerated," Macdara said.

Larry beamed. "Aye. Bought it from a butcher. Figured I'd keep the refrigeration. You never know when you need to keep something cold."

Macdara and Siobhán exchanged a look. "Mr. Lorcan, would you mind stepping away from the truck?" Larry raised an eyebrow, but quickly stepped away. "Was this truck parked here on Monday evening?"

Larry nodded. "It was pulled around back, near the greenhouse."

"Were you here on Monday evening?"

"No. The garden committee was here. Thus all those paint cans I presumed."

"The paint cans belong to Finnoula Connor," Siobhán said. "According to Mr. Lorcan."

"I *swear*."

"Was your truck locked up on Monday evening, and did you have possession of the keys?"

Larry started to fidget. "What does my truck have to do with anything?"

Macdara stared him down. "You're expecting us to believe that you didn't hear how Cassidy Ryan was found?"

Larry gulped. "Rumors. I heard rumors—something about making her look like a statue."

"A gold statue," Macdara said. "A *gold* statue."

"But these were Finnoula Connor's cans. Surely you're not thinking of her as a murderer?" His jaw dropped. "She's won three years in a row!" He chewed on his lip. "There has to be an explanation."

"You haven't answered my question about the truck."

Larry began to blink his eyes rapidly. "I left it unlocked with the keys in the ignition." Macdara groaned. "What?" Larry said. "Who's going to nick an old, refrigerated truck?"

"You're free to go," Macdara said. "But we'll be towing away the truck."

Larry suddenly whirled around and stared at his truck as if he was seeing it clearly for the first time. "Are you saying . . . ?" He gulped and pointed at the inside of the truck. "You think someone murdered Cassidy in the lily pond, sprayed her gold, and put her in the back of my truck?" His mouth dropped open.

"You are not to discuss anything we've talked about with anyone else," Macdara said. "Is that clear?"

"It's very clear," Larry said. "And Monday evening I was with a lady friend." He gestured at Siobhán. "May I borrow your notepad and biro?"

Siobhán handed over the items and Larry scribbled a

name and number and handed them back. "She'll verify my whereabouts Monday evening."

Aretta, who had been standing nearby, stepped up. "Would you like me to follow up on that?" she asked. Macdara nodded and Siobhán handed her the notepad.

"One more thing," Siobhán said. She pulled Aretta out of Larry's earshot. "Emily Dunne said something about a butcher's truck parked on Sarsfield Street when the crate was delivered on Thursday morning. Could you scour the CCTV to see if Larry's 'meat truck' comes into view?"

Aretta reached into her pocket and pulled out her mobile phone. "I'll get a photo of it first." Aretta hurried off.

"I'll be ruined," Larry Lorcan was saying when Siobhán returned to his side. "If something horrible happened here, I'll be ruined."

"One thing at a time, Mr. Lorcan," Macdara said. "Don't forget—there's a killer out there. That's the reason you need to keep everything you've learned today to yourself. Do not even tell your lady friend. You don't want anyone thinking you're a threat."

"Me?" He gulped. "A threat?" He looked to Siobhán as if she could provide some clarity.

"A murder took place on your premises. You may have observed things that seemed innocent at the time, but may turn out to be the keys to unlocking this mystery."

Larry Lorcan nodded, his expression grim. "Am I free to go?"

"Yes," Macdara said. "For now."

"I need to call a taxi," Larry said.

"I can have a guard drop you at home," Macdara said.

Larry nodded. "Thank you, Detective."

Macdara arranged the transportation and soon Larry Lorcan headed for a squad car with the guard. Macdara and Siobhán watched him go. Minutes later Aretta returned.

"His lady friend confirms that he was there all night Monday. She said if need be, the neighbor saw them together. I went ahead and called the neighbor and she confirmed she saw Mr. Lorcan arrive and then leave again in the morning. And he wasn't driving that old meat lorry."

"Excellent follow-up, Garda Dabiri."

"Thanks. I'm off to the station to pull CCTV footage from Thursday morning."

"She's going to see if she can spot Larry's truck parked on Sarsfield Street," Siobhán said, off his quizzical look.

"Brilliant," Macdara said. "Pieces are starting to fall into place."

"I can't believe anyone would have deliberately murdered her here," Siobhán said. "It's too risky."

"So far that risk has paid off," Macdara said. "But unlucky for the killer, we're closing in. Jeanie found another blond hair in the pond. I'm going to have the truck processed for fingerprints. Hopefully, whoever did this slipped off his or her gloves before getting behind the wheel."

"I doubt it leads anywhere," Siobhán said. "Even if we do find prints, I doubt any of our gardeners are in the system."

"We could ask them to give their prints," Macdara said. "But I agree. Regardless. Has to be done."

Siobhán nodded. From having a clean record to being a murderer. Whoever did this was not a seasoned criminal. But this kind of cover-up was also unusual. Why so elaborate? Was this planned far in advance or conceived at a moment's notice, using whatever was on hand to stage the body and haul her away? She'd eventually been placed in a crate, and given this nursery had trees both delivered and shipped, there were crates on the property large enough to do the job. Who would have imagined that this nursery might have been the perfect place to commit murder? In the killer's mind all he or she had to do was change the narrative, obscure the time of death, and distract them with gold. This killer might be an amateur, but one thing was for sure. His or her moves after Cassidy Ryan was killed were downright diabolical.

Chapter 23

"Do I like people better than roses?" Teagan Moore stared directly into the camera. "Yes. Next question?" Before Molly could respond, he continued. "Because they don't talk, how's that for a why? *Now.* They *communicate.* They let you know by the folds of their petals what mood they are in, or what their needs are. Sun. Food. Shade. Water. A calming voice. Or manure." He paused, a thoughtful furrow creasing his brow. " 'Of all flowers, methinks a rose is best.' Shakespeare and arguably John Fletcher knew it too."

"John who?" Macdara said. He and Siobhán sat hunched in the squad car in the car park of Lorcan's Nursery. The implications of what had most likely taken place inside that greenhouse were still reverberating through their minds. But since they had time to kill before their interview with Sean Bell's wife, they had decided to watch Teagan Moore's interview with Molly Murphy, and Macdara had retrieved his iPad from the glove compartment.

The pair were visible on a split screen. On the left-hand side, Molly sat cross-legged on a sofa, a large orange cat curled up in her lap. Teagan Moore was sitting at his dining room table, stirring a heaping spoonful of sugar into a cup of tea, an enormous display of long-stemmed roses sitting on a console table behind him. She had a feeling he had staged them for the interview. They were bright yellow and looked like sunshine in a vase.

"Do you have any other hobbies?" Molly could be heard asking. "Anything at all?"

Teagan straightened his spine and frowned. "If you couldn't tell by my quote—I read."

"What do you like to read?" She thrust up her index finger. "Besides Shakespeare. Irish folklore by any chance?"

Macdara paused the screen. "Interesting," he said. "Why do you think she asked that?"

"Good question," Siobhán said. Was all of this stemming from Molly Murphy? Had she instigated talk of *The Headless Horseman*?

"Curiouser and curiouser." Macdara wiggled his eyebrows at her.

Siobhán laughed. "I see what you did there, Alice."

Macdara grinned. "How are you feeling?"

"Perfectly fine, don't fuss."

"Mission impossible." He rewound the video and pushed Play and they listened to Molly ask the question once more.

"What do you like to read? Besides Shakespeare? Irish folklore by any chance?" Molly's eyes sparkled as she waited for an answer.

Teagan shook his head. "Would a book by any other name smell as sweet?" Teagan said theatrically. Molly could be heard sighing. Apparently she was trying to get him off the subject of roses and he wasn't having it. "Roses," Teagan said. "I read books on roses, or ones that mention them." A wry smile touched the corner of Teagan's lips. He held up his hand as if to stop any further questions. "Why would I read anything else? In roses, there's everything. Poetry. Beauty. *Horror*."

"Horror?" Molly sounded interested once again. "Roses?" Teagan nodded. " 'We can complain because rosebushes have thorns, or rejoice that thorn bushes have roses.' " He paused as if waiting for her to identify the quote. She did not. "Alphonse Karr, *Lettres Écrites De Mon Jardin.*"

"Sure," Molly said. "Although I was hoping for something a little more exciting."

Teagan's eyes narrowed into slits. "And what in your young life would you consider exciting?"

Molly shrugged, then stared at the camera. "I dunno. Something like Dullahan?"

"There she goes again," Macdara said. "We're going to have to follow up on that."

"As soon as possible," Siobhán agreed. "Wasn't she the one who first mentioned Dullahan to you?"

"She was indeed," Macdara said. They turned back to the screen and focused on Teagan Moore.

"Who needs that imaginary nonsense?" Teagan said, raising an eyebrow. "Roses aren't fiction. They're living, breathing things. They have teeth and claws." He tilted his head and stared at the camera as if trying to gauge Molly's level of interest. "Do you understand? Their leaves are their teeth and their thorns are claws." He tilted his head. "Or is it the other way around?" He laughed as if Molly had made a joke. There was no doubt about it; in Teagan's world everything was coming up roses. "Do you know there are well over three hundred species of roses?" His tone was that of a seasoned lecturer. "Roses are not just beauty; they're resilience personified." He held up a rose whose white head was drooping and gently stroked the petals. "People are always trying to take a piece of my prize-winning roses. *Heathens!*" His eyes blazed with rage.

Molly perked up. "If someone were to mess with your roses—what do you think the punishment should be?"

Teagan thrust his rose in the air. "Off with their heads!" he said. "And I'm not talking about my roses."

"Like the Headless Horseman," Molly said.

Teagan's mouth dropped open. "Why do you keep mentioning him?"

"Exactly," Siobhán yelled. "Why?"

Macdara gave her the side-eye; no doubt she'd ruptured an eardrum.

Molly's lips stretched into a smile. "Are you afraid?"

Teagan crossed his arms. "I'm afraid of a lot of things. Early frost. Sneaky townsfolk creeping on my garden with shears. Insects munching on my babies. The Headless Horseman is nowhere on my list, but you've mentioned him twice now, so go on, tell me what that's all about."

"You tell her," Macdara said, no doubt hoping to prevent another outburst from Siobhán.

Molly shrugged. "Alice McCarthy had the book fall out of her stack, and Finnoula Connor had a book of Irish lore, not to mention a horse sculpture that reminded me of the time-old tale. Let's just say—it's been on my mind." She twirled her biro and looked lost in thought.

Teagan raised an eyebrow. "Are you trying to tell me something? Is either of them implementing folklore into their gardens this year?"

Molly shrugged. "I suppose we'll soon find out." Teagan grunted. "What are your thoughts on Cassidy Ryan?" Molly continued.

"What about Cassidy Ryan?" Teagan tried to sound disinterested, but his entire body tensed. He examined a fingernail.

"She's quite the competitor."

The corners of his mouth twitched. "She doesn't threaten me. She's a show pony. Me, I'm a workhorse."

"And here you called him a pony," Siobhán teased. Macdara's response, his usual smirk, filled her with joy.

"Workhorse," Molly repeated as she scribbled something down.

"That's right. A workhorse doesn't have time to worry about a show pony. He's too busy *working*."

"And if you win this year's Top Garden Contest, what would you do with the money?" Molly asked, her pen poised for his answer.

Teagan's gaze drifted to his vase of roses, his expression softening with unabashed affection. "What do you think? Buy more roses."

Molly rolled her eyes, but if Teagan saw her he didn't let on. "So you're not at all upset that Cassidy Ryan—who hasn't lived in Kilbane since childhood—is using this competition to win *another* competition, one with a million euro purse?"

Teagan's eyes widened. "It's true?" he asked. "I thought it was just a rumor."

"I've done my research, Mr. Moore. This contest is simply something she needs to check off—like an item in a scavenger hunt."

"Stirring the pot," Siobhán said. "Always stirring the pot."

"Scavenger hunt," Teagan Moore repeated.

"Any final words?" Molly asked. "Anything more you'd like to say about Cassidy Ryan?"

Teagan leaned into the camera. "I think she'd better watch her back. Because we're coming for her." He paused. "I suppose I should speak for myself. Me. *I'm* coming for her."

Chapter 24

The merriment of Sarsfield Street swirled around Siobhán and Macdara as they made their way past the fluttering bunting and stalls bursting with blooms. A band had set up on a makeshift stage, with chairs arranged in circles for musicians to come and go as they ran traditional Irish music sessions all day long. To Siobhán's delight, Ciarán was already seated, warming up his fiddle. She waved and he waved his bow in return. They found Nora Bell at the agreed-upon meeting spot, a section for children with face-painting and a petting zoo. She stood in a flowered skirt and white blouse, her brunette hair wavy and flowing past her shoulders. She turned slightly as they approached, and pointed to a nearby table.

"I think that should be a good spot," she announced, pointing as she headed for the table.

They sat across from her, and for a moment Siobhán watched the young ones playing: petting goats, showing off their face paint, and twirling with wild abandon in the middle of the street. She caught Macdara watching them as well, and then the two exchanged a smile.

"Mrs. Bell," Macdara began. "Although we're not officially sitting in the interview room of the garda station, this is a police interview. I will be recording it on a small device, and we expect your full and honest cooperation."

The corners of her mouth turned down. "Understood."

Macdara nodded. "Are you currently in the process of divorce?"

"I filed for divorce," Nora confessed. "But Sean wants to work through it. I'm considering it. For our children's sake."

"May I ask when this trouble began?"

She raised an eyebrow. "Is that relevant?"

"It may be. It's best if you just answer the questions and we'll decide what's relevant."

She sighed. "Sean is no longer the same man I married. This competition has him all consumed." *Recent*, Macdara wrote. She scoffed. "Some nights he barely comes home."

Macdara leaned in. "Any nights in particular?"

"Several nights this past week. It was the last few days before the garden tour, and he claimed all of them were pulling all-nighters, but I thought that was ludicrous." She shrugged. "But then he had Finnoula Connor approach me to confirm that she too had been working all-nighters."

"Say more about that," Siobhán said.

Nora waved her hand as if dismissing it. "I suppose it's my fault for yelling at Sean at the Kilbane Inn. The next morning Finnoula came over—she pretended to be checking to see if I was alright, but I know she was digging for gossip. She must have heard me giving out to him for pulling all-nighters, and in a very condescending manner she said: 'We've all been pulling all-nighters, petal, and believe me, we're too tired for any shenanigans.' "

Siobhán nodded. "We're sorry to be personal, but I take it you believe your husband is having an affair?"

Nora shook her head. "I wasn't accusing him of knocking boots with Cassidy Ryan, if that's what you're thinking."

There was a catch in her tone. "Someone else then?"

She sighed and glanced at the recording device. "I can't say for sure. He denies it. But I've seen him on numerous occasions with Emily Dunne." She crossed her arms. "And Molly Murphy, that reporter." She shook her head once more, as if reliving an argument with her husband. "Young ones, both of them. He's so impressed that one of them is writing a novel." She pointed to her children who were now screaming at each other and playing tug-of-war with a baton. "Does it look like I have the time for creative projects? I spend all day minding our children, and he starts flitting around the young ones, admiring what they do with their *freedom*?"

"Is it Molly Murphy who's writing a novel? The reporter?"

Nora pursed her lips; in her mind Siobhán had missed the point entirely. "I don't remember if it was her or Emily. He hasn't even read it and he's 'so impressed.' "

"Wait." Siobhán was having trouble figuring out what this all meant. "Does he at least have a copy of the novel?"

Nora Bell narrowed her eyes, no doubt wondering why on earth Siobhán cared about it. "I suppose he considers himself a mentor. I think he tried creative writing once, but he was terrible. Just over-the-top, ya know? It's only because he loves gory tales. I mean, what is a young woman doing writing such nonsense?" She shook her head.

Nora had ignored a portion of Siobhán's question. *Interesting.* "Where is this manuscript now?" Siobhán asked.

"This again?" Nora's mouth dropped open as she stared at Siobhán. "Are you joking me?"

"I assure you, I am not."

Nora stuck her lip out and crossed her arms. "I only saw one page. I told him if he didn't get rid of it, I'd burn it."

Or cut it to shreds? Siobhán had a feeling she was looking at the woman who decapitated Cassidy's photo. As far as Siobhán knew, they'd found no manuscript whilst searching Sean Bell's house. Then again, they hadn't been told to be on the lookout for one. Siobhán had never heard anyone mention Emily Dunne taking an interest in writing, so this had to be Molly's work. Was that why she was always trying to stir the pot? Constantly bringing up Irish lore and Dullahan? Was journalism her day job but she aspired to be a novelist?

"Do you have any idea what kind of story Molly Murphy, or whomever, was writing?" Macdara asked.

"The Headless Horse*woman*," Nora scoffed. "Utterly ridiculous."

Although Siobhán and Macdara did not look at each other, she knew they were both clocking this information with glee. *Ding, ding, ding, we have a winner.* Molly Murphy was the originator behind all these references to Dullahan, and somewhere along the lines she'd been inspired to rewrite the classic tale. Was she also a killer?

Was she responsible for the golden items placed in the gardens? That innocent-looking freckle-faced girl? Molly had a good excuse to come and go as she pleased, and none of them would have thought it was unusual if they saw her around. It pained Siobhán to think of someone so young having such a dark side. And what motive could she possibly have? Had Cassidy Ryan let something slip about the rare Ghost Orchid? If Molly was the killer, her entire life would be over. Then again, Cassidy Ryan's life was already over. And her family and friends would grieve the rest of their days. No matter his or her age, this killer needed to be caught.

Siobhán placed the evidence bag on the table in front of Nora and watched her reaction closely as she slid it across the table. Siobhán pointed to the blank spot. "Cassidy Ryan's head has been cut out of this photo."

Nora raised an eyebrow. "It must be her then. Molly Murphy. She's really getting into this ridiculous book she's writing, isn't she?"

"Are you saying Molly Murphy did this because she's writing *The Headless Horsewoman?*" Macdara asked.

"Who else?" Nora replied. She held up a finger then reached for her handbag. "After I gave out to him, I saw him ripping this up and throwing it in the bin. I don't know why I taped it up and saved it. I suppose in case I ever ran into the scribbling psychopath." She took out a torn-and-taped sheet of paper and handed it to them. "You can have it. You'll see for yourself she's not the great writer she purports to be. Pure rubbish."

"That's a harsh description," Macdara said. "Psychopath."

Nora gave him a look and a shrug. "You'll see what I mean when you read it."

Molly Murphy was a professional writer. Siobhán found it hard to believe her writing was that bad. Was it actually Emily Dunne who was writing this so-called horror book? Siobhán had to admit, she couldn't wait to read it.

Macdara tapped the newspaper article. "Do you know who did this?"

Nora's brow creased as she studied it. "Why would you think I had anything to do with this?"

"We found that in your flat," Siobhán said.

"In the same drawer as divorce papers," Macdara added.

The shock etched on Nora's face was not easily feigned. "You'll have to ask my husband. I swear. I know nothing about this."

She was holding something back. "I understand women's intuition," Siobhán said. "And if that's the only reason you suspected your husband of having an affair, I believe you. But if there's anything else, anything at all, it would be to your advantage to tell us now."

Nora's gaze fixated on her children. "He didn't just wax on about one of their books, he also watched all of Molly's interviews," she confessed, a brittle laugh escaping her lips.

"Not just his own, mind you. All of them." She held out her thumb and gestured to herself. "I guess the bloom has gone off this rose."

"Have you asked your husband directly about these concerns?" Macdara asked.

"He denies them all. He said he was only reading the manuscript as a favor, and only watching the videos because he wanted to see if he could garner anything about his competition. But that doesn't make sense, does it? He already knows everything about his competitors. The same gardeners participate every year."

"Except for Cassidy Ryan," Siobhán interjected.

Nora crossed her arms and glared. "If you're trying to get me to accuse my husband of being a murderer, you're wasting your time."

She was right. This conversation was going nowhere. Siobhán pulled her notebook closer. "Can you tell us where you were this past Thursday evening?"

"Why?" Nora asked. "Am I a suspect as well, like?"

"It would be very helpful if you simply answered the question," Macdara advised once more.

She scoffed once again. "Sean told you about Thursday night, did he?"

Did she believe he was locked in his shed? Siobhán gave a shrug of her own. "We want to hear it from you."

"Fine. He took me out to the Kilbane Castle for a fancy dinner. But that does not mean he's instantly forgiven."

Siobhán nodded along as if she'd expected the answer. She knew it. *Liar. Big, fat liar.* "You're positive it was Thursday evening?" If he had this alibi why didn't he just admit to being at dinner? *Because he wanted them to believe that as late as Thursday afternoon Cassidy Ryan was still alive.* Unfortunately for him, they knew better.

"Yes. Thursday was the only night we could get a child minder."

"What time did you finish dinner?"

"Half-eight."

"And then?" Macdara asked. "Did you paint the town red?"

"Hardly," Nora said. "Sean was in bed and snoring by nine." She glanced at her children. "Unlike *them* and therefore unlike *me*."

Macdara closed his notebook. "I think that's it for now. Garda O'Sullivan—do you have any additional questions?"

"I think we have everything we need," Siobhán said. Nora fled the table as soon as the words left their mouths. For a moment, they watched Nora's children as they continued to scream and play. "Time to interview the liar?" Siobhán said as she stood.

Macdara looped his arm around her. "You took the words right out of me mouth." He glanced at the torn-and-taped manuscript page. "But first? How about a little story time?"

"I would have preferred a romance," Siobhán said. "But I'll take what I can get."

Kilbane Garda Station—Cassidy Ryan Murder Probe
Marked into evidence: Partial torn-and-taped manuscript

The Headless Horsewoman
Chapter 1
Garden in the Night

The dewy, damp night air clung to Cassandra's moist porcelain skin like a glistening protective shield as she desperately navigated the narrow and dirty country roads that wound dangerously through the rolling green fields of County Cork. Her hot breath formed ghostly puffs in the chilled night air, and the only ambient sound to be heard was the sound of her very own dainty footsteps. *Crunch, crunch, crunch.* And the occasional poignant, jarring hoot of a wise old owl. *Hoot, hoot, hoot.* If only she was as wise as that old, hooting owl. For it certainly wasn't wise for her to be wandering about in the dark of the night, the blackest of black nights, as dark as a black hole in an ever-expanding, infinite universe. But this was the sacred hour she loved the most: the Witching Hour.

Chapter 25

The clock on the wall ticked with methodical precision, each second reverberating in the interview room where Sean Bell sat, his hands clasped together, his eyes restless. Across from him, Siobhán O'Sullivan leaned back in her chair, her gaze steady, while Aretta Dabiri stood by the door, her arms folded across her chest.

"Tell us again about being locked in your shed," Siobhán began. "It was Thursday afternoon, was it?"

Sean's leg began to bounce under the table. "Did you talk to me wife?"

"Please answer the question."

"Did I say Thursday?"

Siobhán tilted her head. "That's what you told me, remember?"

"To be honest, it's a bit of a blur." He turned his head to Aretta to see if she would sympathize. She did not.

"Let me see if I can refresh your memory," Siobhán said. "I found you 'locked in' on Friday morning. It was the reason you didn't show up in the town square to kick off the garden competition."

His fidgets grew more pronounced. Outside the closed door, the distant murmur of the garda station carried on—a symphony of clacking keyboards and hushed conversations, punctuated by the occasional radio crackle—reminding them of the world outside this door that continued to spin. Sean Bell's silence stretched thin across the confines of the interview room. "Have you lot spoken with my wife?" he asked once more. "Someone saw you chatting with her on Sarsfield Street."

Siobhán leaned forward. "What exactly are you worried about?"

"What do you mean?"

"It sounds as if you're worried about something your wife might have told us," Aretta said from the doorway.

"Are you having an affair?" Siobhán asked casually. She needed to gauge what he was and wasn't willing to answer.

"What?" Sean's response came fast. "No. Never." His hands balled into fists, flexing the strong muscles in his arms. "You *have* talked to me wife."

"Mr. Bell. Why did you lie about being locked in your shed?"

His mouth dropped open and he was having a difficult time maintaining eye contact. "Maybe I exaggerated a bit."

"In what way?" Siobhán was tired of his antics. Her tone grew stern.

"It wasn't Thursday night I got locked in. It was early Friday morning."

"In other words, you lied."

"A harmless lie. I was hoping maybe Cassidy Ryan would be disqualified or something." He turned his palms up. "Doesn't that prove that I'm not the killer?"

"Elaborate."

"If I was the killer I wouldn't have wanted to draw any

correlation between myself and Cassidy. How foolish would that be? I wouldn't have needed to throw shade."

"You set the entire thing up, hoping we would take your word for it and immediately disqualify Cassidy Ryan?"

"It seems so," Sean said. "And it proves I'm not the killer."

"The only thing it proves to me is that you're a liar," Siobhán said.

"Women," Sean muttered.

"Excuse me?" Siobhán said. "What was that?"

Sean pounded the table in a flash of anger. "First me wife accuses me of cheating, and now you're accusing me of lying."

"Only you can speak for the cheating, but you have lied. To my face. And now that I know Cassidy Ryan did not lock you in the shed on Thursday evening, who helped you pull of this little ruse?"

"Nobody."

"You're saying that whilst inside the shed you slid that rake across the door yourself?"

"Oh," he said. "That."

Siobhán glanced at Aretta. "Oh," she repeated. "That."

"That," Aretta said. "*Men.*"

Siobhán nodded and shrugged. "We can go on like this all afternoon, Mr. Bell."

He sighed. "Emily Dunne locked me in the shed, alright? And I had nothing to do with it."

"What version of the story is this?" Siobhán asked. "I'm losing track."

"I believe it's the third version," Aretta said. "And not one of them are alike."

"Well, then. We certainly hope the third one's the charm." Siobhán stared at Sean.

"I'm telling the truth. Emily Dunne was a mole. She'd

been instructed to sabotage the players. That's what she told me."

"And yet Friday morning was the day of the competition," Siobhán said. "Shouldn't that have been the end of her sabotaging?"

"It should have never been part of the competition to begin with. It's the only year it ever happened. The year Cassidy Ryan joins. I may not be a garda, but I find that suspicious. Don't you?"

"You're saying it was Cassidy Ryan who told Emily to sabotage the other players?"

"Who else?"

"Why did you meet with Emily Dunne at Butler's Lounge?" Siobhán continued.

He crossed his arms and stared at a spot on the wall. "I don't remember. It was probably about sourcing an item for me garden."

"This was after the competition was canceled," Siobhán said. "And no one needs to meet in a pub to source items for their garden."

"Right. Let me think." He made a show of concentrating. "I was telling her she needs to come clean to you lot about locking me in the shed, and being a mole. That if Cassidy Ryan put her up to it that it might be important evidence for your murder inquiry."

"Some might call that hypocritical," Aretta said. "Pushing her to be honest with the guards, all the while keeping your own lies buried."

Sean dropped his chin and placed his hands on the side of his head. "I was only trying to get Cassidy disqualified. It was an impulsive decision. Molly came 'round to me garden that morning, and the idea just came to me."

"I thought it was Emily who came 'round to your garden

that morning," Siobhán said. "With your golden bell—was that it?"

"My bell was black," Sean said. "You found it in Cassidy Ryan's garden!"

Gotcha. "How could you possibly know that, Mr. Bell?"

"What?"

"Cassidy Ryan's tent was sealed as a crime scene. How could you possibly know that we found your bell inside?" Was this over? Were they looking at their killer? Had he and Cassidy been the only two gardeners at Lorcan's Nursery late Monday evening? Had he been there all night dressing up the body and fixing the broken fence?

His hands moved to cover his face. "I can't help that people gossip," he said. "It must have been someone in the know."

"Someone?" Siobhán said. "Are you saying you don't remember who imparted this particular piece of gossip to you?"

Sean let out a moan. "You're getting me all twisted up."

He was twisted, alright. More than a pretzel. "You're telling me that once I haul Emily Dunne and Molly Murphy into the station, one of them is going to confess to locking you in your shed?"

Sean Bell curled and uncurled his fists, over and over. "It was me wife. Alright? She was browned off, thinking I was flirting with the young ones, blaming the competition for consuming all me time. She must have seen Cassidy Ryan leaving our property right after she tried to peek into my garden. She flew into a rage and locked me in the shed. But don't worry. I'm not pressing charges."

Siobhán stood. "Mr. Bell, I've had it with your lies."

He looked flabbergasted. "What now?"

"You said Cassidy Ryan visited you on Thursday, then returned and shut you into your shed around half-five that evening."

"I've since corrected it."

"You corrected being locked in *Friday* morning. Now you're saying your wife did it—which means we're back to Thursday."

"Liars lie," Aretta said. "Over and over."

Sean narrowed his eyes. He looked as if he wanted to lash out, but he was doing his best to control himself. "My wife *saw* Cassidy Ryan on Thursday—our flat is right there, you know, and I told you she showed up around noon to peek on my garden—but Nora didn't confront me about it until Friday morning. I worked all night and she was furious. Got the wrong idea about me and Ms. Ryan. When she couldn't get me to admit that I was having an affair, she locked me in the shed. Said she'd only let me out if I admitted it. I would not admit to something I did not do, so I remained there until you let me out."

And here it was, time to put Sean Bell in his place once and for all. She'd start with the smaller lie and work up to the biggest.

She reached for an iPad situated on a small shelf behind her and cued up the video. She studied Sean as he watched Macdara break out of the shed on the first try.

He closed his eyes for a moment. "I don't know what to tell you. I tried and failed. Maybe you didn't latch it quite right."

"That must be it," Siobhán said to Aretta. "There must be a right and a wrong way to barricade a shed door with a rake."

"Live and learn," Aretta said.

Siobhán continued to stand, her gaze unwavering as she studied him. "I understand that you watched Molly Murphy's interviews of the other gardeners. One might say with great interest."

"It was a competition," Sean said as he finally removed

his hands from his face and placed them on the table. "Forewarned is forearmed." Just then, through the narrow window in the doorway that offered a sliver view of the outside world, Macdara passed by, followed by Finnoula Connor, their figures briefly framed in the glass pane before moving beyond sight. Sean's eyes flickered toward the fleeting image, his expression hardening. "We're all under the spotlight, are we?" he asked, though it sounded less like a question and more an accusation.

"It is a murder inquiry." Siobhán's hand moved with deliberation as she placed the newspaper article of the now-headless Cassidy Ryan on the table before him.

Sean's gaze fell upon it, and he bit his lip. "I didn't do that."

"Is it just me," Siobhán said to Aretta, "or are you finding it hard to believe a word that comes out of his mouth?"

"He wouldn't know the truth if it were a fox and it bit him," Aretta said.

"I have no idea what that newspaper clipping has to do with me!" Sean said. He was starting to unravel. *Good.*

"Funny," Siobhán said, taking her seat once more. "We found it in your flat, in your desk drawer along with your divorce papers."

Sean crossed his arms. "Nothing was ever finalized," he said. "We are not getting a divorce." He licked his lips. "Did she say we were getting a divorce?"

"If you didn't do this—who did?" Siobhán said, ignoring his question and tapping the newspaper article. Sean glanced down at the clipping again, Cassidy Ryan's face conspicuously absent. His lip twitched as if he were trying to suppress a smile or perhaps swallow back a secret.

"I don't want to get anyone in trouble. She did it for a laugh."

"Who?"

"If I tell you, will you finally believe me?"

Siobhán shook her head. "You're in no position to bargain, Mr. Bell."

"Mr. Bell. Why do you have to be so formal? You've always called me Sean."

"This is a formal inquiry. Who cut Cassidy Ryan's head out of the newspaper article?"

"Alice McCarthy," he said with a dismissive wave of his hand, "for a laugh."

"A laugh?" Aretta chimed in, arching an eyebrow. "And you kept it in your drawer?"

He shifted uneasily, the legs of his chair scraping against the linoleum floor. "I might have put it away in the drawer, but I would have thrown it out eventually." His voice held a note of defensiveness.

"Let's roll the dice and say it was Alice McCarthy who cut off Cassidy Ryan's head."

"It was. I swear."

Siobhán was growing tired of his proclamations. "Did Alice tell you why she did this?"

Sean sighed, the corners of his mouth drooping. "She wasn't happy that Cassidy was using this competition to win another one. Neither of us were, to be honest with you. She didn't even try to hide it! Someone—might've been Nessa—made some kind of 'Off with their heads' comment. I guess that inspired Alice to cut Cassidy out of the group photo. Cassidy Ryan never really belonged."

And she paid for it with her life.

"I heard you did some repairs at Lorcan's Nursery recently."

Sean visibly relaxed. "Now. That's the kind of guy I am. I noticed it was damaged, and Larry was concerned about the potential crowds that would be coming through during the garden competition."

"What day did you do the repairs?"

His tension returned. "I noticed it Monday evening during our committee meeting and returned Tuesday morning to repair it." Despite his attempt at a calm demeanor, sweat was pooling beneath his hairline.

"Are you sure about that?"

"I am positive." He tilted his head. "Why? What on earth does that have to do with your murder probe?"

"If you're telling the truth, where did you go when you left the nursery?"

"What do you mean?"

"If you returned Tuesday morning, that means you were returning from *somewhere*. Your wife was very clear that you were not home Monday evening." It was time to lie to the liar. Nora hadn't said which days he wasn't home, but something went down after that committee meeting and she was throwing a dart at the target, seeing if it would stick.

Sean began to squirm. "I have a woodworking shop not too far from the greenhouse. I was picking up materials, and by the time I finished I was knackered. I slept in me car."

"You took time to do all that when you had your own garden to focus on?"

"I didn't want anyone to lean on it and plunge into the pond."

Interesting. Liars often stuck to the facts. "Did you paint the little bridge as well?"

"No," Sean said. "Nessa O'Neill did."

"How did that come about?"

"She happened into the nursery—we were all there a lot the last week—she saw the work I had done and asked Larry if there was any leftover paint. There was, and she volunteered to paint it. It's a tiny bridge, alright?"

"I heard you've been reading someone's novel?"

He frowned. "Another ridiculous question. I'm done here." He stood and walked to the door.

"Mr. Bell. We know for a fact that you did not see Cassidy Ryan on Thursday."

He whirled around, fury stamped on his face. "I did so. She tried to peek in on my garden."

"I was home Thursday morning, did you know that?"

He tried to look nonchalant, but not before a look of panic came over his face. "What does that have to do with anything?"

"Owen Sheedy. Do you know Owen Sheedy?"

He began to sweat. "No."

"Interesting. He knows you."

Sean shrugged. "I'm in the competition, everyone knows me."

"I wonder if you assumed myself and Macdara wouldn't be home when that crate was delivered."

"I know nothing about a crate."

"Do you want to know what the crate contained?"

Sean shook his head. "Any more questions and you can call my solicitor."

"Cassidy Ryan's body," Aretta said. "You couldn't have seen her on Thursday afternoon because she was already dead."

Sean's mouth dropped open. He seemed frozen in time. He thought his story would work. Even killers made mistakes. And if he was innocent? If he didn't see Cassidy Ryan on Thursday, who did he see? The same woman who Eoin had mistaken for Cassidy on that Thursday morning? But if so, why wasn't Sean insisting that he would have sworn he saw Cassidy that afternoon? Could his wife, Nora, have dressed up in that blond wig, sunglasses, and hat? Was she trying to catch her husband cheating by pretending to be the mistress?

"I'm contacting a solicitor," Sean said. "I have nothing more to say."

But Siobhán had more to say, and he couldn't stop her. "Have you ever seen a Ghost Orchid, Mr. Bell?"

She swore his face turned even paler right before her very eyes. "Only in photographs," he responded after a long silence. "Personally, I don't see what the fuss is about. They're *much* too delicate for me." And with that he walked out the door and slammed it behind him.

Chapter 26

The glow from a red paper lantern cast a warm hue over the secluded nook at Jade's Chinese Restaurant, where Siobhán and Macdara sat in front of six different appetizers. Their iPad, cued up with Molly's interview of Finnoula Connor, had been set to the side along with two pairs of earbuds. Siobhán needed to eat first, or Macdara would be working this case solo. Aretta had declined the invite.

"She's missing out," Siobhán exclaimed as she finished her third egg roll.

"So am I," Macdara said, eyeing the empty plate.

Siobhán threw her head back and laughed. "Liars make me hungry," she said. She had already filled him in on their interview with Sean Bell.

"*For Whom the Bell Tolls*," Macdara said.

"Unfortunately, Aretta and I were doing all the 'tolling,' " Siobhán said. "Nightmare."

Macdara stabbed a dumpling with his chopsticks and then began drowning the poor thing in soy sauce. "Finnoula might not have spit out as many lies as your one, but she was annoyingly evasive."

"Do tell." They paused as Macdara finished his dumpling.

"She'd claimed someone must have stolen her trophies from out of her shed—she had hired Sean to make her a cabinet for them, but of course he would be busy until after the competition, so she had been storing them away."

Another shed. Siobhán was going to start calling this shed-gate. "We didn't see any evidence that anyone had broken into her shed."

"She claims she left it unlocked."

It seemed incongruent with someone as meticulous as Finnoula, especially when you considered what those trophies meant to her. "What about the 'Best Weeds' trophy?"

"She was insulted. Said weeds don't grow in her gardens."

Siobhán smirked as she twirled a piece of chicken satay. "Did she at least admit to firing her garden crew and not paying them?"

Macdara nodded. "She said they were not as methodical as she required and so it was easier just to do it herself. She doesn't think they should be paid when they weren't working, but now that she knows they are complaining, she said she would compensate them."

"And the committee meeting?"

"She said she was the first one to leave that Monday, around half-eight. Claims all the other gardeners were still there when she left. She said she did not see Cassidy Ryan, nor did she know whether or not Cassidy arrived after she left."

Siobhán leaned back in her chair. "That's a lie."

"She said her husband can corroborate her story, that the two of them walked around her garden with their evening scotch."

Husbands didn't always make the best witnesses, but the

fact that she had a witness did bolster her statement regardless. "Even if she did leave early and did not see Cassidy Ryan, there's no way one of the other gardeners wouldn't have mentioned if there was some incident with Cassidy Ryan." *An incident that might have led to murder.*

"You're assuming they all knew about it," Macdara said, emphasizing his words with the chopsticks. "It would have only taken one person to push her over the little bridge and then hold her under."

Siobhán sighed. "True." She held up her hands in a defensive position. "Watch where you're flinging that soy sauce."

Macdara grinned. "Sorry."

"And the book of lores?"

"Right." He started to gesture with the chopsticks then made a show of putting them down. Siobhán laughed and shook her head. "She said Molly Murphy was inspired by her horse statue and got her thinking that she could write a female version of *The Headless Horseman.* So when Finnoula was at the bookshop she decided to buy it as a thank-you for all the interviews."

"And yet she never gave it to Molly," Siobhán pointed out.

"She said she tried, but Molly politely thanked her and declined, stating that she didn't want anyone else's version in her head while she was writing."

"What was your take on that?" Macdara had excellent instincts.

"On one hand, it sounded plausible. But if it's true—why didn't Molly mention it?"

More questions. More possible liars. There were days Siobhán wondered if she should have spent her life running the family bistro instead. "Let's watch the video," Siobhán said with a sigh. A server came to collect their plates, as they donned their earbuds.

* * *

"Gardening is not a mere hobby. It's a science. A serious endeavor demanding meticulous attention—the right balance of nutrients, precise plant placement, organized procedures." Even though her audience was just one—Molly Murphy—Finnoula Connor's tone was that of a college professor lecturing her lowly students.

Macdara turned to Siobhán and mimicked a yawn. She laughed and nodded.

The camera panned across Finnoula's wall of trophies, polished gold reflecting years of triumphs. Siobhán paused the video.

"I thought she stored them in the shed?"

Macdara nodded. "I suspect she lied. But all she has to say is that she moved them after this video was taken and that must be when they were stolen."

"'Stolen' just to dump them in her garden installation and drown them." This case, or more aptly, these suspects, were maddening.

"It seems like plants are like your children," Molly was saying.

"Children?" Finnoula made a face. "They're leaps and bounds better than children. They rarely disobey."

"You seem like a woman who does not like to be crossed," Molly said.

Finnoula stared into the camera and did not reply. Siobhán paused the video.

"Did you ask her about the golden rose that we found in Teagan's garden?"

He nodded. "I nearly forgot. Listen to this. She said she *loaned* it to him, that she thought it would be a wonderful touch for his garden."

"She admitted to helping a competitor?"

He nodded. "I felt the same as you, so I pressed her on it.

She laughed and said her winning streak couldn't last forever, that even if she was *always the best*, that this year she was fully prepared to 'concede the crown.' " They resumed the interview.

"What do you think of Cassidy Ryan entering the competition this year?" Molly asked in a chipper voice.

Finnoula's demeanor shifted as Molly Murphy posed the question, and her jaw tightened. "Rules are there to uphold tradition and fairness. And we will be revisiting them, to ensure that in the future the integrity of our competition remains intact."

"Be that as it may, it's too late for this year," Molly said.

Finnoula pursed her lips. "I am aware."

"How does that make you *feel*?"

"Are you filming an interview or a documentary?" Finnoula asked. Before Molly could answer, she continued. "Let me be perfectly clear. Cassidy Ryan may have ambition, but she will not triumph in a contest such as ours."

Molly tilted her head slightly, her expression unreadable, yet Siobhán knew the cogs were turning. As usual, Molly seemed to be digging for a reaction. "I'm quite surprised to hear you say that, given her clout and experience."

"She's in this competition for all the wrong reasons."

"You've jumped to my next question. It sounds as if you *do* know about the million euro competition?"

Finnoula nodded. "It's an outrage. Larry Lorcan is no fool. He'll do the right thing."

" 'The right thing,' meaning declare anyone else the winner but Cassidy Ryan?"

Finnoula crossed her arms. "If you wish to ask me about my garden entry, I'm happy to answer. Otherwise, you'll get no satisfaction from me."

Molly took it in stride. "Tell us about your garden this year."

"My garden will be fit for an old Irish manor, replete with a central fountain sourced from the very heart of our history."

Before Siobhán could pause the tape, Macdara did it for her. "Irish manor," he said. "I heard."

"Finnoula herself couldn't be the writer of that story. Could she?"

Macdara tilted his head. "Seems there are many aspiring scribes in the world. It's possible, isn't it?" He rubbed his chin. "But why wouldn't she cop to it?"

Siobhán grimaced. "If it was her, I wouldn't cop to it either and she should stick to gardening." She pushed Play.

"My garden will be in a circular shape with shrubs meticulously arranged, and beyond them, flowers will stand tall in assigned grid positions, a spectacle of order and beauty." Her hands fluttered as she spoke. "I will also include a thorough collection of herbs. Where would the field of medicine be without them?"

"An old Irish manor," Molly said, a spark igniting in her eyes. "Now. That would make for a splendid setting in a novel, wouldn't it?"

Siobhán and Macdara made eye contact. Maybe Molly was the writer after all. But how could her creative writing skills be so poor compared to her journalism?

"I'm afraid that's all the time I have for you today." With that, Finnoula walked out of the frame.

Molly slowly turned the recording device on her phone around until her face filled the screen. "There you have it, folks, the front-runner has abruptly ended the interview." Molly shrugged as her beau came into view behind her. It took her a minute but Siobhán finally retrieved his first name from the cluttered spaces of her poor brain. *Brandon.*

"Are you finished now?" Brandon was saying. "I'm starving." One could not miss the whine in his tone. He was pouting.

"Sorry, luv, I have work to do. Why don't we get a take-away?"

"Is this what our marriage is going to be like? Is this going to be our future?" He put his hands on his hips.

Molly rolled her eyes, pointed to his posture, then looked at her engagement ring. "I hope not. But I guess it's true: all husbands nag." Molly made a face into the camera before shutting it off.

Just then the bill arrived on a small tray along with a pair of fortune cookies.

"Speaking of the future," Macdara said with a nod to the cookies. He reached for one.

"Wait." Siobhán commandeered the iPad and fiddled with it until Brandon was back on the screen. He wore a black T-shirt with the logo of DADDY-O, a local pub that catered to the youth. The guards were often called in regard to the pub, the complaints ranging from loud music to actual brawls.

" 'Wack fall the Daddy-O . . .' " Macdara started singing "Whiskey in the Jar" as Siobhán zoomed in on Brandon's hand.

"He's wearing an engagement ring as well," she exclaimed, tapping the screen.

"Young ones," Macdara said. "Always messing with tradition."

"It's not that. *Look.*" She tapped the frozen image of Brandon. "We need to find him and make sure he still has this ring."

Macdara frowned. "Don't we have better things to do than interfering in their love story?"

"Remember the ring we found on Cassidy Ryan? It was a man's ring."

"You're right," he said. "I'd nearly forgotten about that."

"Let's get it out of the evidence room and pay him a visit."

"Like Cinderella's shoe," he said. He handed her a fortune cookie.

"You're unusually superstitious today," she said.

"I just know we have great things in store." His smile said it all, and they shared a moment.

"I'm not sure I want to know," she said, eyeing the cookie.

"Go on, so," Macdara said. "I hear Jade's had them tailor-made for the garden competition."

Siobhán broke the cookie in half and pulled out the white paper nestled within its sweet confines. " 'He who throws dirt is losing ground.' "

Macdara laughed. "Sounds about right." Macdara cracked his open and the curled paper popped into the air and arced before landing on the table. Macdara whooped. "Did ya see that?"

"Remarkable," Siobhán deadpanned. "Read it."

He leaned over and smoothed it out. " 'Bloom where you are planted.' " Once more he grinned. "Hear that? Looks like you're stuck with me."

"I didn't need a cookie to tell me that," Siobhán said. "If you tried to plant yourself anywhere else, I'd just pluck you out and bring you back home."

Macdara grinned. They shared a quick kiss, paid the bill, and walked out, leaving their fortunes to wither on the sticky table behind them.

Chapter 27

The worn oak door of Daddy-O creaked as Siobhán and Macdara stepped over the threshold, and Siobhán braced herself to be greeted by the familiar musty scent of yesterday's stout and busted dreams. To her surprise, it had the aroma of fresh-cut lemons, and the dim lighting had been chased away by new chandeliers, flush to the ceiling. Slim glass vases filled with cut flowers dotted the circular tables spread throughout the space, and a promotional poster for the garden competition hung on the wall behind the bar. It seemed everyone was getting into the spirit of the competition, and Siobhán was hit by an unexpected pang of loss as she sent a silent prayer to Cassidy Ryan, and especially her friends and family. They had arrived in Kilbane a few days ago, their palpable grief adding to the mounting pressure to find her killer. But there was something about the transformation of this old-timey-pub-turned-new that gave her hope.

A few years back, this pub had been a snug cocoon for old-timers, decorated with a myriad of photos on the walls, not of celebrities, but of the patrons whose entire lives, both thrills and chills, had been wallpapered amongst faded jerseys and winning racehorses. But it had been taken over by youth, and now the walls were painted clean, the photos replaced by a mural—done by none other than Eoin O'Sullivan, showcasing a variety of instruments: guitars, fiddles, drums, and squeeze boxes that appeared to be floating midair. Just looking at them uplifted Siobhán. And in a perfect juxtaposition to the age of the ownership, Daddy-O was now *the* place for trad music, and Ciarán was a regular, joining every session he could.

Siobhán and Macdara came sparingly. Ciarán had made it clear that he "saw them enough at home, like," and so they staggered their visits out of respect. Growing up the youngest of the O'Sullivan Six meant that he had been sheltered and babied his entire life, and he needed room to spread his wings. That didn't stop Siobhán from wanting to clip them, and she was relieved that at this afternoon hour, only a few heads had popped in for some day-drinking, and Ciarán was not one of them.

Standing midbar, Brandon O'Leary rubbed a cloth onto the long counter, now gleaming despite the years of elbows and confessions. When there wasn't live music, Brandon was known to play whatever struck his fancy, and today, the thump of rock music vibrated through the floorboards.

If Brandon was surprised to see them, he didn't show it. He bopped his head to the music, flipped his dishrag over his shoulder, and slapped down two coasters. "Detective Sergeant. Garda." His face split into a toothy grin. "What can I do for ye?"

"Just here for the music," Macdara yelled. "We want to see which one of our heads will explode first."

Brandon belted out a laugh, his large frame tilting back as he raised his hand, fingers splayed in the universal rock 'n' roll salute. He then pulled his mobile phone out of his pocket, thumbed the screen, and seconds later the music dimmed and they could hear themselves think.

"Two minerals," Macdara said as they pulled out their stools. "Coke and a bottle of orange."

"Congrats on the engagement," Siobhán chimed in, when Brandon set the minerals in front of them, and she and Macdara switched so that he had the Coke and she had the orange.

"Thanks a million." Brandon's reply came easy, but his eyes narrowed slightly, an acknowledgment that pleasantries and minerals weren't the real reason for their visit.

"Speaking of," Siobhán ventured as she glanced at his hands, now sans engagement ring, "we were watching Molly's interviews with the gardeners, and in one of them, I thought you were wearing a gold band."

Brandon let out a groan, the sound lost momentarily in the swell of guitar from the speakers. "Molly thought it was sexist if she was the only one announcing to the world that she was taken." His infectious grin was back, and Siobhán found herself approving of Molly's choice in a mate.

Siobhán saluted the comment with her orange drink. "Do you take it off for work?"

He grimaced. "Nah. To be honest, it's a bit of a sore subject with Molly." He glanced at Macdara as if trying to garner support. "I had to dig through mounds of goat droppings to see if I could find it." He grimaced. "All those nightmares for nothing. I bet one of those hairy beasts still has it in him."

"You lost it at Nessa O'Neill's?" Although she certainly wasn't the only goat owner in Kilbane, she was the only one in the competition.

Brandon nodded. "Aye. Flew right off me hand." He leaned in conspiratorially. "Since I started keto? Already down a stone. Unfortunately, mostly in me fingers." He spread them out for emphasis. "Isn't that mad?"

"That's gas." Siobhán reached into her pocket, pulled

out the evidence bag, and set it on the counter. "Is this your ring?"

Brandon's eyes widened. "Whoa. You found it!" He raised his hand in a high-five, but just as he went in for the touch, he stopped, then stared at the evidence bag as his hand slowly dropped. "I think I'm missing a few episodes this season," he said, scratching his head. "What's it doing in that bag?"

Macdara held another evidence bag aloft, this one containing an antique gold pen nib. "This was straight from the mouth of a goat," he said. "Molly's a scribbler, isn't she?"

Brandon leaned in closer, squinting at the delicate object. "It was a graduation present from her folks. She's been mental since it went missing." He continued to frown as he stared at the bags, his eyes ping-ponging between them.

"I take it you tagged along with Molly when she visited Nessa?"

He nodded slowly. "Molly was conducting most of them online, but Nessa said she had too much work to do and if Molly wanted to interview her, she'd have to do it in person. She blames the goats, says they have separation anxiety. Truth be told, I think she's the one with separation anxiety." He gave a half-hearted chuckle. "You know?"

Siobhán's expression remained neutral, checking to see that no one was ear-wigging when she went in for the kill. "Any idea how your ring came to be on the finger of a dead woman?"

Brandon's eyes widened. "You're joking me."

"I assure you, we are not," Macdara said. "And this information stays between us—you cannot tell anyone, not even Molly, until this case is closed."

"You're saying this ring was found on"—he gulped—"Cassidy?" he whispered. Something about his tone reminded Siobhán of the Headless Horseman, whispering the name of his victim before he attacked.

"Listen to me, Brandon," Siobhán said. "You're not one of our suspects. But it's strange, isn't it? Because yes. Someone placed this ring on Cassidy's cold, dead hand." She wasn't usually so blunt, not to mention dramatic, but Brandon was teetering on the edge, she could see his wheels turning, as if he was grappling with whether or not to tell them everything.

"It must be her," he said, his words tumbling out in a rush. "Nessa." He shook his head. "Please don't tell Molly you found it. I'm still getting married, mind you, but not with that yoke on me finger." He shivered, no doubt imagining it on her cold, dead finger.

"Consider it done," Macdara said. "But we're going to need to go through a few things." He too looked around the pub. Since their arrival, it had mysteriously emptied out. If one craved popularity, becoming a guard wasn't the profession for them. Brandon's posture seemed to wither. "Do you want to do it here and now," Macdara continued, "or shall we schedule an interview with you at the station?"

Brandon's eyes darted toward the private booths nestled in the far corner. "We can sit there," he suggested. "I'll lock the doors for a spell."

"Good man," Macdara said. He picked up the minerals and they moved to the booth as Brandon turned the sign on the door to CLOSED and engaged the lock. Finally, he turned the music all the way off before sliding into the booth, across from them. He eyed their notebooks nervously.

"Brandon," Macdara began, his voice friendly, "did you accompany Molly on any other interviews? Besides Nessa's?"

Brandon shook his head, his fingers tugging at his ear. "No, that was the only one. As I said, Molly prefers to do them online."

"What about Cassidy Ryan?" Siobhán asked. "Have you ever met her?"

He gulped. "Only once. We ran into her at the bookshop. Molly tried to introduce me, but Cassidy Ryan wouldn't even look at us. I don't mean to speak ill of the dead, but here she was this big-time designer, right? And she's snubbing Molly? It's like a David and Goliath situation, isn't it?"

"Interesting comparison," Siobhán mused.

"You liked it, did ya?" Brandon asked, sounding proud of himself. "Definitely a David and Goliath thing going on alright."

Siobhán nodded. "At the end of that tale David kills Goliath. Stone to the head, wasn't it?"

Brandon's smile faded. "To be honest I've never read it." He glanced at the clock as sweat formed on his brow.

"Speaking of reading, I heard Molly's writing a novel," Siobhán said. "*The Headless Horsewoman?*"

Brandon snorted. "She's always starting novels but she never finishes. I guess all the drama these gardeners are stirring up have her creative juices flowing."

"Have you read it?" Siobhán asked, leaning back against the worn leather of the booth, keeping it casual.

Brandon dismissed it with a wave. "She only has a few pages, like. Always foisting these partials on me. I put me foot down. Enough is enough, like. I said I'd read it *if and when* she finished it."

"You might want to change that tune if you want to stay married," Macdara said. "Any idea why she chose *The Headless Horsewoman?*"

Brandon's eyes widened. "What do you mean?"

Macdara flashed an easy smile. "I'm just always curious about how writers get their ideas."

Brandon's gaze drifted to a point over their shoulders, as if he could visualize the moment of inspiration. "She saw some horse sculpture in Finnoula Connor's house. During an online interview, that is. I guess it inspired her."

It tracked with Finnoula's recollection. When this many suspects were involved, corroboration was essential if they wanted to get to the truth. Brandon had no idea that Finnoula Connor had been asked the same question, and vice versa, so Siobhán was inclined to believe this was the unbiased truth. The horse sculpture inspired Molly Murphy to begin penning her tale. "What inspired her to change the character to a female?" Siobhán was genuinely curious.

"She likes doing that. You know how Shakespeare made men dress up like women?"

"Not quite what he was doing but go on, so," Siobhán said.

"Well, it's her revenge. She likes to take classic tales and change all the heroes to heroines. Class, isn't it?" Pride for his bride-to-be shone on his face.

"We'll get out of your hair," Macdara said. "But I'm curious. Why do you think Cassidy Ryan snubbed Molly?"

Brandon put his index finger on his chin as he considered it. "Molly said she dug up a secret on Cassidy. Nothing crazy, like. Just something about her garden installation."

Siobhán was dying to look at Macdara, but she controlled herself. "Did she tell you what exactly she found out?"

Brandon shook his head. "See? She didn't need to worry. Molly wouldn't even tell me. But apparently, before Cassidy Ryan even came to town, Molly overheard Larry Lorcan on the phone with Cassidy. I guess they were discussing some secret flower, or whatever. Larry was going to try and get it for her. Molly did some snooping—don't tell her I told you that, like—and honestly, she should have left it at that. But she ended up letting the cat out of the bag when she first met Cassidy Ryan. I think she was trying to impress her, like. You know. Show her she was good at her job. Which she is. But after that Cassidy Ryan basically turned into stone around her." He stopped, as a look of shock came over his face. "Not stone like a statue, it was just a figure of speech."

"No worries," Siobhán said. "We didn't read into it."

Brandon frowned. "I'm confused. What was there to read?"

"We believe you, mate," Macdara said. "That's what she means."

"Right." Brandon's face relaxed a bit but he still looked confused.

"You were saying that as soon as Molly told Cassidy she knew about her secret flower that Cassidy's behavior instantly changed around her?" Siobhán prompted. She was starting to wonder if Molly and Brandon were a good match after all. Then again, every person had their strengths and weaknesses.

Brandon picked up the thread. "Next thing you know, Molly's got this letter, right? 'Cease and Desist.' Warning her to stay away from her, no doubt threatening her to keep quiet about her secret flower."

"What exactly was the threat?" Macdara asked.

Brandon shrugged. "Just—stop—or else." He threw up his hands. "We'll never know now, will we?"

"What proof did Molly have that the letter was actually from Cassidy Ryan?"

Brandon frowned. "It was signed."

"You're familiar with Ms. Ryan's signature, are ya?" Macdara asked.

Brandon was starting to sweat. He pulled at his collar. "No. But why would anyone else write it? I just told you Molly knew what her big garden surprise was, and Cassidy did not like that. She didn't even want to meet me. Everyone likes me." He attempted a grin but quickly released it.

"I bet Molly didn't like receiving that letter," Siobhán said. "I mean she was just trying to do her job."

Brandon nodded. "Molly can be hotheaded. And she definitely did not like it. She read Cassidy's letter out loud to me—and then tossed it on the footpath like it was rubbish." *Molly lied. She'd told them she couldn't find the letter.* Brandon's mouth suddenly dropped open. "You're not, like, going to fine her for littering, are ye?"

"As a favor to you, Brandon, we'll let that one slide," Macdara said.

Brandon let out a sigh of relief.

"Where exactly were you when Molly tossed this letter?" Siobhán asked.

Brandon didn't hesitate. "In front of Raven's."

Raven's. Is that how Teagan Moore came to have the letter in his possession? After all, his garden was behind the shop and he lived above it.

"We'll get out of your hair," Macdara said, as he slid out of the booth and held his hand out to Siobhán.

"There is one more thing," Brandon said. He ran his hand through his hair. "I might know why Cassidy snubbed us in the bookshop." In addition to sweating, his neck had flushed red.

"You'd better tell us everything," Macdara said.

Brandon hung his head. "Cassidy overheard Molly gossiping about her, like."

Macdara leaned in. "What day was this?"

"Sunday week. I remember because it's my day off."

They knew Cassidy was still alive on Sunday. Siobhán perked up. "Go on, so."

"Molly was waxing on about how it really wasn't fair a professional was trying to beat out all these locals. She said something about Cassidy being snippy in their interview. Even said she wondered if there was any 'dirt' on Cassidy and maybe she should be the one to dig it up. Padraig kept making funny faces, but she just plowed on. We had no idea Cassidy was in the shop until Padraig's eyes totally bugged out and he mouthed, 'She's here.' We turn around and sure enough, there she is. From the look on her face she'd heard every single word." He chewed his lip. "I wonder if that was the reason for the cease and desist letter, because three days later it was delivered to our door."

That wasn't the reason because Cassidy couldn't have written that letter. But she could see how Brandon came to that conclusion. "Leaving the letter aside for a moment, was that Cassidy's only reaction?" Siobhán asked as she accepted Macdara's offer to help her to her feet. "Her facial expression?"

Brandon scrambled up after them. "No. She whirled around and grabbed a book on the shelf. The title was: *Stalkers.* I guess she thought we followed her in there, like. But we didn't. Molly's always in the bookshop. I don't mean to speak ill of the dead, but I don't get why Cassidy was so browned off. All this over a secret flower? Then? On her way out?" He grimaced again. "Cassidy Ryan looked directly at me and said, 'Run.'"

Chapter 28

Nessa O'Neill came into focus, propped up on a crate near her goat pen, the sound of bleating audible in the background. "Apologies for the noise; the lads are a bit rowdy this morn," Nessa's voice trilled through the iPad speakers. She maneuvered the camera on her phone to show off the goats, cavorting in the background, their coats a motley array of earthy browns, grays, and creamy whites. One audacious fella nosed curiously at the camera before being shooed away by Nessa's gentle hand, its beard quivering with the sudden movement. "Gardens should be wild, free," Nessa began, a hand sweeping across the scene behind her.

Molly nodded, jotting down notes. "Can you tell me more about that philosophy?"

Nessa's eyes sparkled with an almost religious fervor. "Nature knows best how to manage herself without us meddling. A garden, a true garden, isn't manicured within an inch of its life. It's natural, alive, bramble and blossom intertwined." The camera panned slowly across Nessa's garden, revealing a tapestry of wildflowers, their vibrant hues peeking out from among thickets and tall grasses swaying in the breeze. "Each plant finds its place, battles for sunlight and soil, and thrives or fades on its own merits. That's the real competition, not some prize dangled by judges. It's survival. Life itself clawing forth from the earth."

"You certainly present a compelling narrative," Molly said. Chewing a mouthful of wild clover, a goat paused to watch Molly with an almost suspicious gaze, as if sensing her quest for more than just a simple interview. "Speaking of competition," Molly ventured, "this year's event has everyone tittering about Cassidy Ryan. What are your thoughts on her participation?"

"You'd be surprised." Nessa leaned against the worn wooden fence, and she crossed her arms. A wry smile played at the corner of her lips.

Molly waited but Nessa simply stared at the camera. "Well, then. Surprise me."

"Let's just say . . . I know people."

Molly sighed. "I feel as if you still haven't answered the question."

Nessa gave a little shake of her head. "What was the question?"

"How do you feel about Cassidy Ryan crashing the party, so to speak?"

"The more the merrier." Nessa grinned, although there was something forced about her demeanor; maybe it was the clench of her jaw.

"You're fine with a professional landscaper—an outsider with ulterior motives—joining you this year?"

Nessa dropped her arms and spread them out on the fence behind her. Siobhán felt as if she was trying way too hard to look casual. "It's good to have the pot stirred now and again. Keeps us all on our toes, doesn't it? It's better than the same old patterns repeating year after year."

"By 'same old,' do you mean Finnoula Connor winning the trophy every year?"

Nessa paused to scratch behind the ear of the goat that had wandered over, its eyes bright and curious. "There's that," she admitted, giving the animal a final pat before straightening up. "But I can't control the taste of the judges." Her eyes narrowed as if weighing her next words. "I don't really care who takes home some fake gold trophy."

"What about the golden rose?" Molly asks. "Isn't that real gold?"

"Twenty-four carats, maybe?" Nessa said with a shrug. She curled her index finger as she began to move through a vegetable patch. She bent over, the image jerking until she finally straightened up. She held up a carrot plucked from the ground. "But if I don't win? I still have these." Several goats circled Nessa, all vying for the carrot. She laughed and split it between the three of them.

Molly looked as if she was losing patience with this interview. "Are you worried about your goats getting into your garden installation?"

"These lads?" Nessa laughed. "They might be cute, but they're no match for a gate latch."

"Have you heard about Cassidy Ryan's *other* competition?"

Nessa narrowed her eyes. "I'm only focused on our competition."

"I take that as a yes. Does this mean that it doesn't bother you at all that she's basically using all of you as a stepping stone to a million euro prize?"

Siobhán paused the video and turned to Aretta and Macdara. They were hunkered in Macdara's office. "Do you think Molly started stirring the pot because Cassidy basically rejected her?"

"Rejected or threatened?" Aretta said.

Siobhán held her hands up, palm up, as if weighing the options. "Given how rare that Ghost Orchid is, I can see why she was freaked out that Molly had already sussed it out."

"All this drama," Macdara said. "Over plants."

"Like Nessa said," Siobhán replied, "nature can be wild."

She pushed Play.

"It was me, alright?" Nessa said.

Molly, who looked as if she had been falling asleep, perked up. "What was you?"

"I already mentioned, I *know* people. I know people who know people."

"Would you please stop talking in riddles?"

Nessa wasn't happy with that response. She exhaled, blowing a bit of her fringe in the air. "I happened to be speaking with a landscaper in Dublin who began raving about Cassidy Ryan and mentioned her big contest but that she first had to win a local garden competition, and did I know of any?" She shrugged. "I told him she should come to Kilbane. Why not? She lived here as a young one, didn't she? What's the harm?"

"What do your other contestants think of you inviting Cassidy?"

"Are you joking me?" She shook her head. "I'm not telling them, and that's off the record, by the way."

"I think they'd be quite upset, don't you?" Molly probed.

"Upset?" Nessa said. "I think they'd kill me."

Chapter 29

The Incident Room of the Kilbane Garda Station was thick with anticipation. A whiteboard loomed behind Macdara, a tableau of names and connections mapped out for discussion. Cassidy Ryan's name was scrawled at the center, the nucleus from which all threads radiated. Siobhán glanced at the gardeners' section, each name a suspect, then over to the trio of Larry Lorcan, Molly Murphy, and Emily Dunne. It had taken hours just to organize the whiteboard with notes beneath each subject, along with a list of their inconsistencies and lies. If it were a garden, it would be choked with weeds. Only by pulling them one by one could they maybe see the truth hidden within.

"Good morning, gang," Macdara said to the full room. "We're here to sift through our suspects and iron out the inconsistencies we've found." He turned to Garda Dabiri, waiting off to the side. "But before we dig into the nitty-gritty, Garda Dabiri has a few updates about the fire at Cassidy Ryan's cottage. Aretta, do you need the screen down?"

"Yes, thank you, Detective Sergeant Flannery," she replied, "I have several photos to display."

Macdara reached up and pulled down the screen as

Aretta approached, setting her laptop near the projector with deliberate care. A few seconds later the first photo materialized—an image of ash-covered plants. "If you wouldn't mind, I'd like to begin with a proverb my father used to say when I was growing up." Siobhán straightened up, Aretta rarely divulged personal information at work. " 'When the roots of a tree begin to decay, it spreads death to the branches.' " The proverb hung in the air, and every guard was listening intently. Siobhán thought it was a fantastic image, and mentally began imagining all of their suspects' lies as the roots, and the branches—their suspects.

"Once we had a better image of the plants and shrubs found at Cassidy's cottage—Japanese maples, variegated hostas, blue Himalayan poppies . . ." Aretta listed each species with a meticulousness that belied the chaos of the fire-ravaged scene. "There is no doubt that all of these 'top-shelf,' if you will, plants were intended for Cassidy Ryan's installation at the O'Sullivan property."

"If I may interject," Macdara said.

"Please," Aretta said with a nod.

"This aligns with our theory that the killer did not realize Cassidy was creating her garden elsewhere and had planned on delivering and setting it up on the Thursday—the last day before the competition." He stared at the screen. "Our killer must have panicked when he or she, or they, saw an empty tent. That's why the killer needed her alive through Thursday evening. We believe it is a garden contestant, or someone closely affiliated. This killer needed to steal a few items from every other garden to set up in Cassidy's empty tent. It would have been the quickest way to construct a garden in such a tight time frame. We need to press our gardeners on their opinions of how items from each of their gardens were stolen."

"I have a theory on that as well," Aretta said.

"Let's hear it."

"Larry Lorcan confirmed that the gardeners had been allotted use of the greenhouse, meeting room, and back warehouse from which to work and store items. It's reasonable to assume that one could find bits and bobs from each garden in that warehouse to assemble in Cassidy Ryan's tent."

"That fits in well with our other theories," Macdara said. "All roads lead back to the greenhouse."

"It was meticulous," Siobhán said. "Whoever did it did not hurry."

"If Cassidy was murdered in the wee hours of Monday morning, the killer or killers had four days to assemble Cassidy's garden," Aretta said. "But if you indulge me, it lines up quite nicely with my theory."

It was good to see her so engaged and talkative. This was the first time Garda Dabiri had taken the lead. Siobhán couldn't help thinking that she was like a flower, finally coming to bloom. Siobhán was anxious to hear her theory and settled back in her chair. "As we all know by now, the centerpiece of Cassidy Ryan's garden was to be a rare orchid—the Ghost Orchid. It was not found amongst the other plants and flowers at the cottage."

"We believe the Ghost Orchid is the motive behind the murder," Macdara chimed in once again. "And only those in the business, or those working closely with our gardeners, would have known the rarity and worth of that particular orchid."

"Murder?" a guard said aloud. "Over a hothouse flower?"

"Over the fortune the killer believed he or she could make from the Ghost Orchid, Garda," Macdara corrected. "Pure greed. One of the oldest motives in the book."

With another click, the scene shifted to a charred manuscript page.

"We also found what appears to be another passage from

a novel that we've been told was being penned by Molly Murphy. It looks as if this is the second half to the torn passage we collected. I have added, for clarity, the ending line of the one we already had in our possession . . ." Aretta read the passage aloud, as the guards followed it on the screen.

But this was the sacred hour she loved the most: the Witching Hour. She was headed to one Irish garden in particular, one she adored the most because the elderly owner who owned it slept like the dead. Therefore, she could sneak onto the grounds of the manor house—trespassing, she was—and sit in the scrumptious garden, one that only the wealthiest of all the wealthy persons in all of Ireland could afford. She was out of breath when she reached the old limestone wall to the magnificent, lush garden, but she gathered all her strength from every nook and crevice of her body, and she climbed that old limestone wall. If it could talk, that wall, it would have a lot to say. Lucky for her, it knew how to keep its stony mouth shut. She stopped for a moment at the top of the old, limestone wall, and nodded at the now-full yellowish-orange moon, before dropping to the lush garden below. She landed on her hands and knees in a thorny shrub, which hurt very badly, and drew drops of blood so red they were black.

But soon she was soothing herself in the bright lights of the ornate fountain as they illuminated all of the fancy, flowering shrubs, and colorful flowers, and cheery statues, shrouded in the darkest corners of the dark. But on this very night they had transformed into something ghoulish, something as animatedly alive as the voluptuous Cassandra herself.

The manuscript ended there. "That's all we've found so far," Aretta said. "But I believe there have to be additional pages out there somewhere."

"Someone shouldn't quit her day job," a guard piped up, and the room filled with laughter.

"You're saying this was found in Cassidy's cottage?" Siobhán asked.

"Most likely," Aretta said. "But given the state of it, slightly charred but still readable, we cannot discern whether or not this was carried in by the wind—"

"Or purposefully placed," Siobhán said.

Macdara raised an eyebrow. "Are you trying to say it was . . . *planted*?" Laughter erupted once more.

"I think we have to keep that possibility in mind," Siobhán said when the room finally settled down. "Unless Cassidy was our scribbler, why would she have a portion of the story?"

"Copies of the entire passage we've collected so far are being prepared as we speak," Aretta said. "They will be distributed shortly. We've also recovered some personal items from the cottage." Another image splashed across the screen— a pile of melted plastic and charred circuitry. "Her laptop and mobile phone," she continued, her finger tracing the outline of the devices in the photo. "But, I'm afraid, they've not been spared by the fire's wrath."

"Where are we with the mobile phone records?" Macdara called out to a guard in the back corner of the room.

"Still delayed."

"We won't get anything off those pieces of cinder," Macdara said. "Perhaps they were the reason for the fire."

"They are en route to our tech team in Dublin," Aretta said. "But the heat has likely devoured their secrets."

"What else?" Macdara said.

Aretta was prepared to continue. "We have confirmed with Larry Lorcan that the crate used for transporting Cassidy's body is indeed similar to the ones they receive when trees are delivered."

"Similar, or it's exactly the same crate?" Macdara asked.

Aretta flicked to the next screen showcasing a large crate. "There's no way to know for sure, but these are the crates."

"Indistinguishable," Macdara said.

"Could someone have taken one unnoticed?" Siobhán asked.

"Larry Lorcan said that he had given the gardeners and crew full range to the nursery, the greenhouse, and the back warehouse. It's more than possible someone could have taken one, either in the dead of night, or they reconstructed ones they had used for their own garden deliveries."

"Sean Bell had the most trees," someone piped up.

"Any crew member could have taken one," another said.

"We've at least confirmed that our circle of suspects has tightened to the gardeners, the crew members, or our three offshoots—Larry Lorcan, Molly Murphy, or Emily Dunne," Macdara said. "Thank you, Garda Dabiri."

Aretta hesitated. "There is one other thing. . . ." Macdara motioned for her to continue. Aretta clicked the remote, and a collection of their golden items appeared on one side of the screen, and Molly's cease and desist letter on the other with certain words highlighted:

Dear Ms. Murphy,

I cannot comply with your request for an interview, I am in the weeds, as they say. And furthermore, I know what you're really after is gossip, and you had better watch what you say. This assignment isn't for a tabloid. Why don't you pen something meaningful? Believe

me—I will expose you and you will not come
up smelling like a rose. You're young, but that
does not excuse you. My advice? Put your
head down and mind your business. Only then
can you stand up tall. When you finally grow
up and wish to apologize, give me a bell.
Maybe you can photograph me holding the
winning trophy, but until then—stay away
from me and my garden!
Yours truly,
Cassidy Ryan

She began to narrate as she used a laser to highlight not only the words, but the items as she spoke. "Pen—antique *pen* nib—straight from the goat's mouth at Nessa O'Neill's farm, and here"—she moved to one of the golden trophies found in Finnoula's garden—"a trophy inscribed BEST WEEDS, a golden *rose* found in Teagan Moore's garden, a golden *bell* in Sean Bell's garden. As far as *head*, although it doesn't match the golden statue found in Cassidy Ryan's garden—which seems to me as if it's mocking how we found Cassidy Ryan's body displayed, but it certainly correlates with Molly's story: *The Headless Horsewoman*. It is also possible the killer intended on leaving only the head of that golden statue in Cassidy's garden but was unable to accomplish that particular goal." She finished speaking as everyone leaned in, eyes scanning the text and images.

"That is good work, Garda Dabiri," Macdara said. "Excellent observation."

Aretta gave a nod. "Thank you, Detective Sergeant Flannery."

Macdara stood and moved closer to the screen. "I can't believe we didn't pick up on the clues in the letter."

Aretta beamed. "I read it again and again. Took me a while to recognize it too."

"The letter is typed," Siobhán said. "Even her signature. How can we be sure it really came from Cassidy Ryan?"

"With no witnesses to the fact and her laptop singed, we can't," Macdara said. "But now that I see the letter compared with the objects, I feel there's little doubt Aretta has sussed out the secret code."

"It's impossible to ignore," Siobhán said. "But I'm wondering about the *why*. If Cassidy was the one who penned the letter—what does the killer gain by placing all those objects?"

"Maybe it was someone creative who simply derived pleasure out of the wordplay," Aretta said.

"Like a killer's signature," Macdara added.

"There is a common denominator—or shall I say a common person—throughout all of this," Aretta said, her voice unable to contain her excitement. "Molly Murphy." She clicked, and another screen appeared, this one with Molly Murphy's name at the top and a list below it. "Molly had access to not only all the gardeners, but all the gardens. She could come and go, nearly unseen. As we learned last night, the ring found on Cassidy Ryan's finger belonged to Molly's betrothed: Brandon O'Leary. He told Detective Sergeant Flannery and Garda O'Sullivan not to mention the loss of his ring to Molly. But what woman doesn't notice when her fiancé is missing his engagement ring? Which begs the question—why didn't she ever mention the missing ring to Brandon? Molly is also good friends with Emily Dunne, the clerk at the charity shop who *thought* she was sourcing these golden items for the gardeners. But Sean Bell claimed his bell was black, and indeed a black bell was found in Cassidy's garden. Molly would have known how gullible her friend Emily could be and easily exploited her. Then there is the tale itself," Aretta continued. "*The Headless Horsewoman.* In the original tale, the horseman only spoke a single word when he arrived at the victim's house. A name. Detective Sergeant Flannery and Garda O'Sullivan distinctly heard a recording while they were watching Cassidy's cottage burn—a whisper of her name."

"We did," Macdara said. "Gave me the chills."

"Was the recording found in the ashes?" Siobhán asked.

Aretta nodded. "It was an old-fashioned tape recorder. The tape was brand-new, and the only thing on it was the name Cassidy, repeated over and over. Our theory is the arsonist left it playing just outside the fire zone knowing you were expected to arrive any moment."

"What about prints on the recorder, anything like that?" Macdara asked.

"We're sending it for analysis," Aretta said.

Macdara groaned. "That will take forever." He gestured to the screen. "Sorry. You were saying. Molly Murphy?"

Aretta nodded. "Until last night, I had everything but a solid motive," she said. "But when I learned from Garda O'Sullivan that Brandon O'Leary divulged that Molly Murphy had been the first to learn of Cassidy's Ghost Orchid, *and* they argued about it? To the point where Cassidy was flaunting books on *stalkers* in front of Molly? She even told Brandon to 'run.' I believe if Cassidy Ryan were alive today, she would stand up here, and if not shout, then at least whisper the name of her killer. 'Molly Murphy.' "

Chapter 30

Gathering as a family in Eoin's restaurant was the balm Siobhán needed after the eternal department meeting that ended with everyone eager to arrest and charge Molly Murphy with the murder of Cassidy Ryan. Aretta had been invited but the excitement of maybe solving her first case had infused her with an adrenaline, and she'd asked if she could keep working. Siobhán had kept her gob shut because everything Aretta had presented was logical, but it hadn't clicked for Siobhán and she had learned to listen to her gut. James and Gráinne had arrived early this morning and were regaling them with remodeling nightmares, at this stage mostly in the form of getting permits and bargaining with the locals for their status in the community. Siobhán felt a pang of jealousy, wishing they all could be together, and although the seaside town of Lahinch was a little spot of heaven, Kilbane was, and would always be home.

Gráinne switched the conversation to Ciarán's new band, and Siobhán tried not to wince as he waxed on about taking the show on the road.

"What about you, Ann?" James said, his voice already

forecasting a tease. "Any love interests we should know about?"

"No," Ann said. "None that you should know about." There was a moment of silence and then everyone burst into laughter.

"Touché," James said as Gráinne fist-bumped her.

"I need you all to vow to me that you'll come home often," Siobhán said, aware of the panic in her voice.

"Of course they will," Eoin said. "They'll never get a feed like this anywhere else, and they know it." More laughter ensued along with sincere compliments to the chef.

James raised his glass of sparkling water and everyone else raised theirs. "Sláinté."

"Sláinté," they chorused and then clinked. These were Siobhán's favorite moments in the entire world and they were so fleeting that she felt a duty to cling to them. Macdara gave her a look, and she shook her head slightly. She needed more time before they shared the news, for despite what everyone else was thinking, she did not feel like this case was solved. Was she biased? Was she jealous that Aretta had put together a puzzle that had been in front of Siobhán all this time? There was no doubt that there was a correlation between the cease and desist letter and the golden objects placed in the tents. And Molly did have access, and arguably the same motive as everyone else: greed. Then why didn't it sit right with Siobhán?

Everyone helped clear the plates and Eoin delivered a superb dessert, which they did not need, but could not resist. A Guinness chocolate cake served with fresh berries and cream. "A spot of good news on the horizon," Eoin said as everyone dug in. "The Six is booked solid for the next three months."

A chorus of "congratulations" and applause erupted. Gráinne let out a hoot. As the chatter continued, the conversation naturally turned to the case. Although everyone knew better than to ask for details that were not yet public, it was unreasonable to expect the topic not to be on everyone's minds. James and Gráinne were looking forward to perusing the gardening booths on Sarsfield Street and garnering ideas they could use at the inn. After the desserts were consumed, Ciarán was cajoled into playing the fiddle, and soon the restaurant filled with the sound of their voices, joining as one. It was times like these that Siobhán took mental snapshots, prized memories that she would cherish the rest of their lives.

When Eoin rose to clear the dessert plates, Siobhán insisted on helping him. Once they were in the kitchen, they shared dishwashing duty. "I need to ask you about the Thursday you believed to have seen Cassidy Ryan," Siobhán said.

Eoin nodded. "From a distance though . . ." His voice trailed off, uncertainty creeping in. Siobhán knew for a fact that whoever he saw could not be Cassidy Ryan. She also knew it could not be Molly Murphy—they were nowhere near the same height. He stopped as if her words had just registered. "Did you say *believed?*"

"Could it have been someone else? Maybe wearing a wig?" Siobhán probed.

"I never gave it a thought," Eoin said, his brow creasing as he revisited the memory. "I suppose it's possible. If . . . 'other attributes' "—he used air quotes—"could have been . . . embellished."

Cassidy Ryan had been a voluptuous woman. Love her or hate her, she'd been a force of nature. An image of her turned into a golden statue flashed through her mind. Who would do something like that? Who would even think of it?

"Siobhán!" Eoin sounded panicked. She followed his gaze to her hands. The small plate she'd been washing had cracked in her hands, and blood was dripping into the sink.

"I'm sorry, I'm sorry," she said, setting it down and bringing her hands up for examination. Eoin was ready with a towel; he wrapped her hands gently. "Hey," he said. "What's the story?"

"You didn't see Cassidy Ryan," Siobhán said in a rush. "She was already dead."

Eoin dropped his hands from the towel and took a step back. "Whoa." He squinted and looked up and to the left. "As I said it was from a distance, she was wearing sunglasses, and a dress. It was . . . flattering." Someone had played up Cassidy's known attributes to distract from the true person? Alice McCarthy was the same height. "Do you think it was the killer?"

"I don't know," Siobhán said. "But I have to find out." She put her hand on his shoulder. "Her time of death is inside knowledge. I shouldn't have mentioned it."

"I won't say a word, I swear." Eoin held up a finger, disappeared into a storeroom, and returned with a first-aid kit. "Are the cuts deep?"

She removed the towel and examined them. "Barely scratched the surface."

He handed her the first-aid kit. "Bandages ought to do— go on so, off to the jax with ya," Eoin instructed. She kissed him on the cheek and took his advice.

Siobhán and Macdara stood by Cassidy's tent. Macdara knew she was mulling over something and patiently waited until she was ready to talk. "Eoin swore he saw Cassidy Ryan Thursday morning," she began. "That means *someone* was impersonating her and it could not have been Molly Murphy."

"She could have put someone up to it," Macdara said. "We've already known this killer was using people as pawns. Owen Sheedy, Emily Dunne, the gardening crews . . ."

"But who would she have used to impersonate Cassidy, and doesn't that make the person an accomplice?"

"If we arrest Molly, we'll get her to talk." They were waiting on the DPP, Director of Public Prosecutions, to deliver a ruling on whether or not they had enough evidence against her to make a case.

"Alice McCarthy has the build, the height . . ."

"She would have needed a blond wig."

"Easy enough to get."

"But why? Why would she leave her own garden with so little time remaining, and if she was simply a pawn, why wouldn't she have come to us and told us what she'd done?"

"I agree we need all those answers," Siobhán said. "Don't you think we're all being a bit premature to jump on the Molly-did-it wagon?"

"We can still gather facts," Macdara said. "But Aretta's accounting of how it could have gone down has made the most sense of anything so far."

"What about the crew uniforms that are missing?"

"Isn't it possible they were just misplaced?"

"I suppose."

Macdara took her hand. "Are you dreading getting back to your studies?"

"Yes," she said. "But that's not what this is about."

"Siobhán?" Gráinne poked her head out of the restaurant door and yelled for her. She was holding up a mobile phone. "There's a call for ya. Some kind of emergency?"

They met each other halfway and Siobhán nodded her thanks. Macdara stayed at her side. "Hello?"

"Is it true?" a familiar voice said, her voice quiet amidst background noise. *Molly Murphy.* "Do you think I'm a killer?"

"Where did ya hear that?" Siobhán said, her mind racing with how to handle this.

"I'm a reporter. I have sources." A whistle sounded in the background, distant yet unmistakable—the sound of a train.

"Molly. Listen to me. If you're thinking about leaving . . . *don't.*" Macdara tensed beside her.

". . . horseman? . . . escape goat . . . in me life . . . purple rose . . . I'd *never* . . ." Siobhán was only catching every other word as static and the noise obscured the rest.

"Molly, we have a bad connection. Can you hear me?"

". . . honestly . . . escape goat . . . purple rose . . . purple rose . . ." Molly's voice rose with desperation, her speech becoming more and more fragmented.

"Escape goat? Purple rose?" Siobhán repeated as she shook her head. "I don't understand." The line went dead.

"Purple rose?" Macdara echoed straightaway.

"She said that and 'escape goat' several times." She tried to work it out. "Do you think she was referring to Nessa O'Neill and Teagan Moore?"

Macdara frowned. "And here I was wondering if she is a Prince fan."

"I doubt she was taking this opportunity to share her musical taste." Siobhán chewed on her bottom lip. "She sounded panicked."

"Did Teagan Moore have purple roses?"

"Not that I'm aware."

Macdara rubbed his face with his hands. "Any idea where she is?"

"I could hear rattling and a train whistle."

He sighed. "Let's go." She didn't need to ask where, it only made sense to start with the closest railway station. They were headed for Charlesville.

Chapter 31

The Charlesville Railway Station was a small affair with three through platforms and a reduced time schedule. Siobhán and Macdara reached the platform in time to see the last train of the day disappear around the curve. Nearby, the only other soul near the tracks was a man in baggy clothes sifting through a rubbish bin. Macdara took a few euro out of his pocket and handed it to the man, who hurried away with the money clutched in his hands. Macdara stared down the tracks then turned to Siobhán. "We could give chase in the squad car, but we don't know if that was the train she boarded, or even which direction she was headed." A wind had kicked up, sending bits of rubbish bouncing along the platform. Low gray clouds hovered above them, promising imminent rain. No doubt the garden booths on Sarsfield Street were hurrying to pack up before everyone and everything was soaked.

"If only the station house was still in operation," he said. "We could have sussed out the clerk, see if he remembered which ticket she purchased."

"Many have gone the way of phone boxes," Siobhán said. "People can buy tickets on their smart phones."

"Technology." Macdara sighed. "In many ways it has helped solve murder cases, and in other ways, it's derailed it."

Siobhán laughed and shook her head. "That entire segment was just a setup for that pun, was it?"

Macdara grinned. "It was worth it to hear you laugh." His gaze turned soft. "How ya feeling?"

She held up her hand. "We promised."

Macdara brushed a strand of hair away from her face, then ran the back of his hand down her jawline. "I'm struggling with that."

Siobhán took his hands and squeezed. "Please. I want to get this murder probe done and dusted first."

He pulled her into him and hugged her, burying his face in her hair for a moment before pulling away. "Molly Murphy is on the lam," he mused. "More proof that she's guilty."

"Or scared," Siobhán countered. Her mind churned with possibilities. "She's young and determined. I don't see her as a runner."

"And yet . . ." Macdara gestured to the track.

"We hadn't arrested her yet; she was free to go."

Macdara shook his head in disagreement and retrieved his mobile from his coat pocket. He pushed a button. "Bring Brandon O'Leary into the station," he said. "We believe Molly Murphy just fled on a train."

"Is that Aretta?" Siobhán asked. Macdara nodded. "Tell her I'd like Teagan Moore brought into the station as well."

Macdara's eyebrow arched, but he repeated the instruction without hesitation. He finished the conversation and turned to her. "She said she just ran into Teagan at the bookshop's coffee house. I figured you wouldn't have a problem catching him there."

"You figured you could get a few free pastries out of it."

Macdara looped his arm around her as they headed back

toward the squad car. "Teamwork makes the dream work."
Siobhán laughed and gently punched his arm.

The rain began to fall and the pair picked up their pace.
"Why Teagan Moore?" Macdara yelled over the wind as
they started to jog.

"I want to ask him about purple roses, not to mention
how Cassidy Ryan's cease and desist letter ended up in his
flat."

"Wasn't it dropped on the footpath in front of Raven's?
That's what Brandon said."

"Exactly. If Teagan's answer matches Brandon's, Bob's
Your Uncle. Otherwise, one of them is lying."

By the time Siobhán was making her way to the coffee
shop in the back of Turn the Page, it was raining cats and
dogs, and the wind shoved her along with a howl. She
slipped down the alley that granted access to Lift the Cup
without having to drip her way through the bookstore. A
bell dinged as she entered and shook herself off, buoyed by
the scent of freshly ground coffee and delectable pastries.
Oran McCarthy, it turned out, wasn't just a brilliant interior designer, he was also a magnificent baker. The coffee
shop had everything one could want: exposed brick, local
art on the walls that rotated on a monthly basis, comfy seat-
ing, and access to the bookshop with the ability to bring
one's purchases from one to the other. It had only opened
recently, and Siobhán was thrilled that Oran and Padraig's
vision had finally been realized. And given it was just across
the square from the garda station, they were guaranteed to
stay busy, and the ten percent off all baked goods for the
guards certainly didn't hurt.

The whir of espresso machines pulled at Siobhán as memories of running her family bistro flooded her. She ordered a
cappuccino and stepped back to watch the barista's hands
dance gracefully over the machine. Then she requested two

pastries in a take-away bag for herself and Macdara—a lemon tart and a chocolate raspberry brownie. *Heaven.* On second thought she ordered two of each, just in case she regretted not choosing the other, and knowing full well Macdara would pout if she suggested they split them in half and share.

Teagan Moore was a solitary figure seated in a comfy armchair in the corner, lost in the pages of a book. Siobhán sunk into the velvet green chair opposite him and drank her cappuccino as she watched him openly. The book must have been a good one, it took him ages to feel her gaze upon him, and when he finally did, he let out a yelp.

"Garda O'Sullivan," he exclaimed, his book falling to the small table between them and his hand flying to his heart. "I think you just shaved years off me life."

"Apologies," she said cheerfully. She glanced at the book on the table: *Quiet: The Power of Introverts in a World That Can't Stop Talking* by Susan Cain. ·

"Is it good?" she asked.

He frowned. "I'm still working on it."

"I won't take up much of your time, I just had a few questions for ya."

"By all means." He crossed his legs, removed his glasses, which he placed in the breast pocket of his dress shirt, and folded his hands on top of his knee.

"Did you plan on having any purple roses in your garden this year?" Siobhán asked straightaway.

"Purple roses?" Teagan echoed with a frown. "No." He leaned forward, the wrinkles in his forehead deepening. "They're quite rare, so it might have been a good idea, but they can be . . . elusive to grow. Some associate them with royalty, others with mystery. Not quite my style."

"Mystery," Siobhán repeated. *Interesting.* Given she didn't think Molly Murphy had been referencing royalty— was she trying to clue Siobhán in that there was more to this murder than met the eye? But why would she bother speaking in riddles? Especially when she knew chins were wagging, and fingers were pointing at her.

"Why do you ask?" Teagan inquired, a hint of wariness seeping into his tone.

"I overheard someone at the booths mentioning them," Siobhán lied. "It piqued my curiosity is all."

He nodded. "Perhaps I'll grow some next year, just for you."

"Lovely." He glanced at his book, then at the clock on the wall. "There is one more thing. I've been meaning to ask you."

"Ask away."

"How is it that Cassidy Ryan's cease and desist letter came to be in your flat?"

Teagan tilted his head. "You found that? In my flat?"

"The guards who searched it did."

"That is a mystery. I haven't the slightest clue." He continued to stare at her, not flinching a bit. Perhaps he was learning something from his book.

"Any guesses?" she said.

"Where exactly was it found?"

That's what I want you to tell me. "I'm not sure," she said. "Just amongst your things."

Teagan shrugged. "Someone must have placed it there. Maybe Molly herself left it during one of her interviews."

"I've watched her interviews, and yours was conducted online."

He crossed his legs in the other direction and gazed out the nearest window. Rain bashed at the panes, blurring the outside world. "I'm sure she stopped by for a chat at another time. Molly is very thorough."

"She is indeed." Siobhán was somewhat pleased with herself. Teagan would leave the conversation thinking she'd learned nothing of value from him at all. But he would be mistaken. She had just learned two very important bits of information. One, he did not ask: *What cease and desist letter?* He knew exactly what she was talking about. And two, either Teagan plucked the letter from the footpath and now for some reason he was lying about it, or . . . Brandon O'Leary was lying. Which was it? And if Molly was guilty, as both Aretta and Macdara believed, was Brandon an accomplice?

"I don't mean to be rude, Garda, but I have so little time to read." Teagan stared at his book with longing.

"One more question and I'll leave you to it. What can you tell me about the committee meeting last Monday evening? At Lorcan's Nursery?"

Teagan pursed his lips. "As far as I recall, there's not much to tell. Everyone was eager to get back to their gardens, so we were trying to get through the agenda items as quickly as possible." His hands began to tremor as he bounced his knee.

"And what were some of the agenda items?"

"Just housekeeping related to the competition." He waved a dismissive hand as if the very details bored him. When she continued to stare, he continued with a deep sigh. "Organizing the podium for the opening speech in the square, someone needed to check on the delivery of the booths for Sarsfield Street, we discussed how to best utilize the volunteers . . . Honestly, I could go on, but I have the feeling you're after something specific . . ." He put his hands palms-up and waited for her to elaborate.

Before she could prod further, the door opened with another jingle, ushering in a draft of cold air along with laughter that spilled into the room as the two patrons entered. They shook droplets of rain from their coats as they continued their animated discussion.

"Have you read *The Gilded Follies?*" one asked the other, as they glanced in the direction of the bookshop. "Hot off the press. What do you think of that for her gift?"

"I heard it's nothing but purple prose," the second replied. "Let's ask Padraig what he thinks."

Siobhán felt a jolt. *Purple prose. Purple prose.* Molly Murphy didn't say purple rose. She said purple *prose.*

Escape goat . . .

Scapegoat.

And she knew, in that moment, exactly what Molly had been trying to say. Siobhán stood so abruptly that Teagan yelped once again. "Thank you for your time," she said. She ran for the door, leaving the perplexed introvert behind.

Chapter 32

Brandon O'Leary opened the door on the third knock, and rather than look surprised to see Siobhán and Macdara standing at his doorstep, he simply stood back and ushered them in. "She's not a murderer," he said immediately. "But someone is certainly plotting against her."

"Then help us," Siobhán said. "I need to see the story Molly was working on. *The Headless Horsewoman.*"

"Now?" he said, arching his eyebrow. "I don't mean to tell you how to do your job, like, but . . . don't you have more important things to do? Clues to follow, like?"

"Do you have a copy of it or not?" Macdara asked, using his sternest tone.

"I promise you, it's very important," Siobhán said.

Brandon ran a hand through his hair and sighed. "She doesn't like me in her office. But if it's anywhere, it will be there." He led them down a short hall to a closed door on the left. "Seriously, she'd kill me. I'm staying out here. She prints out all of her works because she doesn't like reading them on the screen. Good luck." With that he hurried away, pulling a pack of cigarettes out of his pocket. Moments later they heard the front door slam.

"Let's hope this goes quickly," Macdara said as they took in the small office. The space was a tableau of a creative mind in turmoil—a whirlwind of papers, pens, and books strewn as if a tempest had just passed through, leaving behind the debris of creative pursuits and half-baked plots.

"Let's start digging," Siobhán said, heading for one of the piles on the desk.

"Right." Macdara cleared his throat and headed for another small table underneath the window. He nudged aside a tower of books that immediately cascaded onto the hardwood floors with soft thuds.

"I can't take you anywhere," Siobhán chided. The papers she was wading through were so far all transcripts of the garden interviews. "She was thorough," Siobhán said.

"This feels a bit like an archaeological dig," Macdara answered, lifting another pile. "I expect to find the remains of ancient civilizations buried here. Or at least last week's sandwich."

Siobhán laughed then shook her head. "Less commentary, more searching." She was now on the third and last pile. Finally, something different. Two sheets of paper held together with a paper clip with a yellow sticky note: *The Headless Horsewoman.* Siobhán felt her blood pressure rise. "I've got it."

Macdara hurried over and peered over her shoulder with keen interest. Siobhán carefully removed the sticky note and found herself staring at the first typewritten page:

If you've never had the pleasure, let me assure you that a quintessential Irish garden in the height of summer is a magnificent sight to behold. Vibrant blooms in a kaleidoscope of shapes and colors, shrubbery crafted by artists, playful fairies, gnomes, and angels, all forming a path to an ornate fountain in the center.

*Imagine if you will, a stately manor house beckoning
in the distance. . . .*

"Very different from the other version," Macdara said.
"I like this one better."

"Because it's not filled with *purple prose.*"

Macdara lifted an eyebrow. "Come again?"

"Prose that is so ornate it draws excessive attention to itself. Too flowery, if you will . . ."

"Writers often make multiple attempts," Macdara said.
"Isn't it possible she penned both versions?"

"She was adamant—that's why she kept repeating it—
'purple prose, purple prose . . .' "

"You think someone else wrote the other story?" He
scratched his head. "Why?"

"I think it was written *after* Cassidy was murdered. They
already knew Molly was penning a story about *The Headless Horsewoman* and they needed a scapegoat. I don't
think Cassidy wrote that cease and desist letter either. I
mean there was absolutely no legal teeth to it, and despite
whatever little tiff they might have had, Cassidy wouldn't
want to cut off all publicity. Someone else had to have written that letter in order to drop breadcrumbs leading directly
to Molly Murphy as Cassidy Ryan's killer."

"Say more."

"Once we all knew about the cease and desist letter, because of course Molly would share the details with anyone
who cared to read it, including us, all they had to do was
pick objects to match the words and then drop those items
into the gardens. Think about it. Cassidy Ryan hadn't
planned on copying their gardens at all. She had a very
elaborate one of her own waiting at her cottage. But once
she was murdered, the killers had a problem. If they wanted
to throw suspicion off themselves, they needed to set up

someone else. Throw off the timeline. Drop breadcrumbs leading us directly to their scapegoat. It was complicated enough not to be obvious, but clever enough they hoped one of us would finally pick up on it."

Macdara said the quiet part out loud. "And Aretta picked up on it."

"Indeed."

"If this is all true, Aretta is going to be very upset."

"We'll have to assure her that we're happy she figured out the code, for she was right, it was a code, and it helped us out in the long run. She had everything right except for the killers."

"Are you going to tell me who you think the killers are? I'd like to know before I go completely gray."

Siobhán knew he wanted immediate answers, but she had to talk through her theory step-by-step. "The killers knew that if we discovered Cassidy Ryan was murdered after the committee meeting Monday evening, and *not* on Thursday as we were led to believe, then we'd be looking at all the gardeners as our top suspects."

"They had to know we'd find out eventually."

"Maybe. But they needed to buy time to frame someone else. It was their only hope of getting away with murder." Siobhán wanted to pace but the room was too small. She plowed on. "They needed us to think the murder happened later in the week, when all the gardeners would have a ready-made alibi. Where were they? Why they were working on their gardens. A day before the competition was to open—where else would they be? But there was the matter of the hot air in the greenhouse. Their plan would fall to ruins if the body decomposed too quickly. Lucky for them, Larry Lorcan had just purchased a refrigerated meat truck, and it was conveniently parked at the nursery. But they still had a problem. It must have come as quite a shock when they discovered Cassidy hadn't finished her garden yet. In fact, given she had planned on setting everything up on Thursday, it probably looked to them as if she hadn't even *started* her garden. And if the guards discovered a blank space when they unveiled hers, we would immediately think she'd been killed much earlier. What a pickle. The only thing the killers could think to do in a matter of days was steal a little bit from each of the other gardens to make it look as if Cassidy had purposefully copied all of them. Given the small space they each had to work with, there would have been plenty of *leftovers* to draw from."

"Why exactly did they need the cease and desist letter?"

"Because of course Molly would have had an interview with Cassidy scheduled. She planned on speaking with every one of them the day before the opening. And of course she was dogged. Had they not deterred her with the cease and desist letter—she may have been the first to raise an alarm that Cassidy Ryan was missing."

"I'm surprised Molly was fooled by it," Macdara said.

"She hadn't really gotten to know Cassidy at this point, and the two of them trading barbs was captured on video. Remember that Nora Bell told us Sean suddenly wanted to watch all of Molly's interviews?"

Macdara nodded. "And that's why the cease and desist letter was sent so late in the game."

"Exactly. That letter was crafted after he'd carefully watched all of the videos. It's also why it was late in the game that Emily Dunne was suddenly told she had been selected to be a mole, not to mention Owen Sheedy."

"You're saying Sean Bell is one of our killers. Who else?"

"I'm not sure you're going to believe me."

"I never would have believed gardeners could be so diabolical," Macdara replied.

Siobhán shrugged. "Maybe all that time spent with Mother Nature twisted their minds."

"I don't know how you've figured out who you think did

it," Macdara said. "If you ask me, there's equal suspicion on every single gardener. And I just cannot see some of these gardeners destroying their creations."

"You're right," Siobhán said. "Many of them wouldn't. But that in itself is a very clear answer to why this cover-up grew into such an elaborate production."

"Spit it out."

"I will. But not here. Let's get some fresh air."

Siobhán laid out her entire theory on a run. It helped her think for one, and for two, she didn't have to see the look of disbelief on Macdara's face as she laid out everything she was thinking. When she was finally out of breath, they stopped at their beloved abbey to stretch. The morning sun lit up the grassy floor where monks once tread, making the bell tower on the second story gleam. Although it was a ruined Dominican priory and much of the structure was gone, there were enough remains to feel what it must have been like in its time. Whenever Siobhán was here, she could picture the monks going about their day, cooking, tending the grounds, brewing beer by the river. The carved heads hidden in niches in what remained of the walls seemed to be watching her, and she wished they could advise her on whether or not she was about to make the biggest mistake in her career. This case, and whom she thought the killers were, was one for the books. Even the detective sergeant exams wouldn't have dreamed up such a scenario.

But it was the only answer that satisfied all of her questions. It was the opposite of Occam's razor, for the simplest explanation—that Molly Murphy was the first to learn of the Ghost Orchid and thus murdered Cassidy to get it, then unburdened all of her guilt into a piece of fiction about the Headless Horseman. It might have been the simplest answer, but to stick with their gardening puns, those seeds would never take root and grow.

You reap what you sow. And the killers certainly had reaped. *Overkill.*

"Shall we start hauling our gardeners into the station one by one to question them in light of your theory?" Macdara asked. "Or en masse?"

"Neither," Siobhán said. "We need to catch them off guard."

"I'm listening."

"The winner of the garden tour was supposed to be announced at a closing ceremony at the Kilbane Manor House. The ceremony was to take place in their spectacular garden, of course. Let's see if we can hold a special vigil there instead for Cassidy Ryan, and ask all of our gardeners to kindly attend."

"How could they say no?" Macdara asked. "Are you hoping for a confession?"

Siobhán paused beneath an archway. "We'll keep up the charade that we're convinced Molly Murphy is our killer. She's on the lam, and we're doing everything we can to bring her in. If they believe she's our prime suspect, they'll start to let their guards down."

Around them, the fields in front of the ruined Dominican priory seemed to be holding its breath, as Siobhán awaited Macdara's response. This theory of hers wasn't just risky for her; if she was wrong, it could take him down too. "Let's head for home," he said. "If we want to do this right, we have a lot of work to do."

"Indeed," Siobhán said. Catching one killer would have been hard enough. Catching more than one was going to require skills they would never find in the pages of a book. And in this particular scenario, there weren't enough practice questions in the world to prepare them, no tests complex enough to cover the intricate depths these killers had gone to in order to throw suspicion off themselves. They had shown they would point their finger at anyone but themselves. Turning them against each other might not comport to the spirit of the garden competition, but to catch their killers, it was the only way to go. This year, there would be no winners. Justice was the only thing that mattered now, and if Cassidy Ryan was looking down at them, Siobhán could only hope she would approve of their first and final design. *To Catch a Killer.* It was time to place *losing* ribbons on the killers, ones they would hold for life.

Eoin was waiting by the house when Siobhán and Macdara returned from their run. His face was paler than usual and Siobhán knew immediately something was wrong. "Don't tell me there's been another setback for your opening," she said.

He shook his head. "In my defense," he began, "I have no idea how it got there."

Macdara raised an eyebrow. "How what got where?"

"And how is that a defense?" Siobhán tagged on.

"Please," he said. "No jokes." He turned and motioned for them to follow. "Given we're not officially open, if I'm just popping out for a few minutes, I haven't been locking my doors. And before you ask, the answer is no."

"Well, now I have to ask," Siobhán said.

"The security cameras are not yet operating," Eoin answered.

"Don't tell me you were robbed," Macdara said.

"I was . . ." Eoin stopped. "Whatever the opposite of that is, I suppose." Soon they were entering through the front doors of the restaurant. "At first I thought it was a gift—you know—Jeanie Brady brought me a plant too—I thought—how nice. But then . . . I heard the pair of ye discussing it . . . It might be nothing, but I googled it. It sure looks like it. And if it's not? I mean, why is it in a display case?"

Siobhán felt a chill up her spine. Eoin held the door to the restaurant open, and before Siobhán even laid eyes on it, she knew what she was going to see. But as they approached, mere inches from the miraculous flower, Siobhán was struck by how stunning it was in person. "Cassidy would have won," she said quietly. And there, sitting atop one of the communal tables, in a new case, flaunting its glory, sat the Ghost Orchid. And placed at its base, outside of the case, no doubt carefully dyed by murderous hands, lay a bouquet of a dozen black roses.

"I swear I only stepped out for a few minutes," Eoin said. "I popped into the house for a few minutes." Eoin was staying with them for the time being. "I took a shower, and you know how I installed that speaker."

"I love it," Macdara said. The men were thrilled to play tunes in the shower. Even Siobhán had to admit it was good craic. She wished she could say the same about their water bills.

"Anyway, I wouldn't have heard a car pull onto the property, but obviously someone did."

"I'm glad you weren't in the restaurant," Macdara said. "If it was left by one of our killers, who knows what would have happened."

"Killers?" Eoin said. "Care to say more?"

"I wish I could," Siobhán said. "Suffice it to say, we'll be revealing them soon." She stared at the rare flower, entranced by its beauty but horrified at the lengths some men and women would go to in order to get their hands on it. She patted the case. "And this little guy is going to join us."

Chapter 33

The Kilbane Manor was a testament to history and grandeur, and the walled garden behind it a spectacle of nature. The manor and gardens, once reserved for the gentry's leisurely pursuits, now lay open to the community. If only the garden's ornate center fountain could whisper secrets from its bygone days. This was undoubtedly the setting depicted in Molly Murphy's partial story, and it made sense that this would have been one of her stops while covering the competition. When the manor fell to disrepair many years ago, the town of Kilbane purchased and restored it, then opened it for community tours and events, thus bringing a small ounce of justice to a painful period in history.

Hedges trimmed into geometrical shapes formed a labyrinthine design around the fountain, reminiscent of the order and control that once dominated these grounds. In every corner, flowers and herbs spilled forth in joyful abandon and roses clambered up trellises with an air of elegance. Teagan Moore was the first to arrive, his shoulders hunched, with an expression to match. Dressed in a tan blazer and matching pants, he straightened his green tie and gave a half-hearted wave, averting his gaze as if the guards were the sun and it would blind him to look directly at them. He glanced at the stone benches dotted throughout the garden, and perched on the edge of the one farthest away.

Finnoula Connor followed, her essence one of confidence. She wore a black dress and a small black hat with a bit of lace hanging down as if she was a widow attending her husband's wake. She looked directly at the guards. "Detective Sergeant, Gardas," she said with a smile and a nod. "What a wonderful place for a tribute. I'm sure Cassidy Ryan herself would have approved." Her gaze fell to the blown-up portrait of Cassidy propped up near the fountain. It had been taken after her first big commissioned installation. She stood in front of a showpiece of a garden, hand on hip, smile bright, blond locks blowing in the wind. If only she could step out of the photograph and be the one to point the finger at her killers. It might have been Siobhán's imagination, but after staring at it for a few moments, Finnoula Connor appeared to shiver.

It took Siobhán every ounce of self-restraint not to blurt out that given the way things had worked out, not only would Cassidy Ryan *not* approve, but if she was hanging around in spirit, no doubt she would be out for revenge. Perhaps Molly's story of the Headless Horsewoman had been a premonition. Finnoula took her place on the bench nearest to the guards, as if claiming a winning post. Teagan, already restless, had risen to stand near the trellis of roses, his lips moving as if they were old pals having a catch-up.

Alice McCarthy was the third to arrive, dressed in a white pantsuit and a wide-brimmed hat. Finnoula's gaze flicked over her and she pursed her lips. "I thought black would be more appropriate."

Alice's hand flew to her heart. "I'd rather wear the colors of Cassidy Ryan's angels," she said. "But you do you." Finnoula crossed her arms and exhaled, causing the bit of lace in her hat to flutter.

Nessa O'Neill's presence was announced by sniffling, and she entered in denim overalls and a green T-shirt, looking as if she came prepared to get her hands dirty. She took in the assembly of familiar faces, frowning when she clocked their attire. "I didn't receive a dress code," she said. "Was there a dress code?"

"Yes," Finnoula said. "The Code of Dignity."

Nessa's eyes narrowed and she snorted. Stuffing her hands in her pockets, she began walking around the garden, as if sizing it up for a job. No doubt, if she had been assigned to this garden, she would turn it back into something a bit more wild.

Lastly, Sean Bell stepped through the opening in the limestone wall, also dressed in denims on the bottom, but balancing it out with a black dress shirt and white tie. It was as if he *had* gotten the memo, not to mention a read of what everyone else was wearing, and he'd combined them all in a single outfit. He glanced at his watch. "How long will this take?" he asked. "I have family obligations." He took in the photo of Cassidy and made no attempt to hide the look of derision that crossed his handsome face.

"You might want to cancel those obligations," Siobhán said. "I believe this will take longer than you imagined."

His frown deepened and he plopped himself down next to Finnoula, then leaned over and whispered something in her ear. *Enjoy it while it lasts,* Siobhán thought. Soon, secrets would be unearthed and on full display. She felt a twinge of sorrow that Molly wasn't here to film and report on this event—no doubt it would have been the story of her lifetime. And such a significant personal exoneration, such as the one she was about to receive, would have lived in her memory the rest of her life. The guards had tracked her down by canvassing each of the first three stops off the Charles-ville train, and struck gold at the second stop. She had checked into the nearest inn. And although she would be arriving back in town today, Siobhán couldn't afford to have her in attendance, her very presence would prove that something was very much amiss. After all, who brings a killer to their victim's wake?

The enlarged photo of Cassidy Ryan wasn't the only thing drawing everyone's attention. On the other side stood a pedestal, and upon it rested a display case shrouded in a black cloth, the fabric rippling slightly in the breeze. It was not just the history of the manor that loomed over them now, but the legacy of Cassidy Ryan. As their gardeners grew restless, perhaps triggered by the photo of Cassidy, they began to talk amongst themselves. Siobhán had missed the first part of the conversation but began to tune in as their voices grew louder.

"I told her it was vinca and it is very invasive. Spreads like mint." Finnoula's tone was one of disapproval.

"Not invasive," Alice interjected, "although it does spread by runners. A good ground cover, and nice to use as greenery in places where it can be draped."

Nessa nudged in. "There are also variegated forms. Mints spread both by underground root systems and some, like lemon balm, by seed as well. *They* are truly invasive, but vinca really isn't like mint at all."

Finnoula's eyes turned dark as she glared at Nessa. "I hear from amateur gardeners all the time that they constantly have to clear out vinca because it spreads so prolifically. I call that invasive, and I have been growing many different mints for years, not to mention I've been gardening since you were in nappies."

Nessa held her ground. "I have mint in containers so they grow where I want them to grow. And I've lived on a farm my entire life. My grandfather was a farmer and my granny was a gardener, not to mention a blue ribbon winner, so it is in my blood. I am also a certified herbalist." She crossed her arms and scanned the group as if expecting a confrontation.

"You can't outmint me, Nessa O'Neill." Finnoula's voice had taken on an edge. "I have an abundance of lemon balm, Adam's mint, and pineapple mint. I've used them as companion plants and I've even made tinctures."

"Tinctures," Sean Bell said. "I could use a tincture right about now." He made eye contact with each gardener as if silently warning them against an unknown threat. If only he knew how apropos that was.

"I've been gardening nearly as long as you have, Finnoula," Teagan said. "I can't imagine periwinkle, as I much prefer to call it that than *vinca*, I can't imagine periwinkle with its purplish blue flowers and its lush, dark ovate being that much of a problem, but mints surely are, especially lemon balm. I prefer a lemon verbena, which has a sweeter aroma and is more bushlike. I'd never use a mint as a companion plant." He shuddered at the thought.

Macdara leaned into Siobhán. "Are they speaking English?" he whispered.

"They're speaking plant," Siobhán said. "And they're on edge."

Macdara nodded. "Exactly where we want them to be."

"Vinca minor is bad, vinca major is a pain; it will choke out anything in its way," Sean said, his face hardening.

"It's a good ground cover for a gentle hillside," Nessa said. "And my goats won't touch it."

"Goats!" Finnoula said, unraveling before their eyes. "Enough about your bloody goats!"

The rest of the gardeners froze and their mouths dropped open. Nessa burst into tears. She ran to a bench, sunk down, and began to sob.

"Now look what you've done," Alice said. "Satisfied?"

"Goats are an inappropriate topic," Finnoula said. "I didn't expect her to *cry*."

"Soil and tears," Teagan said. "Our lives consist of soil and tears."

Just then Larry Lorcan strode into the garden, carrying a dozen roses. He placed them gently by Cassidy's photo and stood for a moment in silent reflection. "Rest in peace."

"Rest in peace," the others mumbled, crossing themselves along with Larry.

The air held a tentative calm as Siobhán stood before the gathered ensemble. "We're here today to honor the memory of Cassidy Ryan."

Sean Bell stepped forward. "I don't mean to interrupt—"

Macdara moved to Siobhán's side. "Then don't."

Sean stilled, then nodded. "Apologies, Detective Sergeant. Garda." He looked at his watch and sighed. "But is it true?" He glanced once more at Cassidy's photograph. "Is Molly Murphy her killer?"

The garden hushed as Sean Bell's question dangled in the air. Siobhán felt the weight of all eyes upon her, their gazes sharp. "Someone certainly wanted us to think she was," Siobhán said. "But no. Molly Murphy is not our killer."

Shocked faces stared back at her.

"Thank goodness," Larry Lorcan said. "She was very fair to Lorcan Nursery in her articles and she even photographed my good side."

"I wasn't aware you had one," Finnoula said.

Larry's face flushed red.

The ivy climbing up the limestone wall seemed to press in closer, and the gardeners' expressions flickered with uncertainty.

"I do have some updates on the case, and since you're already gathered, there's no time like the present," Siobhán said. This was going to be one of the most difficult speeches of her life, but she was prepared. "I've known you my entire life. I could have never imagined I'd be standing here today confronting you."

"Confronting us?" Alice said, pulling the brim of her hat so low that her eyes were hidden.

"Yes," Siobhán said. "If only the talents you all so dearly hold wouldn't have been used for such evil deeds." The stillness was palpable, broken only by the distant caw of a rook.

Finnoula Connor clenched her hands into fists. "What on earth are you talking about?" she demanded. "I thought we were here to honor Cassidy. Have we been hoodwinked?"

Siobhán took in Finnoula's stance, the defensive tilt of her chin, the intensity of her gaze. "We are honoring Cassidy," Siobhán said, her voice steady, "by exposing her killers."

"Killers?" Nessa O'Neill shot up from the bench, her tears instantly gone. "Do you mean it was Molly and Emily? Or Molly and Brandon?" she pressed on, desperation seeping through her words. "Or Molly, Emily, and Brandon?"

Alice McCarthy dipped her head even farther. "Yes, was it them?"

With measured steps, Siobhán moved closer to the pedestal. She seized the edge of the cloth and in one swift motion, the fabric whisked through the air—a magician revealing her trick—and there, cradled in the display case like a being of another world, rested the Ghost Orchid. Its spectral-white petals seemed to glow beneath the gray skies. The gardeners stared in horror and collectively seemed to be holding their breath.

"You all look like you've seen a ghost," Macdara quipped.

As whispers began to stir, and several of them eyed the exit, Siobhán turned to Larry Lorcan. "Mr. Lorcan? Won't you join us?" she called.

Larry approached the pedestal reluctantly, his eyes never leaving the bloom that lay before him as if it might vanish. "Can you confirm that this is indeed Cassidy Ryan's show-stopper? Her Ghost Orchid?" Larry nodded.

"It is," he confirmed. "There's no mistaking it." His admission fell upon the audience like a verdict.

Siobhán's gaze swept over the suspects, whose expressions were now etched with varying shades of guilt. "Cassidy Ryan wasn't planning a garden that copied all of yours," she began. "And even though you burned down her cottage, we still found evidence of the true garden she was intending on creating for the competition, one with exotic and rare flowers." She paused, letting the implication of her words sink in. "I kept wondering . . . why would someone burn down Cassidy's cottage? Nothing unusual or incriminating was found inside. You had to know the guards would search it eventually. But you took advantage of the overwhelming number of crime scenes we were attending and set it ablaze in the hopes that we would never know about her true plan for her garden."

"It was Molly Murphy," Sean Bell announced, his voice gravelly. The others began nodding, their movements slow and deliberate.

"We have proof that Molly was set up as the scapegoat," Siobhán said. "*Framed.* I will say, it was a very creative plan. But too many cooks in the kitchen—isn't that what they say?"

"When you say, *you* this, and *you* that," Teagan said, swallowing hard, "to whom, exactly, are you referring?"

"She's getting to that," Macdara said. "Say less and you'll hear more."

Siobhán began to pace. "Let's go over this elaborate cover-up and frame job, shall we? Penning a short story when you heard Molly Murphy was inspired to write *The*

Headless Horsewoman in the hopes that once we connected the golden objects to Dullahan, we'd concentrate on her as our killer. Additionally, you hoped that we would notice that the objects closely correlated with the so-called cease and desist letter from Cassidy Ryan. As if it had caused Molly to fly into a rage. But dead women can't write cease and desist letters, not to mention the fact that Cassidy craved publicity and attention and wouldn't have turned down Molly's interview. You wanted us to think Molly was so incensed by this letter that she concocted her plan to murder Cassidy. Or, maybe you threw in, perhaps she was jealous. If you started enough rumors of Cassidy coming onto married men, maybe we'd assume Brandon O'Leary had been a focus of Cassidy's attention. You peppered the cease and desist letter with specific words: *bell, weeds, head, rose, pen.* What came first? The objects or the letter? My guess, the objects. That's why Sean made a point of insisting he had a black bell, so that we would puzzle over the fact that a gold one was now in his garden. Clever touch moving Sean's black bell to Cassidy's garden."

As Siobhán began to walk throughout the garden, she made sure her voice carried. "Finnoula and Alice made sure to have books referencing *The Headless Horseman* in their second interviews with Molly, but no mention of them in the first interview. Sean had to watch all the videos again to see how you could frame her. You had to create Cassidy's garden because you didn't realize it was being curated at her cottage, and you had to destroy each other's gardens because once Cassidy Ryan was murdered, *none of you had time to finish yours.* This is where you needed a bit of help. This is where one of you phoned Emily Dunne and convinced her that this year's competition was supposed to have a mole, or two, or three. You also needed Owen Sheedy to deliver the crate. But none of you, I'm assuming, had the heart to destroy your own gardens. And that's when you decided you would destroy each other's. All you needed was a few crew uniforms, and a method so that each of you would know whose garden you were selected to destroy. Once more you used Emily Dunne. You would each show up at the charity shop in the crew uniform, and whatever disguise you needed to obscure your face, and she would hand you the name of the garden you were to mess with."

"Each other's gardens?" Teagan questioned.

"Yes," Siobhán said. "Each other's. It was smart if you ask me. First, your reaction upon seeing your garden in disarray would be authentic, and second, I believe none of you could bring yourselves to destroy your own." Mouths dropped open but no one moved or spoke. It was as if they had all been turned to stone. "And who could blame you? There was so little time, wasn't there? Precious ticking hours before the horror of what you'd done would be revealed. Such a short amount of time to accuse someone else and prove it couldn't have been any of you. Which is why you also agreed to each point the finger at another gardener, but not all of you dropped suspicion on the *same* gardener, making sure guilt was scattered equally among you."

"In other words," Macdara said, "you sent us on a wild-goose chase."

"I don't have to stand here and listen to this," Finnoula said. But she did not take a single step forward.

Siobhán's lips parted softly. "We know that Cassidy Ryan wasn't murdered on Thursday evening as we were led to believe."

"I saw her," Sean interjected. "I told you I saw her."

"And you lied."

"Your own brother saw her," Alice said, finally lifting the brim of her hat. "He said as much, didn't he?"

"And how did you know that?" Siobhán said. "Is it because *you* were the one impersonating her?" Alice's jaw dropped, but no words left her mouth. "All you needed was a blond wig, a fancy outfit, and gigantic sunglasses." Several pairs of eyes darted between Cassidy Ryan's photo and Alice. There was no mistaking their similar features. Siobhán acknowledged Teagan. "You threw rose petals in the lily pond where Cassidy Ryan drowned." Not a single gasp sounded; they were all rooted to the spot, rigid with fear. Teagan gulped, his Adam's apple bobbing. Siobhán's gaze landed on Sean next. "You repaired the wooden bridge off which she was pushed." Siobhán turned toward Finnoula, the three-time winner. "You made up an entirely different Headless Horseman story when you caught a glimpse of the one Molly Murphy was writing. If only you had as much experience with words as you do flowers. You see, you fell into something many new writers struggle with: *Purple prose.*" Finnoula's eyes widened and her lips moved as if she was silently repeating the phrase. "And Nessa," Siobhán continued without stopping for reactions, "you made sure to hand me the antique pen nib, hoping it would lead me directly to Molly."

Nessa's expression crumbled, and once more she sunk onto a bench. "Every single one of you played a part in covering up this murder and framing Molly. The lengths to which you went to try and pull this off is quite . . . *impressive* isn't the right word. Not with such evil deeds. You stuck Cassidy Ryan's body in a refrigerated truck because you knew the humidity in the greenhouse would work against you. Is that why you spray-painted her gold and dressed her up like a statue? So we wouldn't immediately know that she had drowned? Because the minute we started investigating all bodies of water and discovered the lily pond, well, it would have brought us to the point where we are now, and you knew that your innocence depended on timing. She died on Thursday evening? It couldn't have possibly been any of you. You were busy working on your gardens. But Molly. She had access. She had means. You just needed to give her motive. I think that was your weakest link. Finnoula, we have Larry's statement that you asked him how to dispose of paint. And when Larry wanted to do it himself for a few bob, I suppose you still didn't think it would ever trace back to you. But we've already collected all the cans of spray-paint. And that brings us to your biggest problem: Cassidy Ryan's garden was bare. It must have come as quite a shock. You had no idea she was curating it all at the cottage she was renting. Mostly because she didn't trust you. If only she knew how apropos that was. And thus you had even more work on your plate, didn't you? She needed to have a finished garden. You each donated items from your own garden to finish Cassidy's. That was the only way to make us think she had lived long enough to complete it. It was also convenient that the nursery had several crates—designed for shipping trees—in which to place the body. Nessa, you found Brandon Murphy's missing engagement ring at your farm and placed it on Cassidy's finger. Maybe if we didn't believe the cease and desist letter would send Molly into a murderous rage, suggesting her husband was having an affair with Cassidy might just do it. You thought you had covered every angle. But I knew there was no way one person could have pulled off a murder, frame job, and cover-up like this. There was no way *two* persons could have done it. It took a village. What a sad, sad twist to that phrase. What happens to you now will entirely depend on how forthcoming you choose to be. Because there is no other logical conclusion to draw than this: Every single one of you is equally guilty for the cover-up, you are all complicit at pointing the finger at Molly Murphy, you are all complicit in stealing the Ghost

Orchid, and you are all equally accused of the murder of Cassidy Ryan."

"Why would we do such a thing?" Finnoula called out. "Just to win ten thousand euro? *Absurd.*"

"Motive matters," Sean said. "And none of us have one."

"You all have one," Macdara said, walking slowly around the Ghost Orchid. "Oldest motive in the book. Greed. Pure greed."

Teagan was the first to crack. "It was an accident," he gasped. "We argued with her and she fell off the side of the bridge. She hit her head on a rock and died instantly."

Nessa was already shaking her head. "Enough of the lies." She stood and faced the guards. "We discovered the Ghost Orchid tucked away in the back corner of the green-house. We knew immediately it was hers." She hung her head. "We decided it wasn't fair that she use her clout and money to win with such a rare orchid. We were just going to hide it until after the competition. We had no idea she was in the greenhouse. Watching us."

"She was only trying to get a million euro!" Finnoula wailed. "She didn't care about us. She didn't care what this competition meant to us. For all we knew, she had stolen that Ghost Orchid."

"I assure you, she did not," Larry Lorcan said. All color had drained from his face.

"We didn't plan to kill her," Alice said. "But when Cassidy suddenly confronted us as we literally were spiriting the Ghost Orchid away, chaos broke out. Teagan was standing on the other side of the bridge, holding the Ghost Orchid. Cassidy went mental. I swear, she might have killed us if we didn't . . . *defend ourselves.* Enraged, she was making a beeline for Teagan, and we had to block her. She turned into a wild animal and tussled with us. We had no idea the side of that bridge was weak."

Nessa hung her head. "It wasn't even a long fall."

"And then, instead of calling the paramedics, and the guards, you took the Ghost Orchid, and conspired as a group to cover up her murder."

"How can you say it was murder?" Nessa said. "We *tussled*."

"The state pathologist found bruises on the back of her neck," Macdara said. "Cassidy Ryan did not die instantly. She was held under the water." One by one, they all turned and looked at Sean.

"It had to be done," Sean said, his voice gruff. "She'd hit her head too hard. She wouldn't have survived, and I didn't want her to suffer."

Siobhán didn't believe him for a second. Humans often told themselves stories in order to cope with the horror of what they'd done.

"We're not *all* guilty of the murder then," Finnoula said. "Only Sean."

Macdara turned to Siobhán. "Care to quote what you learned from your practice exams?"

Siobhán faced the group. "You can all be considered liable for murder if your actions led to Cassidy's action of running away, then being shoved, or pushed or even 'tussled' off the bridge, resulting in her death. And standing and watching while Sean held her down? You all deserve to face the consequences of your actions. It will be in the hands of the Director of Public Prosecutions. Believe me, nothing has saddened me more than this case. Every one of you made a decision that fateful night, and now you will have to face what you've done."

"You reap what you sow," Macdara said. "You reap what you sow."

"She was going to call the guards and accuse us of theft

and intimidation," Alice said. "If you had only seen her, you would have known she was intent on doing just that."

"She might have killed us if we hadn't killed her," Nessa chimed in. They were still trying to justify it, water it down.

"Shut your gobs," Sean yelled at the group. "No one say another word until you have a solicitor. Not one word."

"Enough of your bullying, Sean Bell," Finnoula said. "We listened to you from the start and look where it's gotten us."

Sean seemed to crack visibly. His eyes—dark pools—locked onto the guilt-stricken faces around him. "I know what you're all doing," Sean countered. "You're going to try to pin this all on me. But if I go down? We all go down."

Above them thunder rumbled, and rain began to fall. Macdara whistled and guards who had been waiting in the wings stepped forward. Their hands moved with practiced ease, and soon the metallic click of handcuffs punctuated the air, binding wrists behind backs as Larry Lorcan looked on, horror-stricken.

"I had no idea," he said. "I had no idea."

"We know," Siobhán said. "We know."

Teagan turned his head just as he was being led off. "I returned the orchid to your brother's restaurant," he said. "I hope that helps."

The black roses said it was anything but a gesture of kindness, but Siobhán was done talking to this group.

"Helps?" Finnoula's voice was sharp, the thorn to his roses. "We should have sold the Ghost Orchid and used the money for our defense like we agreed." Her face contorted with bitterness as she stared at Cassidy Ryan's photo.

Nessa shuffled beside her, a cascade of concern knitting her brow. "What about me goats?" Nessa's voice was small and fearful, nearly swallowed by the rain. "Who's going to look after them?"

"We'll find someone to mind them," Siobhán said. "To mind all of your pets. You have my word."

"And me roses?" Teagan asked.

"And your roses," Siobhán said, with a profound sadness for how easy it had been for these good people to do such bad things. How fragile humans, maybe more than plants, how easily it was for them to suddenly snap. "How could we ever forget your roses?"

Chapter 34

Eoin O'Sullivan's grin stretched from ear to ear as he wove between the tables of The Six, his eyes alight with the flickering candles that cast a warm glow over the bustling room. The chatter and laughter of a successful opening night swirled around Siobhán like a jubilant melody. The menu was an opulent affair: seared scallops resting on a bed of black pudding and apple purée, and racks of lamb encrusted with rosemary and thyme, served alongside towers of golden, minted potatoes, and for dessert, a delicate chocolate fondant with a heart of salted caramel, each dish a testament to Eoin's culinary dreams.

Gráinne, James, Ann, and Ciarán were dressed for the occasion, all looking so sharp, their eyes shining with pride. Beside them, Siobhán and Macdara stood together, her arm linked through his, their attire equally elegant. Outside, the sky blushed with the best sunset one could ever witness: ribbons of crimson and gold streaking across the horizon. It was as if the heavens themselves were toasting to Eoin's grand opening.

A tray of champagne went by, and Macdara took one. Siobhán waited, and a second later another server passed with sparkling water for her. Siobhán lifted her glass, and after a few whistles from Macdara, the room fell silent. "I'd like to toast my talented, patient, and extremely hardworking brother Eoin, whose passion for food is only matched by his generous spirit. Congratulations on a smashing opening night!" Siobhán raised her glass amidst the many other toasts that filled the air, the crystal chiming against the others.

"Speech, speech," someone in the crowd yelled. Eoin raised his glass. "Thank you all for coming. From the bottom of my heart, it means the world. But there's one person who deserves all the credit." Eoin looked over his shoulder and nodded his head for Gráinne, James, Ann, and Ciarán to come forward. "None of us would be where we are without the most remarkable woman we know. She gave up everything to raise us, even James who's a year older."

James belted out a laugh. "It's true, I used to be a mess."

"She'd just been accepted at Trinity College in Dublin when our parents were killed. She didn't hesitate to entirely change the course of her life in order to stay home and raise us." Once more they all raised their glasses. "I know Mam and Da would be fiercely proud of you, Siobhán, and we don't know how we could ever thank you."

Siobhán burst into tears, her mascara ruining makeup that Gráinne had taken ages to apply.

"I think we need to call her Detective Sergeant O'Sullivan now, don't we?" teased James, his voice rich with good humor. "Ladies and gentlemen, our brilliant sister just passed her detective sergeant exams."

A loud cheer rang out. "We wanted to get you something," Eoin said. "But we had a hard time figuring out what you would want."

"I have everything I want," Siobhán said. "The best siblings in the world."

"Too bad," Ciarán said. "We got ya a gift anyways." They moved over to a section of wall where something was hanging, but it was obscured by a black cloth. Siobhán hadn't even noticed it.

"Ready?" Ann said to Ciarán. He nodded, and the pair of them removed the cloth, revealing a black-and-white family portrait. It wasn't the kind where people pose, their faces frozen in smiles; it was a candid photo that Siobhán had never even seen. Taken in their bistro, Siobhán was standing by the counter, hand on hip, head thrown back in genuine laughter. The rest of The Six were spread out: Ciarán sitting on top of a table, Ann holding a biscuit, her eyes fastened on Siobhán, Gráinne looking up from a fashion magazine with a smirk, and James and Eoin with their arms looped around each other.

"It's the most beautiful photo I've ever seen," Siobhán said. She meant it. She didn't even remember that specific day, but that was the point. There had been so many days like that, hadn't there? She'd take this photograph over a posed one any day. In one frame, her entire happy world had been encapsulated. A single moment captured in time that meant nothing to anyone else but meant the world to them. Except, of course, for the tall, blue-eyed, messy-haired man beside her; she knew it meant something to him as well. "I wish you were in the photo with us," she said, wiping the tears from her face.

Macdara leaned in as if he had just read her mind, which he might have done. "Who do you think took the photo?" he whispered.

"It's such a great photo," Eoin chimed in. "That I had to order two. One for the restaurant, and the other one is waiting for you at home."

"Thank you," Siobhán said. "Thank all of you." Her emotions threatened to overwhelm her again.

"You're just a waterfall tonight, aren't ya?" Gráinne said.

"Do we call ya Detective Sergeant O'Sullivan now?" James asked.

Siobhán offered a modest nod. "I'm considered a temporary sergeant for the next year. After that, I'll officially be Detective Sergeant O'Sullivan. And thank goodness that ridiculous test and panel interview are behind me." A collective cheer erupted, glasses raised higher in salute. Siobhán caught sight of Molly Murphy seated with Brandon, Emily, Owen, and Larry, grouped together at a nearby table. They too raised their glasses to Siobhán.

"Seriously," Siobhán said, "this is Eoin's big day."

"It's *our* big day," Gráinne said. "One for all and all for one."

"Stay as long as you'd like," Eoin announced as dessert plates were cleared. "Me brother Ciarán and his band will be playing soon. Drink up!"

Macdara took her hand and they walked to the window to take in the first stars appearing in the night sky.

"Will the garden competition ever be the same again, I wonder?" Macdara mused.

"I have no doubt that new seeds will be planted and it will come roaring back next year," Siobhán said.

"Next year," Macdara said, "our lives will be totally different." He took her hand and squeezed it.

They returned to the fold and suddenly Gráinne pointed at Siobhán's glass, her voice cutting through the din of festivities. "Is that sparkling *water?*" The noise in the room halted abruptly and suddenly all eyes were on Siobhán. "What?" Gráinne continued. "Are you pregnant?" From her tone, she thought she was making a joke. But then a silent exchange passed between Siobhán and Macdara, and before words could form on their lips, they were engulfed by the O'Sullivan clan, Gráinne's voice once again piercing the air, this time with delight, "We're having a baby! We're having a baby!"

Macdara's laughter mingled with the excited chorus of congratulations, and when they broke the group hug, Eoin turned to Aretta and pulled her in for a kiss.

"Are you two finally official?" Siobhán asked, her voice tinged with mirth.

Aretta's response was a smile and a nod. Cheers rose up once again.

"Now, how do you like that?" Dr. Jeanie Brady chimed in, her eyes dancing with mischief as she winked at Macdara. "We have romance blooming all over the place. And a baby on the way."

Eoin looped his arm around the pair of them. "I'm afraid you'll be sharing that baby with your siblings, Aretta, and Dr. Jeanie Brady."

"We wouldn't have it any other way," Macdara said. "Right, Siobhán?"

Siobhán nodded. "What is it they say? It takes a village."